BLADES OF BLUEGRASS

What Reviewers Say About
D. Jackson Leigh's Work

Ordinary is Perfect

"There's something incredibly charming about this small town romance, which features a vet with PTSD and a workaholic marketing guru as a fish out of water in the quiet town. But it's the details of this novel that make it shine."—*Pink Heart Society*

Take a Chance

"I really enjoyed the character dynamic with this book of two very strong independent women who aren't looking for love but fall for the one they already love. ...The chemistry and dynamic between these two is fantastic and becomes even more intense when their sexual desires take over."—*Les Rêveur*

Dragon Horse War

"Leigh writes with an emotion that she in turn gives to the characters, allowing us insight into their personalities and their very souls. Filled with fantastic imagery and the down-to-earth flaws that are sometimes the characters' greatest strengths, this first Dragon Horse War is a story not to be missed. The writing is flawless, the story, breath-taking–and this is only the beginning."—*Lambda Literary Review*

"The premise is original, the fantasy element is gripping but relevant to our times, the characters come to life, and the writing is phenomenal. It's the author's best work to date and I could not put it down."—Melina Bickard, Librarian, Waterloo Library (London)

"Already an accomplished author of many romances, Leigh takes on fantasy and comes up aces. …So, even if fantasy isn't quite your thing, you should give this a try. Leigh's backdrop is a world you already recognize with some slight differences, and the characters are marvelous. There's a villain, a love story, and…ah yes, 'thar be dragons.'"—*Out in Print: Queer Book Reviews*

Swelter

"I don't think there is a single book D. Jackson Leigh has written that I don't like. …I recommend this book if you want a nice romance mixed with a little suspense."—Kris Johnson, Texas Library Association

"This book is a great mix of romance, action, angst, and emotional drama. …The first half of the book focuses on the budding relationship between the two women, and the gradual revealing of secrets. The second half ramps up the action side of things. …There were some good sexy scenes, and also an appropriate amount of angst and introspection by both women as feelings more than just the physical started to surface."—*Rainbow Book Reviews*

Call Me Softly

"*Call Me Softly* is a thrilling and enthralling novel of love, lies intrigue, and Southern charm."—*Bibliophilic Book Blog*

Touch Me Gently

"D. Jackson Leigh understands the value of branding, and delivers more of the familiar and welcome story elements that set her novels apart from other authors in the romance genre."—*Rainbow Reader*

Visit us at www.boldstrokesbooks.com

By the Author

Cherokee Falls series

Bareback

Long Shot

Every Second Counts

Romances

Call Me Softly

Touch Me Gently

Hold Me Forever

Swelter

Take a Chance

Ordinary Is Perfect

Blades of Bluegrass

Short Story Collection

Riding Passion

Dragon Horse War Trilogy

The Calling

Tracker and the Spy

Seer and the Shield

BLADES OF BLUEGRASS

by

D. Jackson Leigh

2020

BLADES OF BLUEGRASS

ISBN 13: 978-1-63555-637-7

This Trade Paperback Original Is Published By
Bold Strokes Books, Inc.
P.O. Box 249
Valley Falls, NY 12185

First Edition: August 2020

CREDITS
Editor: Shelley Thrasher
Production Design: Susan Ramundo
Cover Design By Tammy Seidick

Acknowledgments

I owe a huge, sincere thank you to Tracy Dice Johnson. Her open and candid answers to my very personal questions about the loss of her wife, Army National Guard Staff Sgt. Donna Johnson, to a suicide bomber in Afghanistan gave me a much deeper understanding of grief than I could possibly convey in a romance novel. As I explained to Tracy, there are only bits and pieces of their lives in Teddy and Britt's story, but the underlying sense of devastating loss, and having your grief on display for all to see is the same. Tracy was also an invaluable source of information about military life and deployment, and all the things that aren't easily found through Google searches.

And, as always, thanks to my awesome editor Shelley Thrasher. I can always trust her to make my stories better.

Dedication

Somewhere along the way, the United States of America has forgotten its roots. Our forefathers came here to escape government control over their religious beliefs, they came from impoverished slums and debtors' prisons with no hope of escape, and they came here with big dreams of new, better lives.

We've had ups and downs. We birthed the world's great middle class. We fought a war to end physical slavery, then used discrimination to again enslave the same minority in poverty. We put men on the moon, and established our United States as a world power and the leader/protector of Western Civilization.

Now something has gone terribly awry. Our middle class is dying as the gap between the wealthy and the poor widens. Our democracy is endangered by corrupt policies. Our judicial system has been infected with partisan politics. We are no longer united. We have lost our place of respect in the world.

We can only heal if we find a way to overcome the fear that makes us bully, hoard, and arm ourselves against our neighbors.

Non sibi sed patriae. Not self but country.

This book is dedicated to every American who exercises their most important Constitutional right in November of 2020—the right to vote.

CHAPTER ONE

C apt. Britt Story pulled off the two-lane road and stopped with the nose of her truck nearly touching the sturdy metal gate on the other side of the culvert. There was no road beyond the gate, just twenty acres of lush pasture.

A small herd of yearlings and a few mares lifted their heads to watch when she got out of the truck. Some returned to their grazing once they saw she wasn't carrying feed buckets. Others abandoned their snacking to chase and race each other in carefree games, as if her presence had energized them. She smiled at their antics. They'd go to work on the racetrack soon enough.

Britt closed her eyes, listening to their hooves pounding the soft turf and breathing in the clean smell of recently mowed Kentucky bluegrass. Even though the driveway into her grandfather's five-hundred-acre Thoroughbred breeding farm was another half mile down the highway, this gate and the pasture behind it were her portal to the sanctuary she'd retreated to every summer, spring break, and most holidays during her childhood and college years. Having grown up following her father's military career from base to base and then his political career from Kentucky to Washington, DC, she had always considered Pop's farm her real home.

When she opened her eyes, her gaze settled on a tall, silvery-gray mare watching her, ears flicking back and forth. Could it be? Britt put her fingers to her mouth and let out two sharp whistles. The mare snorted and took a few tentative steps in her direction. When

Britt whistled again, the mare tossed her head and charged across the pasture.

Britt slipped inside the gate to greet her favorite from the last summer she'd spent on the farm with Pop. She'd finished college and was scheduled to begin her military career in the fall. Pop had used that summer to school both Britt and Mysty in the basics that readied the foal to go out in the world of horse racing. He'd also prepared her for what she was born to do after she had served her country. A love for horses and Kentucky bluegrass ran deep in the Story bloodlines. When she left at the end of that wonderful summer, she knew she would return.

The eight years that followed had been a whirlwind of training and two deployments. Her father had tried to push her toward the administrative branch, but Britt refused to let his influence tie her to a desk job as some colonel's admin so she would be primed to follow her father's move into politics. She was physically tough and a natural leader, and her command was happy to deploy her with the troops.

Mysty—shortened from her racing name Out of the Myst—slid to a stop, her head bobbing as she extended her nose to sniff Britt's outstretched hand.

"Hey." Britt kept her voice soft, inhaling the familiar scent of horse. She stepped closer to run her hand along the arch of the mare's long neck while Mysty—finding Britt's hand empty—snuffled at the pockets of her shirt and jeans.

"Sorry, but I didn't bring treats. I'm out of practice." Mysty gave a disgusted snort and lowered her head to push Britt back a step. Britt pushed back, laughing. "So, you're still a brat, huh? How'd you do on the track?" She instinctively scrutinized the mare's legs and settled on the long scar running from knee to fetlock on her front right. "Damn. I'm sorry. Looks like you had a bad time of it."

Mysty snuffled at the half-filled sleeve where Britt's left arm should be, and her happy homecoming instantly turned bitter. "Bet my story beats yours."

The rolling hills and red-roofed stables that were Story Hill Farm hadn't changed, but Britt had. She felt like a foreigner in her own country. She'd lost a lot more than her left arm in the Afghanistan desert, and she harbored no hope of ever being the same.

Damn it all. Damn the US Army. And damn the stupidly idealistic patriot she'd once been.

❖

Lt. Teddy Alexander whipped her 2017 BMW 230i convertible into what had to be the last available parking space at the large Veterans Affairs Medical Center. She took a moment to turn her face up to the cloudless blue sky and soak in the warm, early summer sun. God, she loved this car, and she loved summertime. Enough basking.

She twisted the rearview mirror for a quick check—her cover was still snuggly positioned on her head and her tight bun intact—as the car's roof emerged from its nook in front of the trunk and stretched toward the windshield. She checked that it locked down securely, then gathered her briefcase and climbed out of the low-slung sports car.

She felt like skipping into the medical center, where she worked as an occupational-slash-physical therapist. The past month had been a career whirlwind. Her commanding officer, Col. Tom Winstead, had been selected to head a team assigned to liaise with various civilian research projects exploring advanced prosthetics. And, he wanted to take her along as his admin and occupational specialist.

The first steps included attending a week-long conference on prosthetic research and development. It was heart-stopping to see in person what was now possible, and what was almost in reach. Next, they'd traveled to Washington and New York City to meet with other potential members of Winstead's team, and they'd spent an amazing week checking out the labs of the civilian researchers at MIT and Duke University, who were making unthinkable advances in bionic limbs.

The question of where they'd be based once the team was fully formed hadn't come up, but she hoped it would be Walter Reed in DC. The team's mission was to examine the feasibility of bionic prosthetics that could turn wounded warriors into productive soldiers again. They'd also be key in examining the ethics of bionic warriors, a subject that world leaders were reluctant to address. What would keep a military power or terrorists from building an army of soldiers with bionic limbs that contained military technology and weaponry? How would other nations respond?

It was a slippery slope, and she was thrilled to be included. Also, this experience would certainly rocket her up the military career ladder. She'd likely make captain within the year.

When she entered the gymnasium-sized room that was the department's work area, a few patients were already being coached at various therapy stations. Teddy breezed through on her way to her small office, flashing a thumbs-up at a soldier who was grinning broadly after taking his first steps using a new, multi-jointed prosthesis.

Yep, the sun was shining and her future was looking bright... until she saw the single rose on her desk, placed next to a steaming mug of cocoa, and then the envelope on top of the mail in her inbox. It was addressed in a familiar scrawl—*My dear daughter-in-law.*

Teddy set her briefcase down, sank into her chair, and closed her eyes. Guilt and shame flooded her. She didn't have to look at today's date on the calendar. Sure, it'd been five years, but she'd never forgotten before. Never. She'd been so busy, so selfishly happy about this project, she hadn't noticed the calendar date. Truthfully, she hadn't thought or dreamed of Shannon in months. God, she was such an ass. Such a selfish ass.

She was instantly transported to her old office at Fort Bragg. Shannon stood in the doorway, smiling and fingering the buzzed hair at the base of her skull.

"What do you think, babe? That long hair was a pain when I deployed last time. So I thought I'd go short while I'm gone. I kind of like it. If you hate it, I can let it grow out again when I get back."

Only Shannon hadn't come back. Well, she did, but in a casket that remained closed after the chaplain explained the suicide bomber had grabbed Shannon a second before the explosion.

A soft knock on Teddy's open door jerked her from the unwelcome memories.

"Hey. Didn't mean to startle you." Colonel Winstead stood in the doorway, his expression solemn.

Teddy stood and offered a weak smile. "I'm afraid you caught me wool-gathering, sir."

He studied her for a long moment. "I've been so busy dragging you all over the East Coast to get ready for this project, I lost track of the date until Tess reminded me this morning. It's fine if you want the day off, Teddy. I've been working you pretty hard."

Teddy shrugged. She didn't want to go home and dwell on her memories. Not another year. It wasn't like she was still stationed at Fort Bragg and could visit the cemetery. "I've got a lot of notes from our trips to organize. I'd rather work, if that's okay."

He nodded. "If you change your mind, you have my permission to slip out."

"Thank you, sir."

He ran his hand over his graying buzz cut as if he wanted to say something more, then turned to leave.

"Colonel Winstead?"

He turned back to her and smiled. "Change your mind already?"

This time, her answering smile didn't feel forced. "I was wondering if you have a timeline for what's next. With the project, I mean."

He tilted his head, a sign that Teddy knew meant he was considering a decision, then waved for her to follow. "Grab that cocoa Tess made for you and come into my office."

"She really didn't need to do that," Teddy said, picking up her mug and a notepad.

His wave was dismissive. "I told her that, but she wouldn't have listened even if I was commander in chief." He settled into the leather chair behind his desk, and Teddy set her mug on the far corner of his desk, then pulled a straight-backed chair close in front of the desk so she could reach it while she took notes. "I don't have to tell you who wears the stars in the Winstead household. In fact, the general picked that rose from her own garden this morning."

"Does she know you call her 'the general'?"

"Oh, she knows. She even likes it when..." He cleared his throat. "Well, you don't need to know that."

She smiled and shook her head, letting the flush reddening his ears pass without comment.

Their informality wasn't very military, but he'd been her boss and mentor since her army-reserve days. And, while he had an enlisted soldier assigned as his administrative assistant, Teddy was handling anything that pertained to their new project.

"So, our timeline? I know I don't have to, but I'd like to give my landlady a heads-up." Her efficiency apartment above her landlady's detached garage was small and cheap, but living quarters were always temporary and not worth much investment, especially when you were single. The money she saved on housing had allowed her to buy her that fancy sports car.

"Don't start packing yet," Colonel Winstead said. "You know the military doesn't move that quickly unless it's a midnight deployment. I'm estimating eight months minimum before we'll have clinic space allocated and set up and actually begin working with potential candidates." He picked up a folder from the middle of his desk but leaned back in his chair instead of handing it to her. "I do want to have our team identified within the next month so they'll all have time to disengage from their current assignments. I want to persuade an old friend at the War College to join us as an ethics consultant. I'm sure he'll need to complete the current semester there before he can join us."

"I hoped we'd be assigned offices in the Walter Reed complex."

He nodded, fingering the edge of the file in his hands. "We might. But we could end up at Bragg, where there's more room available. It's closer to the researchers at Duke who are developing bionic limbs with sensory perception. Only certain amputees will qualify for our program, and we can have those who do transferred as soon as a week after their amputation surgery. We're looking at an extended relationship with our patients, and DC is an expensive area. The cost of living in North Carolina would make it much easier for our patients' families to relocate to be with them." He tapped his finger against the manila folder. "But we have plenty of time to work that out. I have a priority assignment for you before we pull up stakes here."

Teddy had stopped listening after "we could end up at Bragg," her mind churning with that probability. She loved Shannon's parents. They'd rallied around her like she was another daughter when the world didn't want to recognize her significance in Shannon's life. Later, after the funeral and she'd finally won the court battle to receive federal military survivor benefits, Shannon's mom still hovered to the point that Teddy felt suffocated. She hadn't yet opened the envelope on her desk because she knew it would be the same as every year—details of her visits to the cemetery and pleas for Teddy to visit.

"Lieutenant?"

Colonel Winstead's sharp command for her attention snapped her from her thoughts.

"Sorry. Sorry, sir. What were you saying?"

"I was saying that I have a very important assignment for you, so I need your full attention."

"Yes, sir. I'm sorry...I guess I drifted off for a minute. You have my full attention."

"Good." He laid the file on his desk and opened it. "Female soldier. Combat injury that resulted in amputation of her left arm just above the elbow three weeks ago. She's technically still active duty, but assigned to extended medical leave and released from Walter Reed. I'm designating you to supervise her rehab."

Teddy frowned. This wasn't usual protocol. "Why here?"

"She's elected to spend her recovery at her grandfather's farm, which is about forty-five minutes from here."

That made no sense. Soldiers didn't get to pick where they wanted to rehab. They went where the US Army told them to go. "Why isn't she rehabbing at Walter Reed?"

Colonel Winstead took a deep breath and blew it out before leaning forward and handing the file to her. "This is a special case, Teddy. Very high priority."

"What's so special about it?"

He averted his eyes. "Remember the surgeon who explained the special surgery required for the bionic prosthetic that allows a patient to actually experience sensation?"

Teddy remembered. His research and early results were amazing. "Yes. So…"

"That surgeon was flown to Landstuhl to perform this soldier's amputation the day she was coptered in from the field hospital."

"Wow. Who does she know to get that kind of treatment?"

"Her father is Senator Brock Story."

Teddy frowned. "The guy rumored to be our next secretary of defense if the idiot in the White House is unseated in this year's election?"

"That's him. War hero. Chairman of the Senate Arms Committee. He has high-ranking friends in all branches of the service, powerful political friends, and is near the top in public-opinion polls. Hell, I don't know why he isn't running for president."

She opened the folder and scanned it. "So, what is Captain Britt Story doing on a farm in Kentucky? If she had that kind of surgery, I'd expect her to be rehabbing near MIT or Duke to take advantage of their bionic-limb research programs."

Colonel Winstead stood and walked around his desk to close the door. He returned to his chair but swiveled to stare through the office plate-glass window as though he was watching the therapists work with their patients. After a bit, he spoke.

"There's something about this case the brass doesn't want to talk about." He turned back to Teddy. "It didn't smell right to me either, so I put in a call to a buddy in Landstuhl. He couldn't tell me much, but it was enough. The surgeon wasn't the only one who showed up there. The senator did, of course. He's her father. But Colonel George Banks, an old friend of the senator and commander of the sector where Captain Story was stationed, was summoned. Word is that Senator Story is grooming Banks, who's also from Kentucky, to follow him in politics. So, him showing up isn't necessarily a red flag. But my friend said he was in the hallway outside Captain Story's room before they took her to surgery. He said there was a lot of yelling, and the captain kicked both of them out of her room.

She was so angry the surgery had to be delayed while they sedated her twice to get her to calm down. Before she'd let them take her to the operating room, Story insisted the doctor write an absolutely no-visitors—even family—order on her chart."

Teddy shrugged. "I guess she and her father don't get along."

Colonel Winstead frowned. "Maybe, but there's more. Story was up for re-enlistment three weeks ago, but the army involuntarily extended her enlistment."

Teddy shrugged. "That's normal protocol until the medical-discharge paperwork is processed. What's not protocol is letting her take leave and go home."

He shrugged. "I'm getting pressure to accept her as the first candidate for our project. They want to return her to service."

Teddy scanned the file again. "Is she black ops or something?"

Tom waited until she looked up from the file and met his gaze. "This is just between us, Teddy." He waited until she nodded her consent. "Rumor says she knows something the brass doesn't want her to talk about, something she can't discuss if she's still in the ranks."

Teddy sighed. Seems like they always stuck her with the difficult patients. "So, when's her first appointment here?"

"That's the other thing. She isn't coming to us. You're going to her."

Teddy stared at him. "You want me to drive forty-five minutes there and back every day?"

He shook his head. "Nope. Arrangements have been made to billet you there at the farm until you can evaluate her work challenges and teach her how to overcome them."

"Are you kidding? Who in the world approved that?"

"Orders directly from Colonel, excuse me, General George Banks. He was just promoted."

"But we've got a ton of work to do on our project. Why not give this to someone else?"

"Because you're a medic who went back to school and got double certified in physical and occupational therapy. You should be able to meet all her health and rehab needs."

"But—"

"And, you can work on the project from there. Nobody has to be tied to an office these days. All you need are your notes, your laptop, and your cell phone. But Story is your priority, Lieutenant."

"But—"

"Velvet gloves on this one. Both of those men—Senator Story and General Banks—will have a lot of power over military appropriations in the coming year. Especially funding for special projects like ours. They want Captain Story in our program. They want her to stay in the army. We don't have to know why. We do have to follow orders."

She stared at him. "I don't have any choice in this, do I?"

"Has the army *ever* given you a choice?"

"Good point."

CHAPTER TWO

Coffee on the stove is still hot if you want some. Your breakfast is in the oven, staying warm." He looked up from the newspaper he was reading, his blue eyes peering at her over the top of his reading glasses. "Don't get used to it. Breakfast is at six thirty. Same as always."

Britt grabbed a mug from the drainboard next to the sink and poured herself a cup. She took a sip and grimaced. "Still drinking that cheap rotgut from the grocery, I see."

"Beggars can't be choosers. I like my coffee." He frowned at her. "Where's your arm?"

She ignored his question and carried her mug to the small kitchen table, taking the seat across from him. "You don't fool me, old man. You like the lady that sells the coffee."

He glared at her, then winked. "She's not hard to look at," he said, shoving the sports section to her. "Get that plate out of the oven and eat. You won't be any help around here if you waste away."

Their affectionate back-and-forth had let her block out the past months for a few minutes, but his reference to her physical condition cracked open the door holding back the black mood that had been her constant companion since she woke after surgery in Germany. "I'm not hungry."

Pop put his paper down. "Yes, you are." He rose, retrieved her plate, and plopped it in front of her. "I let it ride last night when you said you were too tired to eat." He tossed a knife and fork down by her plate, then moved the butter and honey from his side of the table to hers before he sat again. "But you're not getting up from this table until I see you clean that plate."

The sausage, eggs, and two fist-sized biscuits did smell heavenly. Maybe she was hungry. She picked up her knife and contemplated her plate. The hospital had served only pre-buttered toast, and these were tall, fluffy, Southern biscuits. Not those dense, squat things that Northerners buttered on top. Southern biscuits screamed for a fat pat of butter to be placed inside. How to do this with one hand? She glanced up at her grandfather.

"You aren't the first to get a wing clipped," Pop said, never raising his eyes from the crossword puzzle he'd moved on to. "Figure it out before your eggs get cold."

Britt grabbed the first biscuit with her hand and dug her fingers in to split it, then used her knife to butter it. She'd skip the honey today. "So, what's on the agenda this morning?"

"Where's your arm," he asked again. "I know they gave you one."

"Are you really asking me that?"

"You know what I mean. Your pro…pro…your fake one? They gave you one, didn't they?"

"Prosthetic arm." She pretended to concentrate on buttering her second biscuit. "I don't like it, so I choose not to wear it."

He peered at her over his readers for a long moment, then returned to her question. "If you're up to it, I thought we'd tour the stables and hit a couple of pastures so I can catch you up on things." He got up to pour himself the last of the coffee. "I'm sure you stopped at your usual place on the way in and saw Mysty."

Her mouth full, Britt only nodded. Had Pop put Mysty in that pasture because he knew Britt usually stopped there? She wouldn't put it past the gruff old codger.

"I bought her back for a song. She injured the suspensory ligament in her right fore, then suffered a stress fracture in the same leg when the trainer put her back on the track too early. It wasn't really his fault. The owner was just too impatient and, after the second injury, was happy to unload her basically for the cost of her vet bill."

"How'd she run?" Britt asked.

"She was coming along really well. When she turned up lame, she'd already won more than her yearling price and racing expenses."

"She has great bloodlines for breeding." Britt mopped up the last of her eggs with her second biscuit.

Pop shook his head. "The first season I bred her, she threw a fantastic colt that brought top dollar, but she had problems with the birth, and I think it must have messed up something inside. Her next two breedings didn't take."

"What do you plan to do with her?"

"I'll put some feelers out to rehome her. The hunter people won't be interested because her previous injuries would rule her out as a jumper." He took her empty plate and put it in the sink, then turned back to her. "Unless you want her."

"What would I do with her?"

"Ride her."

Britt shook her head. Owning a horse was a commitment. "I'll ride her to get the racetrack out of her until you find a home. I don't need any more baggage than I'm already carrying. It's all I can do to sort out my own mess."

He held the door open for her and then followed when she stepped out onto the porch. It was another bright, sunny day. Grooms and horses were already moving through the morning routine around the barns and paddocks. Britt took a deep breath and smiled. Oh, how she'd missed this.

Pop laid his big hand on her shoulder and squeezed. "There's no hurry to make any decisions about anything, kiddo. Horses are in your blood, just like they're in mine. I've been waiting for you to get done playing with the army. Story Hill Farm is yours when you're ready, Britt. But if you feel you have to go back to the army for a while, the farm will always be waiting for you." He slipped his hand from her shoulder to her nape and pulled her to him, rubbing the white stubble on his jaw against her cheek. "I'm hoping you'll stay."

"Thanks, Pop." Her throat tightened at his words and the familiar gesture that had always made her shriek as a young girl.

She wanted to stay. Forever. But was it that simple? Could she just block out the world and everything that had happened? Could she put it all behind her and rebuild her life here? She had to get free of the army first.

❖

Teddy mulled over the information she'd googled on Capt. Britt Story and Sen. Brock Story. If you believed media accounts and the *Army Times'* profile on the two, the father and daughter had a close relationship. Brock Story spoke fondly of his daughter and her accomplishments. Britt Story's regard for her father appeared close to hero worship.

She'd watched the short video that accompanied the online article at least ten times. Captain Story was an androgynous, albeit softer, slimmer, version of her very handsome father. Her smile was quick, and her blue eyes captured the viewer when she looked directly into the camera.

What she saw didn't mesh with her medical file that described a sullen, barely communicative, and short-tempered soldier. Maybe Captain Story was a politician at heart, like her father. Maybe the side she showed the media was a careful façade.

Teddy was betting the real person underneath the conflicting persona was simply a soldier and patriot. In addition to Captain Story's medical file, she'd reviewed Captain Story's personnel file, which was filled with enthusiastic evaluations from her superiors, commendations for valor, innovative thinking, and excellent field leadership.

So, even though Teddy normally would have worn her dress uniform for the initial introduction, she'd dressed that morning in field camos in the hope that Captain Story would more readily relate to that uniform. She smiled to herself. Well, a soldier in field dress and driving a crisp white convertible BMW. Too bad if Captain Story had a problem with that. She wasn't dedicated enough to requisition a vehicle from the motor pool when she could glide along these winding two-lane backroads in her own smooth-handling ride, enjoying another sunny day and the rolling hills.

She slowed when her GPS indicated she was within a half mile of her destination. Dense woods crowded close to the ditch on the left side of the road, but to her right lay a patchwork of freshly mown pastures divided by dark wood fencing. Most of the pastures held small herds—mares with foals at their sides, half-grown colts and fillies. Wow. Was all this Story Hill Farm? More like Story Book Farm. She must have driven down a rabbit hole.

The dark fencing changed to white rails as she turned onto the wide crushed-gravel drive and parked next to a rambling two-story farmhouse with a porch that wrapped around three sides. Not exactly the mansion she'd envisioned, given the fancy Thoroughbred farms she'd driven past around Lexington. Calumet and Claiborne farms were famous for breeding, training, and racing many of the world's fastest horses.

Teddy adjusted her hat, climbed out of the low sports car, and stretched. Downhill from the house, four long stables gleamed in the sunlight. The buildings, like the farmhouse, were white and roofed with dark-red metal. Multiple paddocks stretched outward from the stables, interrupted by a variety of things that reminded her of their rehab gym: several long lap pools, a circular contraption that reminded her of the pony rides at the fair, and several round corrals.

She eyed the house. Front door or side? The steps leading to the side door that faced the barns were worn from use, but protocol dictated she try the more formal front entrance first. Before she could walk that way, a stocky, silver-haired woman opened the side door and stepped onto the porch. Drying her hands on a dish towel, she smiled at Teddy.

"Hey there. You must be the woman E.B. said would be coming from the VA. I don't think he was expecting you so quick. Britt only arrived last night."

Teddy climbed the steps and held out her hand. "Teddy Alexander. I'm assigned to help Captain Story rehab from her injuries."

"Nice to meet you, Lieutenant." The woman's grasp was strong, her handshake like the snap of a salute. "Lynn. I'm assigned to keep this household shipshape. I haven't worn rank in fifteen years, but E.B. still calls me Sarge when I get too bossy."

Teddy smiled. Ex-military? No wonder she immediately liked Lynn.

"I'm sorry if I caught you off guard. I was told I was to embed with the troops here, but the drive was a nice break from the chaos of the city. I won't mind driving out again tomorrow."

"Your quarters are ready. I just hope E.B has prepared Britt."

"E.B. is…"

"E.B. Story, Britt's grandfather and owner of everything you can see from this porch and more. Well, not the road out there. I reckon that belongs to the state." Lynn scanned the area around the barns. "They were out and about before I got here this morning. But that's not surprising. Both of them are early risers."

"So, you don't stay here?"

"Nope. My house is just down the road. E.B. offered me some space when the marines played "Taps" for my Douglas. But after spending thirty years in military housing, I like my own space. Besides, my niece and her two little ones live with me now since her good-for-nothing husband took up with a floozy in Louisville." Lynn paused to look at Teddy again. "I'm sure that's more than you wanted to know. I probably talk too much because the marines only wanted you to shut up and follow orders without letting you know the lay of the land."

Teddy chuckled. "Not just the marines. The army is exactly the same, so I understand."

Lynn's attention returned to the barns. "Looks like they're headed this way. I better get lunch laid out." She turned back to the door.

"Wait!" Teddy pulled her gaze from the two tall figures walking up from the stables. "Something you said…Captain Story doesn't know about the arrangement for her rehab?"

"Senator Story called with the information, but there's some kind of ruckus between him and Britt, so he left it to E.B. to tell her when she got here. Hopefully, he did. Good luck if he didn't. I've known Britt since she was a grasshopper, and she can be an immovable object when she plants her feet against something."

"Great," Teddy said to Lynn's back as she disappeared into the house.

When the two drew close enough, Teddy could see E.B. Story shaking his head and hear the exasperated tone of his low voice. She couldn't make out his words, but judging by the clenched jaw and ball cap pulled low over Captain Story's eyes, he'd finally told her why Teddy was here. Not a problem. Teddy squared her shoulders. Her job was rarely easy.

❖

"He did what?" Britt's anger rose so quickly, her brain sent immediate signals for her biceps to contract and fists to clench. Only she had no fist at the end of her stump, and hot, white pain when her bicep muscle tightened had her grabbing her left shoulder and gritting her teeth. It was time for a pain pill, but she hadn't put any in her pocket. She was determined to avoid the opioid addiction she'd seen in too many recovering soldiers. The pain ratcheted her anger even higher, so she took short, rapid breaths to breathe through it. "Fuck, fuck, fuck."

"I'm glad your grandmother isn't still around to hear you use that language," Pop said. He wasn't one to let her get away with anything. "I don't know why or what's going on between you and Brock, but you're only hurting yourself when you let your anger get the best of you."

He was right, but she wasn't ready to hear it or at a point where she could control the red-hot fury that seemed to burst forth at the smallest provocation. The pain in her arm began to subside to a sharp throb, and she sucked in ten deep breaths like the therapist at Walter Reed had taught her. She hated that therapist. She was perky, and Britt disliked perky, cheerleader-type women. She hated it when the woman would say, "We can get through this," like she was missing her arm, too. But she had taught Britt this one useful thing—breathing through the pain.

"Dad needs to back the hell off," she said as she straightened, still clutching her shoulder. "I don't take orders from him anymore."

"Maybe you don't, but you still take orders from the US Army, and they've assigned a therapist to stay here at the farm while you rehab. I'm sure Brock did pull some strings for that, but I'm glad because I could use your help around here rather than you spending every day driving back and forth to Lexington."

"Like I can be any help. I can't even tie my own shoes."

"Last I checked, horses don't wear shoes that need tying. Anyway, Brock said that's what this therapist is supposed to help you with—how to do things you used to do with two hands." He headed out of the stable. "Come on. It's time for lunch. The sergeant doesn't tolerate tardiness."

Britt followed. The throbbing in her arm had stolen her appetite, but she did need her noon meds, a couple of acetaminophen tablets, and a nap. She wasn't a hundred percent yet, but she didn't want to admit the morning had worn her out. "So, when's this therapist showing up?"

"Looks like your guy is here now," Pop said, squinting as they headed up the hill to the house. "Only it looks like your guy is a female."

"I hate perky women." Britt's lack of appetite was turning into full-blown nausea as they walked up the hill to the house.

"Well, maybe she'll be as mean and stubborn as you are," Pop said.

Britt didn't answer. She was concentrating on keeping pace with her seventy-something grandfather and not moving her painful stump. By the time they reached the porch, she was afraid her legs wouldn't be strong enough to make it up the six steps to the porch. She focused on the door. If she could just get inside, she could sit down. She was so fixated on that attempt, she nearly plowed into the soldier who suddenly blocked her path and saluted.

"Lieutenant Teddy Alexander, Captain Story. I've been assigned to assist in your rehabilitation."

Britt was forced to stop and acknowledge her with a curt salute. She sucked in a breath to try to tamp down her nausea. "Lieutenant. I'm sorry you drove all the way here. I just learned of your assignment, and I'm not prepared to meet with you today."

The edges of her vision were growing fuzzy, and she stumbled as she attempted to skirt around the woman. Lieutenant Alexander grabbed for her, and Britt growled. "Get out of my way."

Teddy was surprised Captain Story was still standing and able to salute. She was pale and sweating. She recognized the signs when Captain Story's eyes lost focus and moved quickly to pull Captain Story's right arm across her shoulders and wrap an arm around her waist to support her.

"Britt..." The man that Teddy gathered was E.B. Story was instantly at his granddaughter's other side but faltered when he realized he was on her injured one.

"It's okay. I've got her. Can you open the door for us?"

"Yes." He opened the screen door and stepped back for them to enter. "Lynn, pull out a chair."

Teddy countermanded him. "We need to lay her down."

"Through there." Lynn pointed to an archway on the other side of the kitchen. A leather couch and recliner were grouped with a fireplace and large-screen television.

Teddy guided Captain Story to the recliner. Patients usually felt less embarrassed by their weakness if they weren't flat on their back with people standing over them. She assisted Captain Story into the chair with practiced ease and lifted the lever that raised her feet.

"What can we do to help?" Lynn asked.

Teddy appreciated that both Lynn and E.B. were calm and steady when confronted by the small crisis. She turned and held out her hand. "I'm sorry, Mr. Story. I didn't get a chance—"

He waved her off. "It's E.B., young lady. Tell us what to do."

She pulled her car fob from her pocket and held it out to him. "Could you go out to my car? I need the medical bag that's in the trunk."

"Sure." He took the keys and left.

"Lynn, I need a glass of water and a small ice pack. A sandwich-sized baggy filled with crushed ice will do."

"We've got a couple of soft ice packs about that size in the freezer."

"Even better. Oh, and a basin or small trashcan in case her breakfast decides to come up."

"On it." Lynn also disappeared, so Teddy returned her attention to her patient.

Captain Story's skin was gray and clammy, her eyes closed. "I'm okay. Just give me a minute." Apparently, she hadn't passed out.

Teddy gently grasped her wrist, noting the slight tremor in Captain Story's hand as she checked her racing pulse.

E.B. strode back into the room and held out the medical bag.

"Thanks," Teddy said, already flipping it open to search for what she needed inside. She found the vial of nausea medicine and quickly loaded a syringe, then swabbed the vein in Captain Story's arm. "Small sting," she warned her.

"No opioids." Captain Story made a surprisingly strong attempt to pull her arm away from the hold Teddy had on it.

"This is just for nausea. It's not a painkiller." She slid the needle into the vein when she felt the arm relax.

Lynn reappeared as Teddy was withdrawing the needle and swabbing the injection site. She slid a small trash can next to the recliner and offered a hand-sized ice pack to Teddy. She stood by while Teddy slid the ice pack behind Captain Story's neck. "What else?"

"She'll need something in her stomach to take some acetaminophen for the pain," Teddy said.

"I was putting together turkey sandwiches for lunch."

"That's perfect, Lynn."

"Mayo. Not mustard."

Teddy and Lynn shared a smile at Captain Story's mumbled input.

"It's been a while, but I haven't forgotten," Lynn said before heading back into the kitchen.

The lines of Captain Story's face were still tense, but her color had greatly improved. The nausea medicine must be kicking in. "Where are your medications?"

Captain Story blinked slowly, but Teddy held her clouded gaze and waited for an answer. Captain Story sighed and closed her eyes again. "Bedside table."

"Want me to go get them?" E.B. asked.

"That would be great. Can you bring down all the bottles on the bedside table? I need to see everything she's taking. If her supply doesn't include any acetaminophen, I have some in my med kit here."

"Be right back."

Teddy stared when E.B. took the stairs like he was thirty years old, rather than seventy. The Story family must have really good bloodlines to be so attractive and athletic. Teddy grasped Captain Story's wrist again and counted while her digital watch ticked off the seconds. She was surprised when she looked up at the brilliant blue eyes, clearer now and watching her. She blinked a few times, then mentally shook herself. "Your heart rate is better, but still fast. Probably from the pain."

E.B.'s noisy return down the stairs interrupted any reply, although Captain Story hadn't appeared to be forming one. Then Lynn reappeared and slid a small plate with a turkey sandwich onto the table next to the recliner.

"Here you go." E.B. held out four prescription bottles and one of Tylenol.

Teddy checked the labels. Antibiotic, an anti-depressant, an anti-seizure drug to manage the nerve pain in her residual limb, and a full bottle of an opioid painkiller. She shook out two of the acetaminophen extra-strength tablets and one antibiotic capsule. "Only the antibiotic at lunch," she said.

"I'm not taking the other stuff." Captain Story held out her hand for the pills, tossed them into her mouth, then accepted the glass of water Teddy offered to wash them down.

"Are you prescribing your own treatment? You know your body belongs to the US Army, and they can order you to take what they prescribe."

Captain Story lifted her chin but failed to hide her slight grimace as she straightened her shoulders in a defiant posture. "Yeah, and I've seen too many soldiers stuck in a circular dependence on the stuff government doctors feed them. I researched each of those drugs. The opioids are highly addictive, the anti-seizure drug is for nerve pain but dopes you up, and the anti-depressant is to counteract the side effect of the anti-seizure pill." Captain Story turned her head away, the muscle jumping in her jaw. "The army isn't going to drug me up to shut me up."

What did she know that the US Army didn't want her to speak about? Teddy's throat closed around the question. Now wasn't the time. She wasn't a fan of the drug protocol prescribed for military amputees, but trying to tough out the pain would hinder healing. "If you don't want to take the drugs, we can explore some alternatives to ease your discomfort."

Captain Story's eyes closed again, and the muscles in her neck visibly tightened.

"In fact," Teddy said, "let's try one of those alternatives now. I'll be right back." She raised the back of the chair without waiting for Captain Story's consent. "It'd be great if you could eat a bit of that sandwich while I go wash my hands."

Teddy headed for the kitchen, waving for Lynn and E.B. to follow. "You guys go ahead and have lunch. I need to massage the tension out of her shoulder and arm, and she doesn't need an audience while I'm trying to get her to relax."

"This is my fault." E.B. stared down at the floor like a guilty ten-year-old. "Britt's just always been so strong, I guess I forgot that she had major surgery only three weeks ago. I walked her all over the danged farm. And then I waited until the last minute to tell her about you. It was too much. She just blew up. I don't think I've ever seen her so angry."

"It's not your fault. Captain Story is an adult and responsible for her own actions. She should have told you she was tiring. And her fits of anger are fairly typical, even from physically healthy soldiers trying to cope with the jarring transition from deployment to home. Imagine trying to deal with that while coping with traumatic injuries."

Lynn slid a plate of sandwiches onto the table and poured iced tea into two of the glasses. "Anything else you need?"

Teddy smiled, then went to the sink to wash her hands. "You can save me one of those sandwiches until I get her comfortable enough to rest."

"You got it," Lynn said. E.B. nodded his agreement, and they sat down to eat.

❖

When Teddy returned to the living room, half of the sandwich on the plate was gone, but Captain Story was clutching her shoulder, her face twisted in a tight grimace.

"Another spasm?"

Captain Story nodded but didn't open her eyes.

"Breathe through it." Teddy moved behind the chair, pressed firmly against a pressure point on Captain Story's neck, and waited while she completed ten deep breaths—in through the nose, out through the mouth. When Captain Story's breathing returned to normal, she dropped her hand into her lap. Teddy released the pressure point and squatted next to the recliner. Even though it was August, Captain Story was wearing a long-sleeved shirt with a T-shirt underneath. Teddy was sure the top shirt was to hide the still-healing residual limb. It often took a while for amputees to let even their closest family see the damage.

"Better?"

Captain Story nodded. Her eyes were no longer brilliant, but a stone-washed blue and shadowed with fatigue.

"I'm glad somebody at the hospital at least taught you how to breathe through the pain."

"A perky therapist did that."

"Good for her."

"I hate perky women."

Teddy smiled. "Me, too. It's like they never took off that high-school cheerleading uniform."

Captain Story didn't smile back. No matter. Teddy didn't really expect the ice would crack that easily.

"Okay. We're going to do a few things to ensure your arm doesn't spasm again, so you can get some rest. First, we need to get you down to your T-shirt."

Captain Story didn't move at first, then fumbled weakly with the buttons.

"Let me help," Teddy said, her voice soft.

"I can do it, Lieutenant." Captain Story frowned but stopped her fumbling.

"I'm sure you can, Captain." Teddy quickly unbuttoned the shirt and carefully helped her remove the shirt. "But I've drugged you up with anti-nausea medicine, so we'll write this off as special circumstances." Teddy gently removed the pressure sock intended to reduce swelling and then the bandage to inspect the wound. "Everything looks good here. She applied a fresh bandage from the supplies in her med kit but left the sock off. She held back a sigh. Although it would be easier to massage hands-to-skin so she could use a warming oil, she needed to first earn Captain Story's trust. She folded the short sleeve of the shirt up.

"I'm going to attach a TENS unit to your arm. Have you ever used one?"

Britt shook her head.

"TENS stands for transcutaneous electrical nerve stimulation. You can actually buy these without a prescription at any local pharmacy now. It uses low-voltage electrical current to relieve pain. It's like a vibrator massage to relax the nerves in your arm. While that's working on the nerves, I'm going to massage your shoulder and neck to loosen the muscles irritating the nerves." Her explanation wasn't scientifically exact, but close enough for her patient to get the general idea.

Captain Story stiffened and grimaced. "Fuck." The sudden spasm was actually visible along her defined musculature.

"Breathe through it, deep breaths." Teddy's words were low and smooth, but she worked quickly to attach the TENS unit, then sent a low current through the muscle to break the spasm's hold.

❖

Britt woke with a start. The house was quiet except for the low murmur of voices coming from the outside. The rhythmic creak accenting the voices told her whoever was speaking was making use of one of the porch rocking chairs. She swallowed, her throat dry. How long had she been asleep? Not long, she decided. The sun was still bright where it pushed between the slats of the blinds. A light throw blanket covered her, and her arm tingled from the TENS unit still attached. She yawned, drew the blanket off, and dropped it onto the floor. She cautiously lowered the footrest so she was sitting upright, then powered down the TENS. The pain was gone, so she removed the adhesive discs that held the electrodes against her skin. She rolled her shoulders and actually felt pretty good.

The last she recalled, Lieutenant What's-her-name was massaging her shoulder. That woman had strong hands, and damn, it felt good. But not good enough to want the army living on the farm. She'd come here to escape everything camouflaged and clear her head. The sooner she made that clear and sent the woman packing, the better.

Britt grabbed a bottle of water from the refrigerator, then stepped out onto the porch. The lieutenant and Lynn stopped their slow rocking and looked up at her.

"You're up."

Duh. "It would appear that I am, unless I'm sleepwalking."

The lieutenant nodded, acknowledging Britt's sarcasm but still offering a slight smile. "How's the pain?"

Britt wouldn't lie. "It's good. Gone for the moment. Thank you."

Lynn stood. "We were just passing the time. Take my chair," she said to Britt. "I've got beds to change and a load of laundry to fold." She stopped with the door half open. "You need to eat more than that half sandwich we got into you earlier."

"I'm not hungry," Britt said.

"I made some of my special soup. I'll warm up a mug of it for you." Lynn nodded to affirm her decision. "That's just the thing you need." She hustled inside as if she hadn't heard what Britt had said.

Britt sighed but didn't sit in the offered rocker. Instead, she propped her butt against the porch railing and looked down at her visitor. "I'm sorry you drove all the way out here, Lieutenant..." She made a show of peering at the name printed on the uniform. "... Alexander, but you won't be staying."

Lieutenant Alexander stared back for a long moment. "My orders came from a rank higher than yours, Captain Story. And I'm not in the habit of disobeying orders, so, yes, I will be staying."

Britt ran her fingers through her hair in exasperation. "Look. I don't remember much of the two weeks after my patrol was attacked, so I feel like I was in the desert last week, then pretty much woke up at Walter Reed and got the hell out of there as soon as they would release me. I came here to get away from the US Army and clear my head." She knew her voice was growing louder with each word, but she couldn't seem to stop herself. "I don't want to eat breakfast every morning and dinner every night while staring across the table at your uniform. Do you get that?" Her shoulder jerked in an involuntary twitch. She closed her eyes and took a deep breath. God knows, she didn't want to restart the muscle spasms. She opened her eyes again after a few cleansing breaths. "I want to be left alone."

Lieutenant Alexander held her gaze and opened her mouth to speak, but Lynn pushed through the door, holding a steaming mug.

Lynn pointed to the rocking chair and barked in her drill-sergeant voice, "Britt Story, sit your ass down."

Despite her righteous anger, Britt's legs were still a bit wobbly. She sat in the rocking chair and accepted the soup mug Lynn thrust at her.

Lynn pointed at Britt, then Lieutenant Alexander. "Work it out. Both of you." She stomped to the door, then turned back to them. "I'll know if you throw that soup out in the yard. Drink it." The door slammed sharply behind her, but they could hear her mumbling to herself as she walked through the kitchen to go upstairs.

They sat in silence for a few minutes, and then Britt took a sip of the soup. The chicken-vegetable recipe was as good as she remembered. She took another sip of the rich broth. It was still too hot to fill her mouth with the bits of chicken and vegetables.

"I can't disobey my orders to rehabilitate your injury, but I can put the uniform away. I did bring a few casual clothes. I'll probably need to drive back and collect some other things anyway, once I see what we might need to help you. I can pick up some more clothes then."

Britt sighed. Apparently, she was stuck with this rock in her shoe. Damn it. She sighed again. Audibly. To clearly express her exasperation. "That would help, I guess."

Lieutenant Alexander nodded and stood. "I'll get my briefcase, if you don't mind answering some basic questions while you finish your soup, Captain."

Britt watched Lieutenant Alexander start down the steps. "Britt."

"I'm sorry?"

"Lose the uniform *and* the protocol. Addressing me as Captain and saluting won't help me forget that the army has infiltrated my home."

Lieutenant Alexander's smile was soft, and her cheeks flushed pink. For the first time, Britt realized her therapist was a very attractive woman. She held out her hand and waited while Britt settled the soup mug in her lap and accepted her offered handshake. "Pleased to meet you, Britt. I'm Teddy."

Chapter Three

B ritt rolled to sit on the side of her bed when she smelled coffee and heard someone opening cabinets and clinking pots in the kitchen downstairs. Pop always rose at five thirty and was cooking breakfast by six.

She'd slept only a few hours and wanted nothing more than to stay in her bed and hide from the world.

When she was in the desert, she'd hated the relentless glare of the sun, constant sweat, and the fine sand that permeated everything. It was in your ears and nose, in your bed and clothes, even in your food if you didn't eat fast enough. But she felt snatched from that world and dumped in another so abruptly that she almost missed the familiar labored wheeze of the air conditioner in the container unit she shared with another female officer. She caught herself listening for the continuous coming and going of military vehicles, and the loud voices of men everywhere at all hours. She'd grown used to snatching short hours of sleep between patrols and other daily duties that kept her busy sixteen hours a day, every day.

The relative silence of the farm at night was unsettling, the soft periodic hum of the central air-conditioning too quiet.

Still, duty called. And if she didn't get up, they'd come find her. She dressed slowly, pulling on jeans and a soft, long-sleeved Henley. She wasn't ready to face the world in short sleeves that would expose her stump. Thankfully, her old ankle-high barn boots had a zipper, rather than laces that would need to be tied. She made a mental note to order several pair before that design went out of style. She was grateful she kept her hair short—pretty much a necessity now that she had only one hand to brush it into order. She regarded herself in the mirror. Nothing she could do about the dark circles under her eyes. She shrugged and headed downstairs.

❖

"Are you sure I can't help?" Teddy wasn't comfortable sipping coffee at the table while a man at least forty years her senior cooked breakfast.

"You'll mess up his system if you try to help," Britt said from the doorway. "Trust me. You are helping by staying out of his kitchen while he cooks."

E.B. pointed at Britt with the spatula he was using to flip the eggs. "You better stay out of my way, too, or your eggs will be the ones full of shells." His threat was softened by the affection in his voice and the way his gaze drank in his granddaughter. Their connection was palpable.

Britt reached for one of the dozen white diner-style mugs from the overhead shelf. "Just getting a cup of coffee."

He pointed with the spatula again. "Lynn put your mug in that corner cabinet. Said I might accidentally knock it off if she left it up there with the others."

"And it can stay there." Britt's curt tone was a knife slicing through the warm mood of the morning ritual. E.B. wordlessly turned back to the eggs he was frying, and Britt's shoulders slumped as she poured coffee. She replaced the coffee carafe but then clasped her grandfather's arm in a brief squeeze. "I'm sorry, Pop. Didn't sleep much last night, but that's not an excuse to be rude."

He nodded. "Go sit down. Eggs are up."

Teddy watched the exchange, cataloging the information revealed during the interaction. Britt wasn't sleeping well. Physical pain, PTSD, or just the general disorientation soldiers experienced after deployment? Or was something deeper keeping her from resting? Also, Capt. Britt Story had amazing control over herself.

She'd witnessed many bouts of volatile anger from soldiers in her situation—suddenly thrown back into their old lives, but with broken bodies—and had never witnessed anyone rein it in so quickly. She wasn't ready to credit the about-face to Britt's relationship to her grandfather. It was possible but unlikely. Friends and family closest to suffering soldiers were usually the ones who became targets when they lashed out at the unfairness of their circumstances.

That self-control, however, was going to be a big fence Teddy would need to climb over to sign off on Britt's case and get back to her own life.

E.B. placed plates piled with bacon, fried eggs, and toast in front of her and Britt, then retrieved his own.

"So, you know much about racehorses, Teddy?" E.B. asked between mouthfuls of food and slurps of coffee.

"Not really. I think they're beautiful. I'm a military brat so we moved a lot, but several of the bases where my dad was stationed had horse stables. He'd had a pony when he was growing up, so he took me riding a couple of times. I didn't get to do it enough to be any good at it."

"My daddy put me in the saddle in front of him before I could even walk, and I did the same for my son." He waved his fork in Britt's direction. "That one never gave her father the chance. Her mama had one of those chow dogs, and Britt here was hanging onto that dog's scruff and using him for a pony when she could barely crawl. She was riding her own miniature pony as soon as she could walk. She can saddle a couple of mounts and show you the farm."

"Teddy is here to rehab my arm, Pop. I doubt she'll have time to stroll about the farm on a horse. We're going to be working through that protocol as quickly as possible so she can get back to her regular duties." Britt's tone was casual, but her eyes dared Teddy to challenge her statement.

Teddy chewed slowly, giving herself time to find the right words before she spoke. "The purpose of physical and occupational therapy is to help you become comfortable again with your career and personal environment after your injury. Taking a ride very well might be part of that treatment. But we'll talk about that after breakfast, while we tackle your first session."

Britt gave a curt nod and stood to retrieve the coffee carafe. Teddy spread jelly on her last piece of toast, and E.B. used his to mop up the egg yolk left on his plate while Britt topped off everyone's coffee.

E.B. popped his last bite into his mouth and settled back in his chair to enjoy his coffee. "So, I'm figuring to pick up a few new mares." He looked at Britt. "Reckon you might have time to do some research on that?"

Britt spooned sugar into her coffee and nodded. "I can. Anything you looking for specifically?"

"I've been talking to David over at Lane's End about breeding to Honor Code. In fact, I like several of the studs they're standing, and their fees are reasonable."

"What's his fee?"

"Forty thousand, same as last year. But I'm betting it'll be higher next year. He's got a pretty impressive offspring doing well in stake races so far this year."

Britt nodded. "Got a mare in mind?"

"Wish I could breed Last Dance to him, but Gail says she threw her final foal this year. She'll keep weanlings next year. So, I want you to look for a Dancer mare to replace her."

"Keep weanlings?" Teddy was lost. It was like they were speaking another language that she didn't understand.

"She'll be put out with a couple of babies when they're weaned from their mothers. Having an older mare in with them helps them cope with the initial separation. They feel safer, I guess," Britt said.

"That makes sense."

Britt looked to E.B. again. "You said a couple of mares. What else are you looking for?"

"You know what I like. Anything from Secretariat's line. He produced the best breeding mares of any sire ever. But I wouldn't ignore something with War in the pedigree. I want to breed for strong legs. I've seen too many breaking down on the tracks the past couple of years. My ideal mare..."

"...would have Secretariat's oversized heart and Man o' War's strong legs." Britt finished the sentence for him. "You and every other Thoroughbred breeder." She took her coffee cup to the sink. "It's late in the year. The mare auctions are mostly over."

"I know. I'm looking for mares that didn't take during summer breedings, so I can breed them early next year."

"I'll get right on it."

E.B. shook his head. "You take care of you first. I've managed without you the past couple of years. You don't need to jump in with both feet until you're all mended."

"Okay." Britt turned to Teddy. "Where do you want to do this?"

"Uh. Well..." Teddy hesitated, still digesting the famous Secretariat having an oversized heart and that being a good thing. An enlarged heart in a person wasn't good.

E.B. answered instead. "After I talked to Brock, I had a couple of guys empty out the small bedroom and put your old weights and bench that were stored in the barn in there. Maybe you won't need them, but they're there if you do."

Teddy smiled at him. "Thank you. We can use the bench for sure."

❖

"What if I don't want a prosthesis?" Britt frowned at the harness Teddy was adjusting across her shoulders. The straps were like wearing a second bra, and Britt's every instinct rebelled against it. She had well-defined trapezius muscles extending from her neck to shoulder. That's why she wore racerback sports bras, soft and with no straps that kept falling off her shoulder. She tugged at one of the prosthesis straps. "This is going to rub my armpit. And my stump is still sore."

"Your arm is a residual limb, not a stump." Teddy sat back, her face a picture of calm.

Britt pointed to her shortened limb, then to herself. "*We* call it a stump." She looked down at it. "Right, Shortie?"

Teddy shook her head but didn't address Britt's declaration. "The harness will feel strange at first, and you likely will experience some tenderness in some areas until your shoulders adjust." She picked up the prosthesis and gently slid it onto Britt's residual limb. "For a few weeks, you'll need to wear this so you can grow accustomed to the harness and the weight of the prosthesis. It isn't functional, but it's about the same weight as the bionic limb you'll be fitted with when your arm is sufficiently healed. You'll have other adjustments to get accustomed to when you get the functional arm."

"It's heavy. It feels like it's pulling my left shoulder down. Won't that hurt my back posture?"

"It's actually weighted comparable to your right arm. It only feels heavy because your muscles have already shifted to accommodate the imbalance caused by the weight of your right arm. If that's allowed to continue, amputees typically develop neck and spine problems."

"How long do I have to wear it today?" Britt didn't try to keep the irritation out of her voice. She'd gotten little sleep after a nightmare woke her, sweating and heart racing, at two a.m. Always the same nightmare. Afterward, she lay staring at the ceiling, waiting for the house to stir. Guilt, frustration, and finally anger built during those few long hours of ceiling-staring until she could barely tolerate her own presence, much less the company of others.

"I'd like you to wear it at least until lunch. We'll take a look at it then to see if it needs adjusting. We can try other styles of harness if you aren't able to tolerate this one."

"You didn't answer my question."

"What question?"

"What if I don't want to wear a prosthesis? What if I'm more comfortable with just my stump?"

"Residual limb, not stump." Teddy pointed to Britt's arm. "You mean other than the neck and spine problems I just mentioned?"

Of course, she did. She wasn't deaf. "Yes."

"The Department of Defense sees your injury as a chance to advance prosthetic technology. You have an additional surgery site on the inside of your residual limb because a doctor your father flew in for your amputation relocated nerves to just under the skin on the inside of your arm. Those nerves transfer the brain's signals for movement to the hand and, hopefully, the sensation of pressure, texture, and temperature from your hand back to your brain. When you're healed enough, you'll be fitted with a state-of-the-art bionic limb that operates nearly as well as a real hand." Teddy's soft, sure fingers that explored the fit of the prosthetic were cool on Britt's swollen skin.

Britt frowned at her. "They can give it to someone else. I don't want special treatment."

Teddy continued to check the fit of the harness. "My orders are to make sure you're in a position to take advantage of that opportunity when it's presented." She finally dropped her hands to her lap. "Whether you ultimately take the chance the army is offering isn't on the table today."

Britt gave a curt nod. "Are we done here?" Their session had begun with massage, then progressed to stretching and range-of-motion exercises. She was tired and agitated, her shoulder hurt, and the prosthesis felt like an albatross she had to wear for punishment.

"How's your pain?"

"Fine." Britt wasn't going to admit to hurting and ignored Teddy's challenging stare.

After a long moment, Teddy seemed to relent. "Okay. I can see that you're tired." She laid a small remote control on the table next to Britt. "Those patches I put on before the sock and prosthesis were wireless TENS electrodes that this remote controls. If you start to experience a spasm or phantom pain again, click it on, then press the up and down buttons to increase or decrease the stimulation."

"Thanks." Britt stood and stuffed the remote control into her pocket. "I've got work to do."

"Take a short nap. At least twenty minutes. Then we can head out for the barns. I'd like to tag along, so I can see what daily tasks you'll need to perform that normally require two hands."

"I'm only going downstairs to the office. It takes a lot of paperwork to run a farm this size."

Teddy gave her another long, studied look. God, Britt was beginning to hate when she did that. It was like she was trying to read her mind, and she didn't want Teddy in her head. "You also need rest to heal. It's been less than a month since your body went through a huge trauma and major surgery."

"I need to work right now." Britt felt like she was about to crawl out of her skin, and her chest was growing tight. She needed to get away before she exploded. She wheeled around but forced herself to walk down the stairs at a normal pace. She went into the farm office, which was adjacent to the living room, and closed the door behind her. Alone at last. She fought the impulse to lock the door, to shut out the world. Only a door couldn't shut out the demons that haunted her. But then maybe she didn't deserve to be free of them.

Chapter Four

Well, that didn't go so bad. Teddy couldn't fathom why Britt was opposed to a high-tech prosthesis, but she had worked diligently through the exercises that were clearly painful at times. Probably because she was anxious to get rid of Teddy. No. That wasn't it. Britt seemed to relish the pain, like she felt she deserved it. Teddy would have to deal with that issue at some point. Her job might be to rehab Britt's body, but she couldn't do that without trying to help heal her mind and spirit, too.

Truth was, Teddy liked Capt. Britt Story. She wasn't sure why.

Britt hadn't gone out of her way to be charming. And why should she? Teddy might be living in her home for a while, but their relationship was purely professional. And Teddy could see that she was struggling mightily to control her agitation. Still, it was hard to ignore those piercing blue eyes and sculpted face. Also, while she might be missing most of one arm, the rest of her body was easy to admire.

Teddy smiled to herself and then closed her laptop.

She couldn't do anything else on the project until some people answered her emails. She'd put out feelers for army surgeons interested in training for the special amputation surgery. That would be the first step to launch the project. Soldiers had been returning for service after amputation for years now, but those who returned to field duty were still exceptions. This innovation could change that trend, giving amputees almost the same choices as healthy soldiers.

The process would be a long one, and the linchpin would ultimately be proving that the talent they were able to retain could justify the dollar-outlay.

She stood and stretched. After lunch, she'd reviewed some stretching exercises with Britt before she disappeared again into the farm office. Now, Teddy was at loose ends. She could drive back to the city and trade the uniforms she'd brought for more casual clothes, but she'd ordered a different shoulder harness for Britt, which should arrive at the hospital soon. It didn't make sense to drive to Lexington today. She could swing by her apartment when she went to pick up the new harness. But she sure could use some fresh air and a walk now. It would give her the chance to see what type of activities went on around the farm. For that matter, Britt should get some air, too.

Teddy stopped, her hand suspended inches from the partially open door, mouth closing on the invitation to take a walk. The high-backed leather office chair was tilted to slightly recline. Britt's eyes were closed, her lips barely parted in sleep. Even so, tension filled the room like a bow strung tight. Britt's brow and the fingers of her right hand twitched at irregular intervals.

Teddy shook her head at the prosthesis lying on the desktop, shoved aside. Britt had worn it the entire morning but complained at lunch that it was rubbing several tender areas on her shoulders. Teddy had expected that reaction. She'd seen the small pink scars along Britt's neck, a few marring her left cheek, where debris from whatever took her arm had sprayed to nick and burn. Those injuries were minor and would likely fade away after a time. For now, they undoubtedly were sensitive, and Teddy could only imagine what scars the harness might be irritating under Britt's T-shirt.

She studied her patient. Despite those scars and the tension, Britt Story really was an attractive woman. But the personal space Britt wordlessly communicated was a wide moat around her. Would the angry Captain Story ever let her cross that moat and see the emotional injuries Britt had suffered? She backed quietly away from the door, silently pulling it closed. Britt needed rest as much as she needed exercise.

❖

Britt woke slowly, stretching her arms—correction, one arm and a stump—over her head. Pop's chair was just too comfortable, especially after her sleepless night. She glanced at the squat black column on the corner of the desk. She'd given it to Pop as a joke, but he'd embraced the Amazon device once he learned he could get Alexa to recite current betting lines, racing results, and sport scores, and also pipe in his favorite oldies tunes while he worked on the farm's finances.

"Alexa, what time is it?"

"It's three twenty p.m."

Good God, she'd been asleep for nearly two hours. She did feel better rested, but now she needed to get up and move. She hesitated when her gaze fell on the prosthetic arm resting atop the desk. No way was she putting that harness back on and dragging around the dead weight of that fake arm. No way.

The urgent call of nature finally got her up and out of the comfortable chair. After a visit to the facilities, she was drawn to the kitchen by the rich smell of coffee. Lynn was chopping vegetables.

"What's for dinner?" Britt poured herself a cup of the aromatic brew and hummed at her first taste. Lynn was a coffee connoisseur, always grinding her beans fresh.

"Chicken pot pie. You need to get some meat back on those bones, and I know you can't resist my pot pie."

Britt grinned, her mouth already watering at the vision of chicken and diced vegetables swimming in a savory sauce and encased in a golden-brown, buttery crust. "You're right about that." She propped her backside against the counter and gazed through the triple windows on the other side of the table. Four long, shed-row-style stables were positioned side by side, parallel to the house. "Pop still down at the barns?"

"Yep. Your friend's there, too."

Britt tensed at the reference. "Not my friend. My physical therapist."

"She seemed pretty friendly to me."

Lynn's tone made it clear she was just yanking Britt's chain, so she took a breath to rein in her defensive reaction. She was feeling good for the first time in weeks and refused to let her father and the US Army spoil her mood.

"She's here to check off a box for the army, nothing more," Britt said, keeping her tone mild and disinterested.

She was anything but disinterested, though. As much as she wanted to dislike Teddy, those green-gray eyes and quick, beautiful smile were mesmerizing. She'd been trying to ignore just how mesmerizing during the few therapy sessions they'd worked through so far.

Two women left the closest barn and walked down the drive to the paddock fence. Britt couldn't positively identify them because of the ball caps pulled low to shield their eyes from the sun, but it appeared to be the manager of the mare barns, Jill, and someone else. Britt cocked her head. The second woman's long blond hair was pulled through the back of her ball cap. Was that Teddy? Britt had only seen her hair held in a tight regulation bun that made it impossible to judge its length.

A gray horse inside the large paddock raised its head and watched the two women. Mysty?

She saw Jill flash the toothy smile that never failed to entice both male and female. Britt and Jill had been running buddies in high school. During that adolescent discovery period, Britt had realized she was decidedly lesbian, while Jill's sexuality remained solidly bisexual.

"Hey, get out of my kitchen," Lynn scolded her when Britt grabbed a couple of the carrots Lynn hadn't yet chopped and headed out the door.

Teddy—if it was Teddy—had her back to Britt's approach, but Jill looked up when Britt strode toward them from the porch.

"Well, aren't you a sight for sore eyes." Jill smiled, but it wasn't the same smile she'd given Teddy moments before. "I heard you were home in one piece." Her eyes dropped to Britt's empty sleeve.

"Well, mostly." She reached out and gave Britt's right arm a squeeze.

"I'd hug my old buddy, but I'm afraid I'll squeeze something that isn't healed yet."

Britt realized that she'd charged down the hill with the intent to...what? Rescue Teddy? Warn Jill off? Teddy wasn't in danger. Jill was a good person. Not to mention that Britt didn't have, didn't want to have any claim on Teddy. Giving herself a swift mental kick, she hugged her friend with one arm. "I'm all right...mostly," she said, echoing her friend's pattern of speech.

She was about to turn to Teddy when a loud whinny sounded, and Mysty pounded across the paddock to where they stood on the other side of the fence.

Jill laughed. "Here comes your girlfriend. How long has it been since you've seen her?" She answered her own question. "Years. That horse has a serious crush on you."

Britt held up the carrots. "I saw her the day I got here, and she's just after the carrots I have in my hand."

Jill laughed. "You always did know how to woo the women."

Britt's face heated when Teddy tilted her head and raised an eyebrow at her. Damn it. After all she'd been through, how could Jill transport her back to their high school dynamic—Britt was the quiet one to Jill's charmer—with one teasing, sarcastic comment.

"As long as they have four legs." Her quip sounded way more nonchalant than Britt felt about being outed to Teddy.

A worker called to Jill from the front of the stables, and she held up a finger to let him know she heard. "Duty calls." She flashed that smile at Teddy again, albeit a few kilowatts less, as though she read something in Britt's sudden appearance. "Nice to meet you, Teddy. I'm sure Britt can answer any other questions." She started to walk away, then turned back to Britt and spoke softly. "I'm so glad you're back here and safe again. When you're ready, make some time for us to catch up with each other."

"Okay. Sure." She'd do that at some point, but some things she wouldn't, couldn't share. Like the wound that still festered inside and resurfaced as nightmares way too often. Britt stared at the ground. She'd made it back, but others hadn't. Especially one soldier she had failed to keep safe. A sharp tug of her shirt nearly pulled her off her feet. Mysty, neck stretched over the board fence, held the top of Britt's sleeve firmly in her teeth as though she was trying to shake the carrots from Britt's hand.

Teddy laughed. "I believe your girlfriend is demanding the bouquet of carrots you brought her."

Britt pushed away the morose memories. She was home, not in the desert. And not in the army as soon as she could process out. She scanned the paddocks, house, and barns to ground herself. She was home.

Mysty tried a different tactic, brushing her big, horsey lips along Britt's cheek and into Britt's hair. She mock-scowled and waved the horse back. "Mind your manners, you shameless tramp."

Teddy's laugh was musical, her smile wide and her eyes warm under the shadow of her cap's bill. When Britt turned a playful scowl on her, she pulled her lips in, a weak pretense of holding in her laughter. She tilted her head to peer at Britt from under her cap, then slapped her hand over her mouth as she burst into uncontrolled laughter again.

"It's not that funny," Britt said, frowning.

But Teddy pointed at Britt's ear. "You've got…uh, you've got green slobber…" Teddy pointed to her own ear in demonstration of the location.

Britt shrugged her shoulder up to wipe at her ear.

Teddy shook her head. "You didn't get it. It's kind of behind your ear, too." She unsuccessfully searched her pockets for a tissue, then looked to Britt, who shook her head.

"I don't have anything either." She was suddenly conscious of the fact that she had only one hand, which at the moment was filled with carrots.

Teddy held out her hand for the carrots, and Britt gave them over, then pulled the sleeve of her Henley down over her hand and thoroughly wiped her ear dry. After that, she looked to Teddy for confirmation that she'd sufficiently cleaned it. Teddy grasped Britt's chin with her free hand and turned her head to inspect the offended ear. "I think you got it all."

Even though Teddy's hands had been all over Britt's shoulders, her good arm and her stump…uh, residual limb, the gentle clasp of her chin felt oddly intimate.

"Thank you," Britt said, her voice raspy from her suddenly tight throat. Their eyes met and held for a long second, until the loud thump of a hoof against wood brought their attention back to Britt's assailant.

"When did you become such a brat?" Britt fussed at the horse but reached to scratch Mysty's neck.

"Is she your horse?"

"No. But her mother was one of the mares under my care the year before I signed up with Uncle Sam. Mysty was shy and skittish as a baby, so I worked with her more than the others assigned to me. I guess she got attached."

"Her name is Mysty?"

"Out of the Myst, spelled with a y."

"Jill was explaining that the babies stay here only until they're a year old. Then you sell them, and someone else trains them to race."

"Yeah. This is strictly a breeding farm, not a racing stable." Britt took one of the carrots from Teddy. "I'll show you how to feed them to her without losing any fingers." She held out the long carrot for Mysty to bite off the end.

"I guess I don't know much about the horse-racing industry."

Britt shrugged. "Some of the more famous farms breed and race, but Pop decided years ago it was less of a gamble to simply breed and sell the yearlings. Other than your operating costs, you pay out stud fees and take in money paid for the yearlings you produce. The only real gamble is making sure the yearlings you sell are successful on the track." When Mysty finished chewing, Britt held out the remainder of the carrot on top of her flattened palm. "Offer the short end like this so she can take it from your hand without nipping your fingers.

Teddy scanned the neat stables, multiple workers moving about their tasks, and manicured stable yard. "Your yearlings must sell pretty well."

"Pop does his homework and has an instinct for mixing bloodlines. Amateurs think if you breed a champion to a champion, you'll get a champion. But it doesn't work that way. Some sires don't seem to be able to pass along winning genes to their offspring. Others, who might not be as well known, might have the ability to produce winning foals because they draw on genes passed to them from several generations back."

Mysty finished the first carrot and began searching them for the next. Teddy held one up and smiled when the mare bit off half.

"How do you know which horses will have winning babies?"

"Research. The racing association keeps meticulous records on every horse from the time they're born until they're retired from racing and breeding. They keep records on the family tree of every horse, so you can trace their bloodlines back as far as the early 1900s, sometimes further. So, when you look for a good sire or dam, you study the racing records of their progeny. Are they sprinters or distance racers? Do certain lines have a lot of leg problems? When you start looking at siblings, half-siblings, three-quarter siblings…it all gets very complicated."

Teddy flattened out her hand and placed the remainder of the carrot on top to offer it to Mysty. "Seems like there should be an app to sort it all out."

Britt chuckled. "Some software can run odds for you, but computers can't walk the barns and learn from grooms that a certain stud is passing along his cribbing habit, his weak pasterns, or a tendency to sulk. A successful breeder has a network of contacts and tracks the horses his stables produce to be on the lookout for weaknesses that don't necessarily show up in racing results."

"Sounds like a lot of work to me. Is that what you're helping your grandfather with?"

"Yep. It might sound boring, but I take after Pop. We love the hunt to find that gem in a jungle of bloodlines."

"What did you and E.B. mean when you were talking about Secretariat having a big heart? I've watched the Derby on television several times, and the announcers talked about a horse having heart. It sounded like they were referring to the will to win."

"That probably was what they were referring to," Britt said. "Secretariat, however, literally had an oversized heart organ. It's theorized that his larger heart pumped enormous amounts of blood to his legs and lungs and was a factor in his legendary performance. As a sire, he's known for passing that trait down through females of his line, who, in turn, have produced many winning colts."

"Wow. Do you have a degree in genetics?"

Britt chuckled and shook her head. "Business. I always figured I'd one day step up to run the farm for Pop. What I need to know about horse genetics, I learned from the master. No college professor could teach me more than Pop about that subject."

The last carrot eaten, Teddy wiped her hands on her jeans, then petted Mysty's long neck. "She's beautiful. No baby for her?"

"Her breeding didn't take the past couple of times. She had a foal two years ago but had a bad time with the birth. Pop's thinking she's not going to work out as a brood mare. Her legs wouldn't hold up on the hunter-jumper circuit. I'm not sure what we'll do with her."

Teddy's mouth dropped open. "You wouldn't sell her to the knacker, would you?" Her expression was incredulous and her tone accusing. Even so, Britt couldn't stop the laughter that bubbled up or let the opportunity pass to tweak Teddy's naive conclusion.

"Knacker? God, I haven't heard that word since I saw *Black Beauty* at the movies when I was a kid. The knacker came for animals already dead, and I think you're asking if I'd sell her to a slaughterhouse. Mysty would make a lot of dog food, but no. God, no." Britt wagged her finger at Teddy. "And you might go to hell for even thinking that while standing in the bluegrass state."

Teddy frowned, then stuck her tongue out at Britt. "Don't laugh at me. I'm just learning about all this."

"Oh. Okay. That's good to know."

A loud clanging drew their attention to the house, where Lynn stood on the porch, vigorously ringing an honest-to-God dinner bell. E.B. emerged from one of the barns and began walking toward the sound.

"Lynn doesn't wait for stragglers. She puts dinner on the table, then heads home to feed her own family." Britt motioned for Teddy to join her in heading that way. "Come on. Her chicken pot pie is fantastic."

"I love chicken pot pie!" Teddy's smile was brilliant, and Britt shoved her hand into her jeans pocket to quell the overwhelming impulse to take Teddy's hand in hers as they responded to Lynn's summons together.

CHAPTER FIVE

*S*he looked up at the quick raps on the door frame. Shannon stood in the doorway of her office.

"Hey, babe. Thought I'd drop in to say good-bye."

Teddy stood and rounded her desk, flinging herself at her wife. "No. I don't want you to go. Stay here. Stay with me."

Shannon's arms were strong, hugging her close, then pushing her away. "You know I have to go. Orders are orders. It'll be okay."

"No, no, it won't." Teddy reached for her again, grabbing at Shannon's desert camos to hold her there, but it was like grabbing at air.

Shannon was smiling, backing away, waving. "Gotta go. You'll be okay."

Knocking sounded again. Not Shannon's jaunty knock, but an ominous rap-rap, long pause, rap-rap.

She was standing in her living room, their living room. Rap-rap, long pause.

Two uniformed men were visible through the double windows. Rap-rap, long pause.

No, no, no. Rap-rap, long pause.

Maybe they'd leave if she didn't go to the door. Rap-rap, long pause.

She couldn't stop her feet from carrying her across the room. Rap-rap, long pause.

Don't open the door, don't open the door. Go away. The words she wanted to scream were stuck in her throat. Her hand reached for the doorknob. Don't open the door. Don't open the door.

The door swung open, and the uniformed men stared at her.
The older man's mouth was moving. "We're sorry to inform you..."
She looked past them, where sunlight spilled across the yard,
their yard. Shannon was there, waving and backing away toward the
street. "Gotta go, babe. You'll be okay."
No, no, NO!

Teddy jerked upright in the bed, her pulse hammering, her face wet with tears. She sucked in a breath. She put her hand to her chest, willing her heart to slow. Movement in the semi-dark caught her attention, and she realized she wasn't alone. Moonlight silhouetted a figure in the doorway. Shannon?

"Are you okay?" Britt spoke low and soft.

"I didn't wake you, did I?" Teddy's heart slowed, then sank a bit as her confusion evaporated and Shannon was gone. Gone forever.

Britt's eyes were dark in the half-light. "I wasn't sleeping."

Teddy wished she hadn't been. Then she wouldn't have fallen into the same horrible dream.

Britt repeated her question. "Are you okay?"

"Yes." Teddy used the bedsheet to dry her face. "No." She sucked in a deep breath and blew it out slowly to stop the sob that wanted to surface. Another breath. "But I will be. I'll be okay."

Britt stood in the doorway another long second, then silently pulled the door closed, leaving Teddy alone with her ghosts.

Breakfast was a quiet, tense affair. At first, Teddy made an effort to be pleasant, but she lapsed into silence and made a show of eating once Pop served up the food. She looked tired. No, she looked haggard, and she wouldn't meet Britt's eyes. Was she afraid Britt would tell someone about her nightmare? Or was she just embarrassed?

Britt looked up from her eggs and realized Pop was eyeing Teddy. She could see the questions in his eyes. When he opened his mouth to speak, Britt was consumed with an overwhelming urge to protect Teddy's privacy.

"Word is that a Tapit filly might be coming off the track and up for auction at Keeneland in a few weeks. You know that line has good legs." Horse talk could always distract Pop.

"What's in her dam's bloodline?" Pop asked, his attention immediately diverted from Teddy.

"Hits all the speed marks—traces back to Terlinqua."

"Is that good?" Teddy asked, drawing out of her funk. "I mean, I don't know a lot about horse racing, but I've been to plenty of Derby parties. It's sort of like going to a Super Bowl party for the fun and not because you care about who wins. Still, I don't recognize any of those names."

Britt felt pleased, though she couldn't imagine why, that Teddy seemed genuinely interested. "Her sire, Tapit, had a modest racing career, but made his name by passing down great genes from farther up his line—Seattle Slew and War Admiral and, ultimately, Man O'War, who was known for his racing record and for passing along his gene for strong legs."

Teddy smiled, and the dullness in her eyes seemed to fall away like scales. "I've heard of them...well, Seattle Slew and Man O'War."

Britt found herself smiling back. "On her dam's side, Terlinqua was directly descended from Secretariat and recognized as one of the most successful brood mares ever. She was great-great-grandam of the 2015 Triple Crown winner American Pharoah."

"I saw American Pharoah win the Kentucky Derby. Wow. What would a mare with those bloodlines cost? Or is that impolite to ask."

Pop shook his head. "Not impolite, but maybe too much. What's her race record?"

"Not that great. Her trainer was Russ Bailey, so it's no shock that she's gate shy," Britt said. "Won her first race, but she was disqualified for her second race because they couldn't get her in the gate. Bailey tried a third race, but she injured her leg jumping around once they got her in the gate."

"That son of a bitch. What idiot owner gave him that horse to train?"

Britt shrugged. "It won't hurt to at least go and see if we can bid on her. Maybe she hasn't drawn much attention since she hasn't done well on the track, and maybe the idiot who put her with that trainer will sell her cheap."

She waited, aware that Teddy's gaze was bouncing between the two of them, while Pop spread jam on his toast and mulled over the information. Finally, he nodded. "You up to it? If I show up and bid on her, it might draw too much attention and up the price. You haven't been around for a while, so maybe you won't get noticed."

"Sure. I'm up to it. I'll keep an eye out to see if my source was right and her name turns up on the auction registry."

Teddy gently worked the scar at the end of Britt's residual limb, lightly tapping and rubbing to desensitize the scar as she massaged the truncated bicep. "Your surgeon did an exceptional job on your arm. It's healing really well."

She almost swallowed the words as soon as she said them. Every time she mentioned the surgeon that Britt's father had flown in to perform her amputation, Britt slipped into a dark mood. Teddy wasn't sure if receiving special treatment not available to other wounded soldiers made her angry, or if it was the fact that her father had made decisions for her while she was too drugged up to protest.

She was surprised when Britt, lying on the portable treatment table Teddy had set up, simply hummed a faint acknowledgement. The scar massage had to be uncomfortable. Some patients sweated through it. Was she in a meditative zone, or was she just that happy about finding the horse they'd talked about at breakfast?

Teddy studied her patient. Britt's eyes were closed, but her face appeared so relaxed in the sunlight that cast a soft glow across the table. She wouldn't call Britt pretty. Girls were pretty. Britt was... more. She was mature, her visage noble. Teddy could easily picture her as an Amazon warrior with a bow and quiver slung across her back or a Celtic shield maiden dressed in silver mail and armed with a long sword or...

Britt opened her eyes and stared at Teddy as if she'd heard her thoughts. Her pupils contracted in the sunlight, leaving her eyes impossibly, brilliantly blue. Teddy was transfixed, snared by those azure pools. Holy Mother, Britt was beautiful.

"Do you want to go with me?"

Teddy blinked. "Go with?" She sounded like an echo chamber.

"Me. Go with me. To the auction at Keeneland. If that mare shows up on the roster."

Teddy peeled her eyes away from Britt's. "That sounds like fun." Too much time in the sun can burn. Too much gazing into those eyes was already melting her insides. She helped Britt sit up and fussed with replacing the compression sock on Britt's arm. "I mean, the more I can learn about what you do, the better we can tailor your functional prosthesis to meet your needs." She looked up when Britt didn't respond. They stared at each other for a long minute before Teddy forced herself to again look away, anywhere but into those eyes that bored into her soul. "Take off your T-shirt."

Britt's eyebrows rose. "I'm sorry. What?"

Teddy cleared her throat and tried for a less hoarse, more professional tone. "You need to wear the prosthesis for at least four hours today. But before I help you put it on, I need to check your shoulders and chest to see where it chafed you yesterday."

"First you want to see my stump, and now you want to check out my chest?"

"Residual limb. Not stump. I can make adjustments in the harness that might help the chafing." Despite her best efforts to remain professional, she felt her neck, ears, and cheeks heating. Wait. Was Britt teasing her? Was she...flirting? Teddy mock-scowled. "Or I can make adjustments that will chafe places you wouldn't want rubbed raw."

Britt chuckled. "You blush so easily, I couldn't resist." She pulled her T-shirt over her head, revealing a white sports bra that did little to hide her erect nipples.

Teddy's mouth went dry. She circled the table under the pretense of examining Britt's back, the muscles flexing as Britt looked over her shoulder at Teddy. "Seems fine except for where this strap goes under your other arm. I've ordered a different harness that I think you'll find better suited to your physique. I'll go pick it up when my boss lets me know it arrived. Until then, you still need to wear the old one. I can add some foam padding to that pressure point in the meantime." She circled back around the table, making a show of examining other potential pressure points without staring at Britt's nipples.

Britt sighed. Her eyes were darker since she'd turned her back to the sunlight, but still beautiful. "If I must."

Teddy nodded once in a curt affirmative. "You must." She held up Britt's T-shirt but let her pull it on by herself. Small tasks like that were all exercises that stretched the residual limb muscles and kept them from shortening and limiting the range of motion. She watched and coached a little as Britt obligingly added the harness over the T-shirt, fitted the prosthetic arm onto her residual limb, and hooked it to the harness. "What's on your agenda today?"

"I'm going down to the stables to check on a few things."

"Excellent. I'll tag along."

"You can go down there any time you like. You don't have to wait for me to give you a tour."

Teddy frowned. How many times would she have to explain this? "I'm an occupational therapist as well as a physical therapist. I'm here, rather than you coming to my office, so I can observe and figure out how you can complete your usual tasks with one hand that previously required two. You might need a modified tool in addition to simply rethinking the way you do something."

Britt stared at the floor. Teddy felt Britt, like most amputee victims, was struggling with her pride more than her injury. But she couldn't let Britt lose her internal battle.

"And maybe I could talk you into giving me a riding lesson?"

Though Britt didn't look up, Teddy could still see the small smile. Good. She felt like she was walking a tightrope with Britt, like any small thing she might suggest could tip the scales between them from friendship to instant rejection.

"I reckon I can do that."

Teddy had no doubt that Britt saw through the ruse to push her out of the office and back onto a horse and was grateful that Britt seemed at last ready to take that step under the guise of giving her a riding lesson.

"I know just the horse for you. Pop's got an older mare from the Whirlaway line." Britt pulled a long-sleeved cotton shirt over the T-shirt and harness but didn't button it.

"Whirlaway? That doesn't sound good. The name's not descriptive of how the horse behaves, is it?" Teddy followed when Britt stood and headed for the door without answering. "You know that if you damage me, they'll just send someone else out."

Britt looked back over her shoulder as she started down the stairs. "Really?"

"Somebody not as good as I am."

Britt laughed.

"In fact," Teddy said. "It probably would be Bruiser. Big guy... not very smart."

Britt stopped at the bottom of the stairs and cocked her head as if considering this threat. She tossed Teddy a quick smile and a shrug. "I'll have to keep that in mind."

Teddy pointed at the screen on the portable ultrasound. "I see it. Right there." She turned to the veterinarian, Gail Dodge, who was manipulating the instrument.

"Yep. Everything appears good," Gail said. "Looks like Story Hill Farm will have quite a crop of babies come spring." She extracted the vaginal probe from the mare and wiped her down before Britt led the mare back to her stall.

"I've got questions if you get a chance." Gail kept an eye on Britt's location while she whispered her request.

Teddy gave a quick nod but didn't answer because Britt was on her way back to them.

"You staying around?" Gail asked Britt as she neared them. "The old man could use some help these days." She raised her voice to make sure E.B., who was muttering as he came in behind them, heard her. "He's getting senile, you know."

"Watch who you're calling senile," E.B. growled. "You're no spring chicken yourself. When are you going to retire and let that boy of yours run things?"

"I'm ten years younger than you, and when I quit working, my idiot husband has got it in his head that we're going to buy one of those big RV buses and tour the country. Until he gets a clue, I'll keep working. I've spent my whole career driving from farm to farm. If Wade wants me to retire and go somewhere with him, he'd better buy me a plane ticket and book a fancy hotel room."

It was obvious to Teddy that the barbs were good-natured, but she looked to Britt for an explanation.

"Gail is Pop's cousin," Britt said. "They've been picking at each other since they were kids."

"How would a young whippersnapper like you know that? Your daddy wasn't even a gleam in E.B.'s eye when we were kids."

"Grandma used to tell me and anyone who'd listen about you two."

Gail's smile was soft. "Grace would know." Her eyes followed E.B. as he ducked into the tack room. "Her favorite story was about my daddy telling our teacher that if she wanted E.B. and me to quit picking on each other and pay attention, all she had to do was sit on a horse while she taught class."

E.B. emerged from the tack room with a halter in his hand that he shook at Gail. "Don't be running off my help, Gail. I just got her to come home." He pointed to Britt. "I need you for a minute." When Britt hesitated, he clarified. "I want your opinion on something."

"I'll help Dr. Dodge get this stuff in her truck, then come find you," Teddy said when Britt looked to see if she was going to follow.

Britt spared one last glance at Gail. "I'm home for good if I can get the army to agree to it." She turned and followed E.B.

Gail stared after her, then turned to Teddy. "Is she okay?"

Teddy considered the question. "Physically, she's recovering fine."

Gail nodded. "E.B. says missing that arm isn't her worst hurt. Something else is going on. That girl has always worshipped her father, Brock, but E.B. says there's some really bad blood between them now, and neither of them will talk about it."

Teddy rubbed the back of her neck. Colonel Winstead had the same suspicion. "I don't know anything about that. I haven't met Senator Story, and even if Britt had confided in me, I couldn't ethically tell you or her grandfather."

"I understand." Gail packed up the ultrasound machine and handed Teddy a stainless-steel bucket of soapy water she'd used to wash her hands and instruments. "Empty that in the wash stall, will you?" She began to fill the arm-length plastic glove she'd worn for the examination with the detritus of her work, then tossed it into the empty bucket, along with some small instruments. Gail could have easily carried both the ultrasound and the bucket, but she handed the bucket to Teddy, who obediently followed her to the veterinary truck.

"I know we can't expect her to be the same after all she must have seen over there in Afghanistan, but she brought back a heavy burden on her shoulders. Those of us who know her can see it. All we're asking is that you let us know if we need to watch out for her after the damn army's done with her."

Teddy caught herself nodding agreement before she'd even thought through the possibilities. "I'm part of that army, and I promise I won't be going anywhere until I'm sure she's not bleeding anywhere—physically or emotionally."

Gail gave her shoulder a squeeze. "Good enough. If she and Brock don't patch things up between them, she's got me and E.B. to watch over her." She stored her instruments away, closed the back of her large SUV, then gave Teddy a long look. "We just need to know what to watch for."

CHAPTER SIX

B ritt studied the yearling her grandfather pointed out. Although the young horses wouldn't begin their race training until they were sold, they needed a lot of general training before they went to the yearling auction.

The youngsters learned how to lead properly in a halter, walk in a line with other horses, submit to baths and daily grooming, and remain calm no matter how much activity was going on around them.

Walking in an automatic walker for twenty minutes daily and swimming in a long, trough-like pool conditioned them. Swimming, rather than running, built muscle without stressing their still-developing bones. The fillies, whose hormones were geared to plump them up in preparation for bearing foals, got extra time in the pool to keep them trim.

This colt, however, was E.B.'s top prospect for the yearling sale. He had impeccable bloodlines and a long stride, but an unpredictable temperament.

"What do you think?" E.B. asked.

"I don't know why you're asking me, Pop. You taught me everything I know about horses. Is this a test to see if I remember?"

"Of course not." E.B. rubbed the light stubble on his chin. "You do this long enough, and you forget some things. I'm just asking you to look into this with fresh eyes and second-guess an old man."

"You're not just trying to give the gimp something to get her back in the game?"

"No, but maybe you do need this to get back in the saddle." Pop cupped her chin and turned her face to his. "You came back with one less arm than you had before you went to that God-forsaken desert, but you also came back with a lot more than some other soldiers did. If you're looking to be coddled, you can go stay with your mother in Louisville. I hope you won't do that because I want you here." He released her chin but clasped her hand in his callused ones. "This farm is your birthright. Since the day you climbed up on your first pony, there was never any doubt Story Hill Farm would be yours when you were ready to run it. I'm telling you I need help with this colt. And you're going to have to promise you'll tell me if you need my help…with anything."

"Okay, Pop." She looked down and sighed dramatically for his benefit. God, she loved her grandfather. "Just don't make me stay with Mom. She's worse than putting up with the babysitter the army sent here."

He tilted his head, a slow smile sliding into place. "I'm getting kind of fond of that army filly. She's got class and spirit. If you aren't interested, maybe I'll take a run at her."

She gave him a playful slap on the arm. "As if. She'd be too much for your old ticker. And she's here so the army can make sure I'm not a thread they left hanging, nothing else."

They both turned to see Teddy approaching, hips swinging as she navigated a downhill slope, her blond hair swirling in a sudden breeze.

"She'll be gone in another few weeks." Strangely, Britt felt a twinge of remorse at the thought.

Teddy seemed to hesitate, then continued toward them when Britt waved her closer. Before Britt could analyze her reaction to Teddy's inevitable departure, Pop squeezed her shoulder to regain her attention.

"I'm serious, Britt. Don't turn down what you need to get well because of whatever's going on between you and Brock and the army."

She frowned. "He didn't tell you?"

"Nope. I figure you will when you're ready. Until then, it's not my business. But you, my granddaughter, are my business." His gaze held hers. "And if I have to take sides between you and my son, I will. I'll always have your back."

❖

Teddy slowed because it appeared that Britt and E.B. were having a serious discussion. When they glanced her way, Britt waved her toward them.

E.B. clasped Britt's shoulder, and then they turned their attention to the tall, sleek colt sprinting the length of the long paddock and back as though for the sheer joy of running. It wouldn't have surprised her if he just jumped the fence at the other end and kept going.

"I'll talk to his groom and see if I can come up with some ideas to tweak his schedule or training and calm him down," Britt said as Teddy joined them.

"Which one is that?" Teddy asked, pointing to the colt.

E.B. slung an arm over her shoulders. "That, my dear, is this year's money horse."

"Money horse?"

"He means this colt is expected to bring a top price at the Keeneland auction next month," Britt said.

"So, you're never tempted to keep and race one yourself?"

"I won't say never." He withdrew his arm and propped his elbows on the fence to watch the yearling. "A colt like this one would make any man think hard about it."

"How many are ready for Keeneland?" Britt asked.

"We've got a good crop this year—fifteen colts and twelve fillies. We have a record of four with the potential to bring seven figures at the auction," he said.

"Really?" Britt looked surprised.

Teddy was still counting in her head. "Seven figures? That's… that's…"

"At least a million dollars." E.B. smiled as he supplied the number still reeling in Teddy's brain. He nodded toward the colt in the paddock.

"Wow...just wow." Teddy had no idea. Story Hill Farm was large and obviously well-funded, but not ostentatious. "What's his name?"

"Most are named by whoever buys them at the yearling auction because they have to pay the fee to register them with the Jockey Club. But the breeder can pick the name if he's willing to pay the registration fee." E.B. nodded toward the colt. "I did for this one. His sire was War Front, so I named him Home from War. I prayed for that every night after she..." His eyes reflected every worry-filled night and every hopeful prayer uttered as he looked to Britt. "...shipped out to Afghanistan."

"Aww." Teddy tried to keep it light, even though her throat tightened at the sentiment. She bumped her shoulder against Britt's. "That's sweet."

Britt ducked her head, her cheeks flushed. "That colt bringing home the big money will be what's sweet," she said. "I've never known you to pay a quarter-million-dollar stud fee before. Not ever. Not even for a stud like War Front."

"Do you know the top price paid at last year's sale?" E.B. asked.

"Of course, I do." Britt propped her elbows on the fence. "I might have been in another country, but we had internet at the base."

"I don't." Teddy joined them at the fence. "How much?"

"Eight-point-two million dollars," E.B. said. "For a filly."

"Wow." She seemed to be saying that a lot around these two. "Wait. Are you insinuating a girl horse has less value than a boy horse?"

"She does." Britt answered for her grandfather. "It's simple math. A top mare can produce one offspring a year, most selling for way less than that filly. A stallion with a hundred-thousand-dollar stud fee can bring in a guaranteed ten million a year, or more."

"Okay. I'll give you that. As long as you remember there would be no boy horses without horse mommies."

"Horse mommies?" Britt gave Teddy a shoulder bump and look of mock indignation. "There are mares or dams, but no horse mommies in Thoroughbred racing."

Teddy was surprised by Britt's playful banter and bumped her back. "I can call them what I want."

Jill waved at them from the neighboring barn and headed their way. "How's Homey doing?" she asked. "No problems, I hope."

"No real problem," E.B. said, not commenting on Jill's nickname for Home from War. "But he's moody, which isn't a good thing if he wakes up in a bad mood on race day. And you know it doesn't take much for word to get around about something like that. It could bring his price down. Britt's going to look into it, though."

"Great. You'll sort him out," Jill said to Britt. "You got a minute to talk about mares with me? E.B. said you were looking to pick up a couple at Keeneland."

E.B. pushed off the fence he'd propped himself against. "I've got some phone calls to make, now that I've got you out of my office," he said to Britt.

Britt hesitated. "I sort of promised to give Teddy a riding lesson."

"Not a problem. We can saddle Mysty and maybe Turn Away while we talk." Jill looked at Teddy. "Do you mind?"

"No, not at all," Teddy said. The longer she could keep Britt out and active, the better.

"Great." Jill's wide smile made Teddy shift a little uncomfortably. She was enjoying Britt's good mood, and the last thing she wanted was Britt thinking that she was interested in Jill. Wait. Why should that matter? She wasn't interested, but…it was unprofessional. That's why. She was here to do a job, not pick up women.

CHAPTER SEVEN

The afternoon was warm but filled with the wonderful scent of fresh-cut grass and spruce from the surrounding hills. The unseasonably mild day reminded Teddy that autumn would come soon.

"You look pretty comfortable in the saddle," Britt said. "I thought you didn't know how to ride."

"I've never ridden in an English saddle. It feels a bit like being bareback because there's nothing to hold onto." Her chest, and legs, tightened as her brain reviewed the precariousness of her perch and her horse shifted into a slow jog, but Teddy could feel Turn Away's powerful muscles gathering for more. "Whoa. Don't run, don't run." She hunched over and grabbed a handful of mane.

"Relax your legs. She's responding to leg pressure." Britt was calm.

Teddy was not.

"Sit back in the saddle. You're giving her all the wrong signals by hunching over her neck. Sit back. You won't fall off. Trust that you have good balance. That's right. Use your stirrups to balance your weight."

Turn Away returned to a leisurely walk, and Teddy let out a long breath. "That was close." Her heart was still pounding.

"You were always fine, although I'd rather not have had to rescue you from a full run. These ladies can go very fast."

"Thanks for reminding me. My heart was almost beginning to slow."

Britt chuckled.

"I don't know why I'm nervous. I started my military career as an enlisted medic, and I've been with patrols that were hit with enemy fire. I didn't panic then. I don't know why falling a few feet off a horse throws me into a panic."

"Because you were trained and instinctively knew what to do on patrol. We'll schedule a few sessions in the large round pen to help you get comfortable with posting a trot and build your confidence." Britt seemed to hesitate and then shrugged. "You can always come back occasionally after you and I are done with my rehab. In case, you know...if you want a lesson or just to take a ride."

"I'd really like that, Britt." Teddy was unreasonably thrilled but mentally slapped herself at the unintended low, warm tenor of her voice. She tried for a lighter, friendlier tone. "I'd always call first, to make sure it was convenient for you."

Britt cleared her throat and looked toward the mountains in a gesture of nonchalance, but Teddy didn't miss her nervous fingering of the reins in her hands. "If I'm not around, Jill would be happy to take you out for a ride or give you a lesson."

"Jill's nice, but I'd prefer to stick to just one instructor." Oh my God. Had she just said that? "Uh, you know, so I don't get conflicting advice." She stumbled around for something else to pry her foot from her mouth. "I mean, I know you better. You've already seen me panic like a dork."

"Good." Britt smiled and met Teddy's gaze for a moment. Damn, she was gorgeous in the sunlight, the wind feathering her short, dark hair and blue eyes like pieces of the cloudless sky. *Patient. This is a patient.*

Sure, it was hard not to get close to your clients, especially the amputee patients who had lost so much. The moments when you touched them, removed bandages to reveal their ugliest wounds, and massaged their deepest scars were intimate, even if it was a nonsexual intimacy. But once patients graduated past their therapy, they usually wanted to move on with their lives. She knew Britt might change her mind on the offer, but the invitation unexpectedly fueled something hopeful in her. Hopeful for what?

Keeping to a slow walk, they turned down one lane after another dividing the large paddocks and even larger pastures that ringed the series of paddocks. The stroll would have been relaxing if Teddy's mind hadn't been working so hard to get back to business, instead of rolling like a horse in heather at the romantic setting and the attraction crackling between them. *Patient. She's a patient.*

The horse discussion when they joined Jill in the mare's stable had been brief. Jill felt one of the older mares should be retired from breeding but was a great mother. She wanted to keep the mare on the farm to be available as a surrogate when a baby's real mother rejected or neglected it. Like people, not all females were great moms. Also, Jill wanted Britt to know that she disagreed with E.B. about not trying to breed Mysty again. Her bloodlines were just too good to pass up another attempt.

Then they were saddling horses for their ride, which gave Teddy a chance to see what challenges Britt would have around the barns. Story Hill Farm had plenty of hired help who could do everything for her, but Teddy instinctively knew that wouldn't sit well with Britt. Her military file had noted that Britt was a hands-on leader and pulled her weight rather than just ordering people around. Teddy wasn't here to change Britt's natural tendencies, but to adapt Britt's environment to her new, different capabilities.

The English saddles were manageable with one hand, since the girth was a buckle, rather than a tie-off like a western saddle. Also, Mysty was well trained to lower her head for the bridle and accept the bit when it bumped against her teeth. But not all horses would be that easy. Teddy had already noticed that all the grooms used both hands on the lead ropes when walking the yearlings around.

Teddy had anticipated her lesson would be in one of the paddocks or one of the round corrals in the training area. But Britt had boosted her into the saddle and—after a brief hesitation to figure how to adjust to a one-handed mounting technique—launched gracefully onto Mysty and settled those long legs around...*Stop it! This is a patient.*

"This is starting to feel relaxing, as long as we just walk," Teddy said. That sounded lame but drew another smile from Britt, one of those smiles that made Teddy's insides flutter.

"Once we get you comfortable with a trot, you're going to want to canter, which is a much easier gait to sit, then run."

"Oh, I doubt I'll ever want to run." A racehorse galloping full out while she clung to its back was right near the top of her too-scary list. Right next to giving rein to her insane attraction to Britt, a high-profile patient with a need-to-know-only backstory. And Teddy wasn't included in that need-to-know circle. What she *needed* was to do her job and move on.

Teddy glanced over at Britt's profile. Damn those eyes and the sexy way she sat a horse.

❖

"Saw you two were out riding today. Pretty day for it," Lynn said as she put a bowl of baby butterbeans in the middle of the table. She wasn't normally there for dinner, but her niece was putting in some extra time at work, so Lynn had brought her great-niece and great-nephew with her for the day. The situation apparently wasn't uncommon, because when she and Teddy headed for the house at the sound of the dinner bell, E.B. came from one of the lower barns with a young girl on his shoulders and a boy hopping and trotting alongside him.

"It *was* beautiful," Teddy said. "I had a great time. Britt's a very good teacher."

"I want to ride a horse," Cameron, the five-year-old, declared, around a spoonful of mashed potatoes.

"You're too little," her brother, seven-year-old Ethan, said.

"You wait until everybody's seated and we say grace, Miss Cameron, before you start eating." Lynn waved a large spoon in empty threat before adding it to the bowl of butterbeans. Cameron put her spoon back on her plate but shot a look at Britt, who'd just taken a big bite of biscuit.

Britt sat at the end of the table opposite her grandfather, and Teddy settled on her right, across from Lynn because the two children had already claimed the seats flanking E.B. Britt put her biscuit down and shifted uncomfortably under the girl's scrutiny.

Children made her nervous because they had no filter when they asked questions...or stared at strangers.

"Who's going to bless the food?" E.B. asked.

The children both shrank in their seats, suddenly shy with the addition of two adults they didn't know.

"I'll do it," Teddy said, smiling at the children, who immediately each slid their hand into E.B.'s.

Cameron held out her hand to Teddy as Ethan took Lynn's in his other hand. He stared at Britt.

"You have to hold hands for the blessing," Ethan said.

Teddy held out her hand for Britt's. Hell, it wasn't like Teddy hadn't already massaged her shoulders and arm, practically carried her inside the first day she arrived. Somehow, though, holding hands seemed different, more intimate. Britt laid her open hand on the tabletop, and Teddy's warm fingers wrapped around hers while Lynn laid her hand on Britt's left shoulder. Teddy's eyes—more green than gray now—held hers. Then long blond lashes lowered over those eyes, and Teddy bowed her head.

"We are thankful for the plants and animals that have provided this meal for us, and for Lynn, who prepared it, and for the people gathered at this table to share it with us. We hope for the safety of the men and women who work to keep *us* safe, both at home and overseas. And, above all, we are reminded to be kind to everyone every day. Amen."

"Amen," the children chorused before diving into their plates.

Teddy looked up at Britt and smiled, then slowly slid her hand away. Britt realized she was smiling back at Teddy and cleared her throat. "That was nice."

"Thank you," Teddy said, her voice as soft as Britt's. It was a small moment, but it was theirs. The others were already passing bowls, teasing Cameron while she made a convincing case for why she should ride a horse.

"Doesn't matter," Ethan insisted. "You're too little for one. It might stomp on you, or you might break your head if you fell off." He thumped his own head with his fork in demonstration.

"I wouldn't fall off," Cameron insisted. "You'd fall off because you can't sit still."

"Can too."

"That's not what Mama said. Is it, Aunt Lynn?"

"I'm not getting in the middle of this," Lynn said. "Eat your dinner, or you don't get dessert."

Their eyes grew wide. "What's for dessert?"

"Cupcakes."

"Wow! Cupcakes!"

"Eat your dinner first."

They tucked into their meals, and the table was quiet for a bit, until Teddy's cell phone chirped. The children stopped eating when Teddy pulled her phone from her pocket and laid it on the table to read a text she'd just received.

"Time-out." Cameron pointed at Teddy.

"You have to go to time-out," Ethan confirmed solemnly. "And no dessert for you."

They looked to Lynn, waiting for her to confirm the sentence.

Britt coughed to cover her laugh at the deer-in-the-headlights look on Teddy's face.

"Uh, Teddy, honey," E.B. said quietly. "We have a house rule against having cell phones at the table."

"Phones at the table has 'quences," Cameron said, nodding.

E.B. clearly was struggling to look firm. "That's right. There are consequences for breaking the rules." He held up a finger. "However, Miss Teddy didn't know the rule and has a very important job though...like a doctor...and might be getting a message about an emergency."

"Like Miss Gail," Cameron said.

"'Cept her 'mergencies are about horses, not people."

"Are your 'mergencies about people?" Cameron asked, looking at Teddy.

Teddy nodded. "Sometimes." She tucked her phone into her back pocket again. "But not this time. So, I'm just going to put my phone away. I don't want to miss cupcakes."

Britt's chuckle was cut short by a kick to her shin. Okay, maybe more of a nudge than a kick, but Britt tossed her roll at Teddy in answer.

"No dessert for you," the children crowed with delight.

This time, Lynn backed up their prediction. "None for either of you. Eat your dinner, and quit picking at each other."

Ethan began to recite an admonishment they'd apparently endured themselves many times. "'Cause she did'unt slave all af'ernoon over a hot stove for you to play with your food."

❖

Britt clicked on the electric tea kettle to heat and stepped into the pantry in search of the remaining cupcakes they'd missed at dinner. The kids were cute, except when their rules deprived her of cupcakes—especially these. Lynn had briefly entertained the idea of opening a bakery, then discarded it as too much work when she was supposed to be retired. And cupcakes were her specialty. Ah. Found them. And she nearly wore them when Teddy stepped into the dark pantry and collided with her. Instead, she dropped the cupcake container that was precariously balanced on the palm of her one hand.

"Oh my God. What are you doing here in the dark?" Teddy grabbed onto Britt's upper arms to catch herself as she stumbled into Britt's chest.

"What are you doing down here?" Britt's heart pounded with an instant flight-or-fight instinct. This was not Afghanistan. Teddy wasn't the enemy.

"I thought I heard a noise." Teddy stepped back and released Britt's arms. "That's why I came downstairs."

Britt's heart slowed to normal, and her brain rebooted. She narrowed her eyes in the semi-darkness. "No, you didn't. You came down to swipe a cupcake."

Teddy pointed a finger at Britt. "Says the woman caught with her hand in the proverbial cupcake box."

The cupcakes. They both looked down at the upended container and squatted at the same time to retrieve it, nearly bumping heads. Their very close proximity, the pale gray of Teddy's eyes, and the faint scent of Teddy's minty breath had Britt teetering on her haunches. She grasped Teddy's shoulder with her right hand and instinctively reached to grab a nearby shelf to regain her balance with the hand that was no longer there.

"Careful." Teddy's alarmed warning was loud in the confined space of the pantry. "You'll bruise your stump."

"Shush." Britt felt like the kid she used to be, sneaking into the pantry with her cousin to swipe snacks after her grandparents and parents went to bed. "You'll wake Pop, and he'll send us both back to bed without cupcakes."

Teddy giggled. Actually giggled. "You realize we're both adults and can eat what we want, right?" Nonetheless, she lowered her voice back to a whisper.

Britt stared at Teddy. Damn, she was cute. "You said stump."

Teddy looked confused. "What? No, I didn't." But the note of uncertainty weakened her denial.

"Yes, you did." Britt grinned, no longer whispering. The moonlight filtering in from the kitchen was too dim to see the blush she imagined coloring Teddy's cheeks, but she spotted other tells of embarrassment—Teddy averting her eyes, then ducking her head while she made a show of picking up the dropped cupcake container. Thankfully, it hadn't popped open.

Britt stood and offered her hand to pull Teddy to her feet. Teddy rose easily, needing Britt's hand only for balance. Or was it more? Neither let go after Teddy stood. Britt's heart began to pound again. Teddy looked up at her, eyes uncertain, face close. The tea kettle beeped that it was ready, and Britt released Teddy's hand. "Water's hot. I was going to have some herbal tea," she said.

Teddy hesitated, then stepped back, handing the cupcake box to Britt. "Can we go out on the porch? If you take these, I'll get tea for both of us."

Britt nodded. She knew she should take her cupcake and tea to her room. But, for the first time since she woke up in the hospital without her left arm, she desired the company of another person. Actually, she wanted time with *this* person.

She pulled a small table over between two straight-backed rockers and set the cupcakes on it. Teddy was already pushing through the screen door, careful to close it quietly, and added two steaming mugs to their late-night dessert. Britt smiled when Teddy hummed with pleasure at her first taste of Lynn's apple-spice cupcake with cream-cheese icing. They were her favorites.

They ate, sipped, and rocked in peaceful silence for a full ten minutes. Story Hill Farm snuggled in for the night's rest under a nearly full moon that softly illuminated the stables and grounds. The wind carried a hint of autumn from the surrounding mountains, and the only sounds were a hooting owl and the occasional horsey snort.

Teddy's voice was quiet. "I have so many unanswered questions. Do you think we can stop dancing around and talk about some of them?"

"Late-night therapy session?"

Teddy shook her head. "Two people who are becoming friends getting to know each other." She turned to Britt and held her gaze.

Britt considered this statement. Were they becoming friends? Was this a door she wanted to open? Maybe a crack. She'd felt so alone lately. "When I was a kid, I asked lots of questions. It nearly drove my parents insane. But Pop, he'd patiently answer each one. He'd point to a pasture and say, 'Britt, questions are like all those blades of bluegrass. You cut one down, and two more are going to spring up.' Maybe we should just leave some questions alone."

Teddy ignored her. "What's your favorite color?"

"What?"

"Your favorite color. It's not a hard question."

Britt turned to hold Teddy's gaze. Ignoring the red warning light going off in her head, she decided to play along. She was curious about the big question Teddy obviously was working toward. "Gray."

"Really. Why gray?"

"Because it's a clean, neutral tone that makes primary colors around it pop."

Teddy tilted her head as if considering this choice. "I hadn't thought of that."

"My turn," Britt said. "What's your favorite movie?"

"That's easy. *Avatar*."

Britt nodded. "Good choice, but why?"

Teddy stared out at the stables and spoke softly. "Because sometimes I'd like to be someone other than myself."

Whoa. Britt waited, but Teddy didn't offer more. She opened her mouth to ask for an explanation, but Teddy jumped in with another question.

"First kiss—how old were you, and was it a boy or a girl?"

Britt chuckled. "That's two questions, but I was twelve. It was a girl. She wanted to practice so she could kiss boys, but I just wanted to kiss her." Following Teddy's ploy to move them back to safe ground, she kept her next question light. "Why do you drive a 2017 BMW 230i?"

"So, you know cars." Teddy grinned. "You like my baby?"

"She's flashy. But most women I know in the military drive trucks to up their macho factor with the guys."

"I own my car because it's an exceptional machine that's fun to drive."

"It's expensive. I happen to know lieutenants aren't paid that well. Family money?"

"Hardly. Because I grew up a military brat, I'm used to not having a real home like most people. I always take advantage of available military housing or rent a cheap apartment. That leaves me disposable income."

That wasn't so unusual for career military, but Britt knew men were much more likely to go that way. Women, even when they were forced to move a lot, were natural nesters.

"And, I don't need a truck, because I prove my macho in the ring."

Britt's brain stuttered, searching for the appropriate image to conjure. "As in martial arts?"

"Boxing."

Britt stared at Teddy. No way. Sure, Teddy had an athletic vibe, but the way she moved was so graceful it was decidedly feminine. "Are you hiding a cauliflower ear under that blond hair?" Dancer, yes. Boxer, uh-uh.

Teddy threw her head back and laughed. "Don't you think you would have noticed, since I usually pull my hair back?"

"Well, I probably would have been polite enough to ignore the disfigurement." Britt liked that she'd made Teddy laugh so freely.

"My father was career marine and teaches fencing and boxing at West Point." Teddy ducked her head and smiled. "Are you surprised?"

"I had you figured for a dancer or a gymnast. Maybe a tennis player."

"Boxing is an elegant dance when performed correctly— slipping and sliding, feinting and lunging to strike. Sugar Ray Leonard was the best. I loved to watch him box."

Britt could see that. She remembered him as an exceptional pro. "So, you fence, too?"

"I'm better at boxing. I started pulling on gloves at six years old." Teddy shrugged. "My parents wouldn't even give me a toy sword until I was old enough to hold a real one, for fear I'd poke the family dog's eye out."

Britt tried to imagine a six-year-old Teddy waving a toy sword at a puzzled Labrador retriever. "You must have been a terror as a child."

"My parents tactfully referred to me as a challenge." Teddy tilted her head, giving Britt a pointed look. "Surely you aren't going to claim you were a quiet child."

Britt shook her head. "You've already heard enough stories from everybody around here to know better than that. I wasn't mischievous—just adventurous."

"Fearless, according to your grandfather."

Britt sipped her tea, struggling to stay in the moment, at the farm. Flashes of weapons fire. Figures in desert camo running, ducking, weaving, diving for cover. The whine of an incoming shoulder-fired missile. She tapped her middle finger against the wooden arm of her rocker, concentrating on counting the pattern. Tap-tap-tap, tap-tap. Tap-tap-tap, tap-tap. Tap-tap-tap, tap-tap. "I'm not fearless." She closed her eyes at the telltale rasp in her voice.

Silence hung between them, broken only by the creak of their rockers. But it was a silence filled with so many words, so many memories, so many regrets.

"We all are afraid at times, Britt. Fear can keep you safe. Fear also can cripple you."

"You work in a hospital." She didn't voice her real thought— you haven't known real fear. Tap-tap-tap, tap-tap. Tap-tap-tap, tap-tap.

"You're wrong."

Had Teddy read her thoughts or heard it in her tone? Distracted by that possibility, Britt stopped tapping.

"I was an enlisted medic before I pursued my degrees and officer school. Two tours. Well, one long tour. I caught a piece of shrapnel in my thigh, but it was minor enough that I was right back at the base after a couple of months in Germany to heal." Teddy rubbed her right thigh absently as she stared out into the dark.

"I'm sorry. I shouldn't have assumed. Of course you know fear." Medics were some of the bravest soldiers Britt had served with, dodging bullets to reach the wounded and refusing to leave until the last had been evacuated. She'd seen one medic load two critically injured soldiers on a helicopter, only to catch a bullet in the throat when he ran back for a third. She shuddered that something like that could have happened to Teddy. "I'm glad you aren't still a medic." She wasn't even sure where the thought came from.

"It's not because I was afraid."

Britt turned to her. "I didn't say that, didn't even think it." But Teddy had made a decision that took her off the battlefield. Britt felt she was in a similar place in her life, and she needed to ask. "So, had you always planned to work as a medic, then go back to get your degree?"

"No. Not really. I just…" Teddy's fingers were white where they gripped the arms of her rocker. Britt was about to withdraw the question when Teddy finally spoke again. "If I wasn't gathering them up in a body bag, I was sending them back with pieces of their bodies missing. Even worse, pieces of their souls gone." Her eyes were bright with defiance, her jaw tight as she spoke. She stood, avoiding Britt's gaze. "I'm sorry. That was insensitive to say to you, of all people."

Britt reached across and caught Teddy's hand. "No. Don't censure what you were going to say." She tugged Teddy back down to her chair. "I'm listening…as a friend, not a patient."

Teddy was quiet for a while, but Britt didn't release her hand while she waited. Finally, Teddy squeezed Britt's hand.

"The cost is so high. I couldn't watch bullets and bombs destroy lives any longer. Not just the lives on the battlefield, but the lives of their families and friends back home. I still want to serve my country, though. I just need to be on the healing end of it." Teddy slipped her hand from Britt's and stood again. She rubbed her face with both hands. "Breakfast comes early. We'd better go to bed before E.B. starts banging pots at daybreak."

Britt smiled up at her. As beautiful as Teddy was in the moonlight, emotional fatigue was evident in the slope of her shoulders and the depths of her storm-gray eyes. "I'll be up soon. I want to enjoy a little more of this quiet night."

Teddy nodded, then slipped into the house.

Britt contemplated everything Teddy had said. Mostly what she didn't say. There were missing pieces to that story. Maybe they were need-to-know, just like the hidden pieces of Britt's. The army wouldn't let Britt share her story, but she sure wanted to hear the one that put that fire, and sadness, in Teddy's eyes.

CHAPTER EIGHT

Teddy put down the ultrasound probe she was using to soften the scar on Britt's residual limb and reached for her phone. The succinct text made her smile. "Good," she told Britt. "The new harness I ordered for you is here. Well, not here, but at the hospital in Lexington. Are you up for a road trip?"

She handed Britt a clean towel to wipe the sweat from her face. They'd begun strength exercises today, and Britt had to be sore and likely in some pain from the workout.

Britt wiped her face, but her attempt to smile back was weak. "Sure. If you let me drive your car."

"How about you take a pain pill, and I'll drive into Lexington. We can visit the hospital, have lunch, and pick up some more jeans for me at my apartment. Then your pain pill will have worn off, and you can drive back."

"Deal. But Tylenol, no opioid."

"Britt." Teddy shook her head in exasperation. "I know you macho butch types feel heroic when you grit your teeth and bear the pain, but pain hinders healing."

"Macho butch?"

"If the saddle fits…"

Britt's eyebrows shot up. "Oh, so you think you're a regular jock after one horsey ride?"

"Maybe not ready for the racetrack. I am ready for my next lesson, by the way. Maybe when we get back." She touched Britt's chin to draw her gaze. "I trust your judgment when it comes to horses. I need you to trust mine when I tell you to medicate."

"Opiates make me nauseous. Do you want me to throw up in that nice car of yours?"

Teddy narrowed her eyes and tried to discern if Britt was being honest. "Truth?"

Britt met her eyes and nodded. "They really do. And I'm not hurting that bad. Tylenol, along with the TENS unit, will take care of it."

Convinced, Teddy gave in. "Tylenol then." She shook out two tablets from the bottle in a nearby cabinet and handed them to Britt with a bottle of water. She began putting their makeshift treatment room back in order while Britt obediently swallowed the tablets. "I need to change into uniform." She glanced at Britt. "Sorry."

Britt shook her head. "It's okay. I want to shower before I dress. I'll meet you downstairs in a bit."

❖

Teddy's breath caught when she looked up from texting with her boss. Capt. Britt Story, dressed in her desert camos field uniform, stood in the doorway of the kitchen. Sure, Teddy worked around uniformed soldiers most of the time, but Britt wore her camos like a second skin. Tall and erect, but not stiff. Teddy fought down the impulse to stand and salute.

Britt held up the prosthesis in her right hand. "I didn't know if I needed to bring this…or wear it?"

Teddy noticed her empty sleeve was already neatly cuffed to just below the end of her residual limb. "You don't have to wear it. I'm a little concerned about the place under your arm the harness is rubbing. But bring the prosthesis. We'll need to try it with the new harness."

"Okay. I'm ready when you are."

"Hold up," Lynn said, coming out of the pantry. "If you have time, stop by the farmers' market on your way back and see if they have the things on the list in this bag."

Britt took the cloth shopping bag Lynn held out and tucked it against her body with her residual limb. "Got it covered. Let's roll," she said, sounding as if she were commanding a convoy.

Teddy couldn't resist coming to attention and snapping a salute. "Yes, ma'am. Your transport is ready."

Britt played along, lifting the hand of the prosthesis to her brow in a mocking return salute. "Stow that cell phone, Lieutenant. There's no texting while driving in this state."

"Yes, ma'am." Teddy flashed a grin at Lynn as she trailed Britt out of the kitchen.

Lynn winked and gave Teddy a thumbs-up at Britt's playful response. Yep. Capt. Britt Story was finding her feet again.

The day was a perfect seventy degrees and sunny, so the drive over the mostly empty county roads was amazing in the sleek convertible. Once they hit city traffic, not so much. The smaller car was crowded between exhaust-spewing trucks and bulky SUVs on the major artery running to the Veterans Affairs Hospital. Teddy had never minded the city before, but she'd become spoiled by the past few weeks of clean country air.

"I meant to ask earlier. Why are you posted at a VA hospital while you're still active duty?"

"I'm part of a small special team assigned to research and recommend our path forward in prosthetics. Many new advances are making the hope of returning valuable personnel to duty, even to the battlefield, a real possibility. We've identified several potential candidates for our research in this area and decided to locate here temporarily while we wait for funding to be approved for permanent quarters."

"So, you got diverted from your mission to play nursemaid to me." Britt's mood had soured the minute they parked at the hospital, and Teddy felt the wall she'd spent the past weeks tearing down rising between them again.

"I wasn't sidelined. You—the method of your amputation—is our first chance to test the most recent advance with a soldier right off the battlefield."

"So, I'm a guinea pig for your program?"

Teddy tugged Britt to stop and faced her. She needed to choose her words and approach carefully. "This isn't just about you, Captain. This is about your duty to your fellow soldiers. If you will withhold judgment until we finish here today, I'm hoping you'll see it as an honor, not just duty."

Britt gave a curt nod. "You've got today, Lieutenant."

They began walking toward the hospital again.

"I was texting with the team commander, Colonel Winstead, when you came downstairs. We picked the perfect day to come in. A doctor from Duke University is here and would like to see you. He's part of their team that's making phenomenal breakthroughs in the field of prosthetics. If you agree, they want to work with you on their latest project."

"I'm not staying in the army, Teddy."

"You don't have to in order to be part of this."

They stayed on the ground floor but walked through a maze of corridors until they reached double doors that opened into a gymnasium-sized room, where several-dozen therapists worked with patients at various stations.

"Hey, Lieutenant!" A woman sitting on a treatment table waved them over.

"Rachel, hi. How's it going?" Teddy asked, leading them to the young woman's table. Teddy gave a covert thumbs-up to a therapist working with a patient two stations away. They'd conspired to have Rachel—one of their hardest working, most upbeat patients—at the rehab center to meet and hopefully influence Britt.

Rachel held up her left hand, the bionics whirring as her thumb and index finger formed an *O*. "A-okay," she said. "I love this hand. They said it just might be my ticket to get off medical disability and back in the army again, now that I'm bionic." Her arm had been amputated mid-forearm, and she continued to demonstrate the hand's capabilities by touching each finger to her thumb. She picked up a tennis ball from the tray next to the treatment table and tossed it from her bionic hand to her real hand and back again.

"Wow. Your eye-hand coordination has really improved. I can tell you've been working hard."

"It'd be a lot easier if I could feel the fingers." Rachel held the bionic hand up and wiggled the fingers. The futuristic limb showed some of the mechanics through the red and black semi-transparent covering. "My brain can make the fingers move, but it still wants to pick stuff up with the end of my arm because that's where my feeling stops. If I'm not looking at the hand and the object when I try to grab something, I always misjudge the distance. But it's nothing that should keep me from doing my job if the army would take me back."

Britt's eyes followed the ball as Rachel tossed it from one hand to the other. The bionic fingers didn't move as quickly as real fingers. "What was your MOS, soldier?"

Rachel grinned. "Sniper, ma'am. I was lucky it was my left hand that got blown off when our transport hit that IED. Not even this super hand could get me back in if it'd been my right one. I need to be able to feel the trigger."

They watched as she tossed the tennis ball to her bionic hand but missed catching it. The ball joined a few others scattered around the floor, but Rachel just reached for another on the tray and tried again. She turned hopeful eyes on Teddy. "Do you think there's a chance for me?"

"Colonel Winstead is working to get a protocol written for returning someone to combat service. This isn't something they've done before. We're breaking new ground, but keep practicing so you'll be ready."

"I want to go back to work, Lieutenant." Rachel scowled. "I was near the top of my MOS in hits. In the army, I'm important. I hate being a civilian. I'm nothing out here. I've got a high school diploma and one hand. I can't even get a job as a waitress or a dishwasher."

"You're getting your medical-disability checks, right?"

"I don't need money. I need to work, damn it." They all flinched at the loud pop when Rachel's bionic hand squeezed the tennis ball too tightly. She dropped it back onto the tray. "Even if they don't want to put me back in the field, I could help train troops at the gun range."

Teddy patted Rachel's thigh. "Try to be patient a little longer. We're pushing this as fast as we can."

"Okay. Sure. I'll wait." Rachel looked at Britt, her eyes traveling for the first time to Britt's empty sleeve. "Oh. I thought you were another PT. Sorry. I didn't see the sleeve at first."

"No problem."

"The lieutenant will fix you up."

"That's the plan," Britt said. "Hold on a second." Britt walked over to a desk on the other side of the room. Teddy shrugged at Rachel's questioning look. They watched as Britt bent to write something, then headed back to them. She held out a yellow note to Rachel.

"This is the address for a gun shop and shooting range near here. Ask for Rick, and tell him Britt Story said he might need some help."

Rachel's face transformed. "Hey, thanks! I'll go see him now." She hopped down and headed for the door, then trotted back to them and held out her hand for Britt to shake. "Really. Thanks, Captain." With that, she was sprinting for the door again.

"You made her day," Teddy said, smiling at Britt.

Britt shrugged. "Rick's a veteran, too. He'll understand and at least give her something to do other than rehab. I'm surprised she got that high-tech hand. I can't imagine what it cost."

"Not as much as you think. The parts were three-D printed, which drastically lowers the price. Our hope is a future where prosthetics like Rachel's will be routinely available to all veterans and active military."

Britt nodded, her gaze roving the large room filled with amputee veterans—some young enough to be recently discharged, others old enough to have lost limbs to disease. Teddy tried to caution herself against being too hopeful, but Britt seemed to be softening toward the project. Getting her on board to work with the Duke doctors would give them a running start.

❖

Britt hesitated in the door of the treatment room when two men—one in uniform, the other in casual slacks and a golf shirt—looked expectantly at her. Doctors. She knew the look. The Tylenol pills that had taken the edge off her pain were long used up, and her arm was aching. She wasn't in the mood for being poked and prodded. A hand brushed her back, and Teddy, who stood behind her, spoke softly.

"I'll be back in one minute. Don't let them start without me."

Britt nodded but wanted to catch Teddy by the arm and haul both of them out to the parking lot. She fought to stuff down her rising temper. She'd always been an even-keel kind of person, but Afghanistan and the army had significantly shortened her fuse. She stepped into the room and came to attention to address Col. Tom Winstead. "Sir."

Colonel Winstead stood from where he'd been propped against a counter and held out his hand. "Captain Story. Come in. I'm Tom Winstead." He looked past her. "I thought Teddy, uh, Lieutenant Alexander was with you."

Britt shook his hand but remained stiffly at attention. "Lieutenant Alexander diverted for a minute and asked that we wait to begin." She wasn't sure, though, what they were here to do, and her irritation was growing too big for the room. She felt crowded by the two men, the way she felt crowded by her father and everybody else who'd been pushing at her. Sweat trickled from her temple and along her jaw. She was crawling out of her skin and about to excuse herself before she exploded.

Then Teddy was there, pressing a cold bottle of water into her hand. Despite the fourth body crowded into the room, Britt felt like the walls moved back a few inches so she could breathe again.

"Sorry," Teddy said to the two men. "I didn't want to get off schedule with Captain Story's medications." She turned her back to them to face Britt, effectively placing herself between Britt and the men. She took the bottle of water back and pressed a small white pill cup into Britt's hand instead. "No arguments, Captain. It's just Tylenol and Tegretol for the nerve pain. Down the hatch."

Britt immediately missed the bottle that was cooling her hand and her head. She tossed the pills into her mouth and traded the pill cup for the now-opened bottle that Teddy held out. Britt gulped down half of it, wishing she could pour the rest over her head. "Thanks," she said, taking one more swallow before handing it back to Teddy.

"You okay?" Teddy's question was soft, her gaze following the bead of sweat Britt could feel still sliding along her jaw.

"Yeah." Britt looked away from Teddy's worried eyes, then gave a small sigh. Teddy deserved an honest reply. She held Teddy's gaze and casually wiped the sweat away. "I'm okay now. A bit of phantom pain was getting the better of me, but it's already fading. The pills will take care of it."

Teddy stepped away and nodded to Colonel Winstead. The men had waited, apparently deferring to Teddy since she'd been treating Britt for the past few weeks. That was saying a lot because colonels, especially men, rarely stepped aside for a lieutenant. It raised Colonel Winstead's stock as far as Britt was concerned.

Colonel Winstead cleared his throat and indicated the other man. "This is Doctor Will Thomas, from Duke University."

Dr. Thomas smiled and held out his hand. "Please. I'm looking forward to working together in the coming year, so it's just Will."

Britt shook his hand. "Britt Story. Uh, just Britt."

"And we're going to ignore rank while we're working, so I'm Tom."

Teddy blazed a smile that lit the room and held out her hand to Will. "I'm Teddy, and I'm really excited to learn more about your project, Doctor Thomas."

"Will," he said, matching Teddy's smile.

Britt frowned. He was handsome and a little too friendly. Time to move this along and get the hell out of this hospital. "So, Dr. Thomas, I'm afraid you've been misinformed. I haven't signed up to be your test subject."

"Yet," Teddy said, frowning at Britt. "Will…" She emphasized the use of his first name. "maybe if you told us more about your project."

"Sure," he said, grabbing a laptop computer from the counter and opening it to a video waiting to start. "This explains how we connect the nerves still viable in your residual limb to sensors in the fingers of the prosthetic hand and allow you to feel sensation."

"Sensation?"

"Hot or cold, and pressure," Will said. "We're still trying to master texture, like the difference between touching silk and cotton."

Britt didn't appear convinced, so Teddy jumped in.

"Any type of feeling is a big step, Britt. It will solve two of the largest problems—the spatial perception Rachel was talking about and grip. How to hold something without squeezing it too tight."

"May I examine your residual limb?" Will asked.

Britt started to refuse. It still throbbed. But she caved after just a glance at Teddy's pleading expression. Her cooperation would reflect favorably on Teddy, maybe even earn her a promotion. She was uneasy, though, still uncertain of her next step in facing what had happened in Afghanistan. Her loyalty to family and country, her disillusionment with the chain of command, and a promise she'd made a young woman under her command were getting tangled up with her growing relationship with Teddy. Today, however, didn't feel like the place to take her stand. She'd go along for now. "Yeah. Okay."

They waited while Britt unbuttoned her camo shirt, handed it to Teddy, then hopped up on the exam table.

"You're still having a lot of pain?"

"Not really."

"She's actually ahead of schedule in her rehab." Teddy elaborated since Britt was being rather nonverbal. "We began strength exercises this morning, so she's experiencing more residual limb pain today than usual."

Will was gentle as he probed and tapped. She jerked when he hit where a nerve was apparently near the skin.

"Sorry, but I needed to test that." His smile was broad. "The surgeon did an excellent job. Once you're healed enough, you'll be an excellent candidate to work the bugs out of our prototype."

Britt stayed silent. There was nothing really to say. She was in a holding pattern until the army decided her fate. But they couldn't keep her in their service forever. She qualified for medical retirement. Hell, all she wanted was to be released. She didn't need their hush money, and she'd get an army lawyer to explain that to her command if necessary.

Will studied her. "You have to *want* to participate, Britt." He looked at Colonel Winstead. "The army can't just order her. I can connect nerves to electrodes in the prosthesis, but I can't make her brain finish the connection. She has to want to move the fingers badly enough." He turned back to Britt but stopped when Teddy put her hand up.

"Captain Story is still recovering from her wounds and has been back from deployment less than a month," Teddy said.

"The earlier we can orient her brain to the arm, the greater our chances of success," Will said.

Teddy whirled on Colonel Winstead. "Colonel, she needs time. I don't have to explain to you the psychological shock of returning from deployment."

"If she needs time, she'll get it." Everyone turned to the man standing in the doorway. Dark-haired and blue-eyed, his features left little doubt he was a close relation to Britt.

Britt had had enough of the arguing over her. She turned to Sen. Brock Story. Her father had interfered in her life enough. "You don't actually have a say in that, Senator. You are no longer in my chain of command, and I'm an adult competent enough to make any decisions the army doesn't make for me." She faced Colonel Winstead and stood at attention with her eyes focused over his shoulder rather than on his face. "Is there anything else, sir?"

Colonel Winstead glanced at Brock, then studied Britt for a long second. "I'm glad to see you healing so well, Captain. I trust Lieutenant Alexander is taking good care of you?"

Britt relaxed a bit and met his gaze. She was already aware of Teddy's admiration for her boss, but something about his demeanor—his warm eyes, his open expression—put Britt at ease, too. "She's a hard taskmaster, but yes, sir. She is."

"Good. Then you're dismissed, Captain Story. I want to see you back here in two weeks to review your progress."

"Yes, sir." Britt whirled and stepped around her father to leave the exam room.

❖

Britt nearly collided with a woman who looked like she must have a van full of children outside, waiting for her to drive them to soccer practice. "Sorry. Excuse me."

"Captain Story?"

Britt stopped her move to step around the woman and met her gaze. "I'm Captain Britt Story." She didn't recognize the woman, yet something seemed familiar about her. Maybe she was a civilian VA employee and had some information for her. "Can I help you with something?"

The woman looked relieved yet anxious at the same time. "I hope so. I'm Julie Prescott, and I'm here on behalf of Senator Amanda Elsbeth. Is there somewhere we can talk in private?"

The request surprised Britt, but her curiosity overruled her caution. A lot of people in Washington seemed interested in her. "I saw a family-counseling room that looked empty just down the hall." She gestured to the hallway she'd emerged from, then began retracing her steps. She stopped at the doorway and let Julie enter first, then altered the sign on the door to indicate the small room was in use before entering and closing the door.

"Can we sit?" Julie asked.

"I've only got a few minutes before my therapist will come looking for me. Will this take long?" Britt sat in a chair opposite the couch Julie chose.

"Not long, I hope." Julie twisted a tissue in her hands, her dark brow furrowed as she seemed to search for words.

Britt jump-started the conversation. "I'm not personally familiar with Senator Elsbeth, so I'm not sure how I can help you."

"I guess I should back up a bit. Prescott is my married name. My maiden name is Avery. Jessica Avery is...was my sister."

Britt stiffened at the admission, her mind instantly back in the camp with Cpl. Jessica Avery choking back sobs as she named the soldier in her unit who had sexually assaulted her. Britt closed her eyes for a long moment. When she opened them again, she found it hard to meet Julie's stare. "I'm sorry, very sorry for your loss. I tried—"

Julie waved away Britt's condolences and sat forward on the edge of the couch. "I know you tried to help Jess, Captain. I Skyped with my sister on a regular basis and know she was sexually assaulted in camp." She paused. "I also talked to her hours before her last patrol. The army's report simply lists her as a combat casualty, but I believe she was a walking casualty before she went on that patrol."

Britt dropped her chin and stared at her hands. She wanted, needed to tell someone. Didn't Corporal Avery's sister deserve to know? But she'd been explicitly ordered not to talk about the whole situation. "I can't tell you more than the army already has, Julie."

Julie's eyes flashed with anger, leaving no doubt that she'd met the same wall of silence from others. "Can't or won't, Captain?" She spat the words like an armor-piercing bullet.

Her sudden anger took Britt aback. This soccer-mom type had a bite. She was glad to answer this question honestly. "Can't."

Julie stood and stared down at Britt. "Senator Elsbeth is leading a Congressional inquiry into the surprising number of sexual assaults and constant harassment female soldiers suffer at the hands of their own troops. She was hoping...I was hoping I could convince you to testify about my sister's case."

Britt stared at the floor and said nothing.

"But I guess I can't." She gathered her purse to leave but stopped when she reached the door. "I still want to thank you for trying to help Jess. She felt like you were her only ally in that God-forsaken place."

Flashes of Jessica Avery tore through Britt's mind—eager to prove her toughness, always on time for duty, laughing and joking with other troops, then sullen and always scared when the soldier she accused wasn't relieved of duty.

She stopped Julie as she opened the door to leave. "I've requested a medical discharge, but it hasn't been approved. Only a subpoena could compel me to testify while I'm still an active member of the armed forces."

Julie stared at her.

"I believe in honor and duty, Ms. Prescott. Tell Senator Elsbeth to get a subpoena."

Julie nodded. "Thank you, Captain."

Teddy caught up with Britt halfway down the long hallway to exit the hospital. "Britt, wait."

Britt faltered, but then resumed her long strides. Captain Story could be a difficult person to deal with. But Teddy wanted to connect with her new friend, Britt, not the military officer. She caught up with Britt and grabbed her right hand to tug her forcefully around and to the left when they reached a cross hallway. "Come with me."

Britt nearly lost her balance and took several steps in the direction Teddy was tugging her, then stopped. Teddy knew she was exceptionally strong for her size because of her boxing workouts. But Britt, who was taller, was an immovable object when she dug her heels in. "Please. The new harness I ordered is in my office. If it doesn't fit or you don't like it, I'll need to send it back today."

Britt glanced back over her shoulder.

"The parking lot is the first place your father will look if he tries to catch up with you."

Britt's rigid stance softened, and she gave a quick nod. Teddy released her grip on Britt's hand, surprised to see Britt's lips curl in a quirk of a smile.

"What?"

"Nothing." Britt's smile grew. "You're a natural horsewoman. That little spin you executed to stop my charge down the hall is exactly what you should do to redirect a horse trying to drag you."

Teddy huffed. "Well, it's not like you had a left hand for me to grab to drag you down this hall."

Britt stopped again, her expression incredulous. Then she laughed. A surprised but genuine laugh. "I can't believe you said that. It's got to be some kind of therapist violation."

Teddy shook her head and chuckled, too. "It's not my usual protocol." She searched Britt's blue eyes. "But you're more than my usual patient."

"Because of your project?" Britt's question was soft, not accusing.

"No. Not because of the project." Teddy started to say more, but several noisy medical personnel were headed past on their way to lunch. "Come on. Let's do this quickly and go grab some lunch. I'm starving."

Britt followed obediently to Teddy's office, sat in the chair Teddy indicated, and began unbuttoning her camo shirt. Teddy pulled the lightweight, soft shoulder harness from the box and held it up.

"No chest strap?" Britt stared at the harness while she laid her shirt over the back of the chair.

Teddy offered a quick smile. "No straps. This is a relatively new style that I find more adjustable and comfortable for female clients." It was time to stop referring to Britt as a patient. "It's easy to slip on with one hand and doesn't have a strap across the chest that interferes with the plunging neckline of your favorite cocktail dress."

Britt smirked as she took the harness and fingered the material. "It's soft inside."

"Less rub," Teddy said. "But the gray mesh on the outside is strong enough to hold the prosthesis in place. Because it is softer than woven straps, it's not as durable, and you'll want to replace it with a new one about once a year, depending on how much you stress it. Once you put it on, though, I think you'll find it's worth the trade-off. Go ahead. Right shoulder first."

Britt slipped her right arm into the harness, and Teddy guided her in how to maneuver her residual limb into the other side, then adjusted a few Velcro tabs so it fit comfortably across Britt's shoulders.

"I like it," Britt said, shifting her shoulders. She looked around Teddy's office. "Crap. I think I left my arm in that exam room."

Time for a baby step. "How about I find you one with something better than a dummy hand."

"Like Rachel's?"

Teddy shook her head. "Not that advanced. You've still got too much swelling. But something a bit more functional. I'll be right back and see what you think."

Britt stood after Teddy left and shifted her shoulders several times in the new harness. It really was much more comfortable. She walked in a small circle, continuing to test its flexibility, and noticed the framed credentials and photos hanging on the wall. Wow. She had been a serious student—a bachelor's degree in psychology, double certified in physical and occupational therapy. But she focused on the photo of Teddy kneeling in the Afghanistan desert, a helmet shadowing her face and her medic pack by her knee while she held an M4 carbine against her chest. The days were long gone when medics wore an identifying red cross on their helmet and carried only a sidearm weapon. "Kabul 2013" was written in the corner of the photo.

She saw other photos of Teddy with her unit, but only one picture sat on a corner of Teddy's desk. The tall blonde in the photo had laughing blue eyes and wore desert camos with a military-police patch on the sleeve. Britt picked up the photo to study it. The nametag on the front of her uniform read S ALEXANDER. A sister? Other than the blond hair, the soldier didn't resemble Teddy. A cousin, maybe?

"I had to go to the storeroom...." Teddy stood in the doorway when Britt turned toward the voice, placing the photo back on the desk.

"Sorry. I was just looking around when you didn't come right back." Britt deflected by returning to the photos hanging on the wall. She pointed to the photo of Teddy in Afghanistan. "How'd you rate a M4?"

Teddy appeared relieved at Britt's redirect. "They were becoming more plentiful in 2013, but most of the guys preferred to keep their M16s. You know, the size of my truck, hands, feet, gun reflects the size of my...you fill in the blank. It was fine with me because I love the smaller, lighter M4. And it had the same firepower as an M16."

Britt nodded and glanced back to the photo on the desk. Teddy ignored the question that hung in the air, holding up a different prosthetic arm that was jointed at the elbow and had a hook on the end.

"I know this appears to be an ancient design, but it's actually still around because it's simple, reliable, and capable of performing dozens of tasks. It's a step toward a more high-tech arm."

Britt frowned. Wasn't that hook-looking thing the stereotype of an armless person?

"It's better than lugging around a non-functioning prosthesis." Teddy pinned her with an impatient look. "Just try it. For me?" Teddy pointed to a chair for Britt to sit.

Doing things to please Teddy was becoming a habit Britt was sure she didn't want to develop. She had too much going on in her life to worry about someone else, even if she was just a friend... she'd almost kissed over pilfered cupcakes. Damn it, though. Teddy was hard to resist. And Teddy's uncharacteristic impatience told Britt that she'd pushed too far, and the photo was something very personal. "Okay."

Teddy pulled a foam socket from one of her pockets. "I picked up a smaller-size socket. Your swelling has reduced significantly enough that the one on the other prosthesis was becoming too loose."

"I thought sockets were custom fitted. You know, you go in a lab, and some guy makes a cast of your stump and uses it to make a socket that fits your stump perfectly."

"Residual limb. We don't say stump."

"You said stump the other night in the pantry." Britt grinned at the exasperated glare Teddy shot her way.

"When you heal enough that your limb stabilizes, then you'll get a custom-fitted socket."

"Arizona got one before she got her first prosthetic."

"Who is…oh, you watch *Gray's Anatomy*," Teddy said as she fitted the soft socket into the prosthetic arm, adjusted Britt's shoulder harness, and attached the new arm.

"Well, yeah. Doesn't every lesbian? Both Arizona and Callie are hot." Oh my God, she hadn't actually said that out loud, had she? Britt had become so involved in watching what Teddy was doing, the filter between her mind and her mouth had gone missing. Teddy stopped, and they stared at each other. Then Teddy burst out laughing. The undercurrent of tension between them drained away. Britt grinned again. Yeah. She did smile a lot when Teddy was around.

"Well, I'm glad you're getting your medical advice from an authoritative source," Teddy said as she wiped a tear from the corner of her eye.

They shared another look. They'd leave their demons buried for the moment.

"Let me show you a few things, and then we can get out of here," Teddy said. "How about we grab some takeout, eat at my apartment while I pack a few more clothes, then head back to the farm. If you're up for it, I'd like another riding lesson."

A late-afternoon ride would be the perfect end to the day.

"Sounds like a good plan," Britt said.

CHAPTER NINE

R eel, reel, reel...that's it. Keep the line taut. Every time he swims closer, take up the slack."

"It's huge. I swear it's going to drag me into the water."

Britt's laugh echoed against the mountains that flanked the wide stream. "We're fishing for trout, not whales."

"But I think I've hooked a whale," Teddy said, reeling again. "Or maybe a hundred-pound turtle." She stopped when a sleek rainbow trout broke the water about thirty feet downstream. "Wow. Did you see that?" Teddy knew she was yelling, but she was so excited. She'd caught a fish. She was pulling in her first fish ever.

"Don't stop. He's headed for the rocks. Don't let him get to the rocks." Britt's voice rose to match Teddy's. "He's going to..." The line went suddenly slack, and Britt's tone returned to normal. "... going to cut your line on the rocks."

Teddy threw her fishing pole down on the stream's bank and stomped around in a circle. "My first fish. I almost caught my first fish. Gosh dang it."

Britt's laughter rang out again at Teddy's child-like show of temper. She bent over and clamped the hook of her new prosthesis on Teddy's pole, then braced the pole against her hip and reeled in the severed line. "Lieutenant, I had no idea you had such a temper. I'm going to have to cover my ears if you keep up that foul language."

Teddy put her hands on her hips and tried to glare at Britt, but she couldn't pull it off. She smiled instead. "My language was so foul the first time I came back from deployment, my sister refused to let me near her kids until I managed to clean it up. It took me a while, but I learned to substitute softer words. The habit unconsciously kicks in when I experience real pain, like a hammered finger or frustration." She waved her arm at the stream and raised her voice. "Like losing my first-ever trout from a danged mountain stream."

"Don't be so disappointed. You almost caught it. That fish has probably been hooked before. It headed straight for the rocks."

Teddy didn't mind that Britt's tone was placating. Her real mission hadn't been to catch fish, but to put Britt in an environment where she began to unconsciously use her prosthetic arm to perform daily tasks. And this had worked. She watched Britt reel in the line, then hold the rod with her hook while she used her right hand to tie off the line and dismantle the rod to fit in the tube that was part of a canvas fishing-equipment ensemble. Teddy was amazed at how fast Britt was adapting after one short week.

"We're leaving?" After a morning of sitting in their therapy room while Britt practiced opening and closing the metal hook on the prosthesis, picking up things and holding them without dropping them, the afternoon outdoors was a wonderful reward. Teddy had suggested a ride because being around the horses seemed to both rejuvenate and relax Britt. Heck. It relaxed her, too. She could easily understand why horse-therapy programs were so successful.

"We'll come again. But unless you want to gallop all the way back, we'd better leave now, or we'll be late to dinner." Britt lifted the strap of the fishing bag over her head so that it crossed her chest and held the kit securely along her back and hip.

Loath to leave, Teddy stood a moment longer to take in the stream and the mountains surrounding them. The warm sun was dipping lower toward the mountain peaks, and the cold of the stream wafting up felt like an early hint of autumn. She felt Britt come up behind her. "I feel like I'm in that movie *The River Runs Through It*. Have you seen it?"

"At least three times. Pop has a DVD of it."

Britt's voice grew closer, and, for a moment, Teddy wished for Shannon's arms to come around her. She imagined leaning back against Shannon's chest, and Britt's lips—No. Not Britt. Shannon. Teddy shook herself. "Let's get going. Lynn said she was cooking beef stew, one of my favorites."

Britt shook her head as she cupped her hand to give Teddy a leg up into the saddle. "Everything she cooks is a favorite of yours."

Teddy settled into her saddle and forced herself to smile. "I won't deny it."

❖

The evening followed what was becoming their daily ritual. Lynn left the beef stew ready to serve, while she took her own pot of stew home to her little family. E.B. and Britt discussed farm business over their dinner, which gave Teddy the chance to ask questions and learn more about the Thoroughbred-racing business. E.B. also wasn't shy in asking what he wanted to know about Britt's rehabilitation.

After dinner, E.B. retreated to the living room to watch his television shows, while Teddy and Britt cleaned up the dinner dishes. Britt's dish-drying was going a little slow tonight because she was carefully picking up the plates with her hook and holding them while she wiped with her good hand. So, Teddy grabbed a dish towel and helped dry after she'd washed everything.

"Ready to shed that arm?" she asked when they were done. "I'm impressed that you wore it all day, but you don't want to overdo it."

Britt shrugged off the denim shirt she wore over a T-shirt and the harness. "This harness is a lot more comfortable, and this prosthesis is at least semi-functional."

Teddy resisted the urge to help as Britt loosened the harness, detached the prosthesis from her residual limb, then removed the harness from her shoulders. The minute Britt set the prosthesis and harness on the table, Teddy was rolling up Britt's sleeve and checking her limb for redness and new swelling. It looked good, but she gently probed the pressure points. "Any soreness or pain?"

"No real soreness. It's more like the relief of taking your shoes off after being on your feet all day."

"Pain?"

"Still getting some phantom pain. It's like an electric shock that leaves me throbbing, but the acetaminophen and the Tegretol are making it bearable."

This was good. Very good. Teddy rolled the sleeve of Britt's T-shirt back down and openly studied her. "I appreciate your hard work and commitment to rehabbing." She spoke softly, a little afraid her question could take them two steps back after this significant step forward. "Does this mean you've decided to be part of our digital-prostheses project?"

Britt stood and put her denim shirt on again. She avoided Teddy's gaze and went to the cupboard to pull down two coffee cups. "No." She placed the cups on the counter and held up the carafe of fresh-brewed coffee. "Coffee?"

"Yes, please."

The last part of their ritual was retreating to the porch rockers for an after-dinner cup of coffee to wind down the day. Neither was big on watching television, preferring to retire early with a good book.

Teddy followed Britt to the porch. They rocked and sipped their coffee in silence, letting the night settle around them. The crickets' rhythmic trill had grown louder as the nights became cooler, and they were in full voice. A snort from a horse, the hooting of an owl, or the howl of a coyote occasionally accented the chorus. But on the porch, the only sound was the creak of their rockers. Teddy finally broke their silence.

"So, you haven't decided, or you have decided that you don't want to participate?"

Britt let out an audible sigh. "The army should spend their money on someone like Rachel, who deserves the chance and wants to return to active duty."

Teddy watched Britt's gaze travel over the stables laid out in neat rows downhill from the house. "It's not set in stone, but Rachel is a top candidate for the project. Her injury is different. We need you, too, Britt. Tell me why you feel you don't deserve to be part of the project."

Britt stood, drained her coffee cup, and placed it on the porch banister. "If you're done with your coffee, I want to show you something."

Teddy set her cup beside Britt's. "Okay." She followed Britt down the stairs and around to the side of the house where they parked the golf cart that E.B. sometimes used to ride down to the stables. "Where are we going?"

"To the hay barn," Britt said. "Hop in. I'm driving."

The hay barn was a long, single-story building much like the stables, but the siding was some type of manufactured board. When Britt hit a switch by the sliding door, a row of overhead lights illuminated the inside. Bales of sweet-smelling hay were stacked in neat rows on top of wood pallets about a foot off the ground, a gap between each row.

"I always thought hay was kept in lofts on top, but I guess your stables don't have a second floor."

"Actually, the stables do have a partial upstairs, but you won't find any hay there. The horses in our stables are very high-dollar. Overhead hay lofts are a fire hazard and create dust that's not healthy for the horses to breathe."

"So, all the hay is kept here?"

"And in another barn identical to this, located on the other side of the stables compound. These barns have fire-retardant siding, and the bales are stacked so air can circulate underneath and between rows."

"Is that important?"

"Hay is very combustible. If it's damp when it's baled, too green or too high in nitrogen content, the bales can heat up inside and spontaneously combust. These bales are tested every couple of weeks to monitor their temperature."

She followed Britt down the center of the barn. "So, you wanted to show me the hay barn?"

"I wanted to show you this." Britt stopped, pulled a can of tuna from her pocket, and peeled back the pop-top to dump the contents into a saucer sitting in the middle of the aisle. "Come on out. I've brought someone to meet you."

A petite gray tabby glided out from between two rows of hay and circled Britt's legs, mewing her thanks. Then she hunkered down and dug into the tuna. Britt walked back a few rows and pulled two of the top bales down into the aisle. "Come have a seat," she said, dragging the bales closer to the cat. She sat on one and indicated for Teddy to sit on the other. Then Britt put a finger to her lips in a signal for Teddy to remain quiet.

After a moment, a tiny mewing came from the place where the cat had emerged. The cat answered, then went back to eating.

"Wait for it," Britt whispered, her eyes bright under the lights.

A tiny, round head appeared, then a second. Teddy covered her mouth to suppress her gasp when a third kitten poked his head out, then bowled over the first two in his rush to get a share of the tuna. The others followed, and soon the little family was noisily snacking and making small mewing sounds of pleasure. Two gray tabbies like the mother, their tails curled around them, squatted around the saucer. The third, larger kitten was orange with a stump of a tail.

"The little ginger kitten. Where's his tail?"

"His daddy must have been a Manx. They don't usually have tails, or if they do, it's only a stump." Britt threw up her hand at Teddy's warning glance. "Not a residual limb. It was never long."

"Stub of a tail, then." Teddy shot Britt a satisfied glance. "A stump is a—"

"Yeah, yeah. I know." Britt looked to the ceiling and recited, "A stump is a sawed-off tree."

"Well, at least you're learning something." She returned her attention to the kittens, which were cleaning their paws and faces now that their meal was done. "They're adorable." Something, however, didn't seem to fit. She never saw cats about in the stables during the day, even though she often spotted them darting between the barns at night, mostly shadows along the edges of the security lights. "Why don't I see more cats around the stables during the day?"

"We have a fairly large feral-cat population that a local nonprofit group maintains for the farm. Pop gives them a sizable donation each year to pay for food and vaccinations, and they come out to routinely feed and trap them to neuter and vaccinate the colony. And the colony keeps the mice population down in the fields and around the barns."

Teddy considered this information. "I've always wondered about those feral-cat people. You'd think that if the cats were all neutered, the colonies would eventually die out."

Britt shook her head. "It's cats like this little mama that constantly add to the numbers. She's not feral." To prove her point, Britt held out her hand. The mama cat turned a suspicious eye on Teddy and avoided her as she slunk over to Britt. She loudly purred her thanks, brushing her cheek and then her body against Britt's hand. "When people want to get rid of a cat and the shelters are too full to take any more, it's not unusual for them to drive out to farm country and dump them. They wrongly figure that the animal will show up at a farmhouse and be taken in. We get stray dogs here all the time that their owners have dumped out."

Teddy was horrified. "That's awful."

Britt shrugged. "People can be mean and cruel." She picked up the mama cat, who settled in Britt's lap and kneaded Britt's thigh as she stroked her. Britt frowned, and the muscle in her jaw worked. "Dangerous, even."

Teddy stayed quiet, hoping Britt would finally reveal what was at the root of her reluctance to join the project. Teddy was sure it had something to do with the apparent rift between Britt and her father.

"Anyway," Britt said, "Mama Cat was probably dumped out here when her owner, who hadn't bothered to have her neutered, realized the cat was pregnant. Jill found her hiding out here, probably terrorized by the territorial feral cats, and we've been feeding her. Turns out, she's a pretty good mouser, but you can tell she's not feral because she never eats them. She leaves them near the door for us to find." Mama Cat playfully batted at Britt's empty sleeve, and Britt's grim expression evaporated. "She's barely more than a kitten herself."

"So, you're going to let them stay in the barn?"

"No. As soon as the kittens are about a month older, I'll get Gail's son—he does some small-animal work—to neuter Mama

Cat, and we'll find homes for the kittens so they don't become feral. I've already talked Lynn into taking one for her household."

Teddy tentatively offered her hand for Mama Cat to sniff and was rewarded with a cheek rub. "What about her, after she's neutered?"

"My grandmother used to have a cat that was supposed to be hers, but it followed Pop everywhere. Grandma died, and then the cat died of old age the next year. Pop's never brought another in the house since then. Lynn and I are conspiring to introduce Mama Cat into the house and try to make a match between her and Pop."

Teddy laughed. "I would have never pegged you for a romantic, Britt Story."

Britt smiled and tilted her head in acknowledgement. "I guess I'm a soft touch when it comes to animals and the people I love. Pop has always been here for me. Always."

Teddy felt a tug at her shoe. "Hey, those are my laces, you little rascal."

While the two gray kittens were tussling on the floor a safe distance away from them, the ginger kitten had edged up to attack the laces on Teddy's sneakers. He batted at the finger Teddy shook at him, then climbed up her leg to sit in her lap. She slowly reached up, careful not to scare him, and stroked his chest, then his cheek. He looked up at her with huge green eyes, then lifted his paw and touched her cheek. The pad of his foot was baby soft on her skin, and he was gentle, no claws extended.

"Looks like another kitten has found his match."

Teddy smiled but shook her head, unable to tear her gaze away from his green eyes. "He's a charmer, but I travel too much to have a pet."

"Cats take care of themselves, pretty much for several days at a time. They're really low-maintenance. And you could always bring him back here if you get orders to deploy."

"The chances that I'll deploy ever again are slim. Since getting my degree and certifications to specialize in amputee work, I'm sure I'll serve out my career in the army's larger hospitals."

"Good. That's good." Britt sounded relieved. Did she worry that Teddy could be sent back to the war zone? "You'll make a great cat owner."

The kitten seemed to agree, patting Teddy's cheek again before jumping down to run and pounce on his siblings.

Teddy laughed at his antics, then stood when Britt did. Teddy called a good night to the cat family and slid one door forward while Britt pulled on the other to close them in the middle. As they climbed into the golf cart, Teddy wished they'd walked instead. The night was so cool and the stars so bright. She loved this sweet side of Britt that cuddled kittens. She wanted to loop her arm in Britt's and lean against her as they strolled back to the house because they were friends. Just friends.

Still, it hadn't escaped Teddy's notice that the kittens had been an effective diversion from her unanswered question. Why didn't Britt want to be part of their digital-prosthesis program?

CHAPTER TEN

Teddy was surprised to find Lynn, rather than E.B., preparing breakfast. Lynn was removing a pan of fat biscuits from the oven, while country ham and chicken-fried steak cut in biscuit-sized squares sizzled on the stove.

"What's going on?" Teddy asked, pouring herself a cup of coffee. "Where is everybody, and why are you here so early?"

"Down at the yearling barn. Inspection day," Lynn said, deftly turning the meats cooking in multiple frying pans. "Didn't Britt tell you?"

"She did mention something about an inspection this morning, but she neglected to say it'd happen at the crack of dawn." Literally, because the first rays of sunlight were peeking over the mountains.

"The inspectors won't be here for another couple of hours," Lynn said. "But there's a lot of work to be done before they arrive." She pointed to a huge platter covered with paper towels. "Can you hand me that. I need to let some of the grease drain from these steak pieces before I put them in a biscuit."

"Are these for the inspectors?"

"No, for the staff." Lynn shoveled steak squares onto the tray, then plopped a second round in the pans to fry. "We'll feed the inspectors at lunchtime. My famous rotisserie chicken salad, some roast beef that's slow cooking in the oven, and lamb wraps with cucumber sauce." She gestured to two large pans of biscuits. "Can you cut those open for me? I'll come behind you and insert the meat."

Teddy took the knife Lynn handed her and began slicing through the middle of each biscuit. "Wow. That sounds incredible. So, we're planning to bribe the inspectors?"

"Don't let E.B. hear you say that. The inspector group that came four years ago had a young guy who'd never been here before. He saw the lunch spread and declared that he'd brought his own lunch because he couldn't be bribed." Lynn threw her head back and let out a hearty laugh. "I wish I'd had a video camera. When E.B. stepped up to that young man, the other inspectors stepped back from the new guy like a crew abandoning ship. E.B. said, 'Son, if you inflate your scores on my horses, I'll make sure you never inspect in this state again. I've been breeding racehorses since before you were in diapers. If my yearlings aren't scored accurately and a buyer pays too much for a horse that can't reach his expectations, my reputation and my business will suffer.'" Lynn held up her hands, her fingers forming two large *O*s. "That boy's eyes were this big. Then E.B. said, 'You go right ahead and eat that peanut-butter sandwich you brought if you want, but the rest of us are going to dive into the best sandwiches you ever put in your mouth.'"

"What'd the guy do?"

"He put his lunchbox back in the truck and lined up for a sandwich with the rest of them."

They laughed together as they filled and stacked biscuits into two huge baskets. When the baskets were full, Lynn covered them with red-and-white checked cloths.

"Do you mind taking these down? The yearling barn is the second one you'll come to."

"Sure. Whatever I can do to help."

"Thanks. Set them on the desk next to the coffee pot, and tell them I'll be down with a second round in about ten minutes."

❖

Teddy had almost reached the first stable when Lynn stepped out onto the porch and rang the old dinner bell. Men and women swarmed out of the other two barns to converge on the breakfast. By the time she reached the office in the yearling barn, an orderly line had formed. Britt was waiting and took one of the baskets from her, while E.B. stood at the barn entrance to address everyone.

"For those of you who are new, we have ham biscuits and steak biscuits. Take only one so everybody can get served right away. For those who want a second, Lynn will be down…" He looked to Teddy.

"Ten minutes," Teddy said to him.

"…in about ten minutes with a second round. There's juice in the ice chest and coffee in the big urn. Sorry, no decaf. Ernie, I won't tell your wife if you don't." Everybody laughed. "We're a bit ahead of schedule, so don't rush. If the judges are slow, it might be a long time before lunch is served, and this will be a long day."

Everyone started to talk and step closer to the person in front of them in anticipation of Lynn's fluffy biscuits.

"One more thing," E.B. shouted, and the crowd quieted. "We've got the best crop of yearlings this farm has seen in years, and a lot of the credit goes to your care and careful handling of each and every baby."

A man standing in line near Teddy groaned and muttered under his breath. "Come on. We're hungry."

An older man standing next to him elbowed the complainer in the ribs. "Show some respect. You know the boss man likes to make speeches."

Teddy suppressed a smile and returned her attention to E.B.

"Whether you were the person who made sure their stalls were clean or the person assigned to one of my babies as a primary groom, you are all just as important in making this year a success. If we do as well as I think at the auction next week, you'll each see something extra in your pay checks."

A cheer went up.

"Now let's eat," Britt yelled over the cheers.

The line went quickly, and Lynn showed up with another huge tray of biscuits. Teddy was astonished that by the time everyone was back working with the horses, every last biscuit was gone. She was lucky she'd grabbed one of the steak biscuits, wrapped it in a napkin, and put it in her pocket while she kept the line moving by filling paper cups with coffee and fishing juice drinks from the ice chest for people.

Now, she stood at the end of the yearling barn that let out to the paddocks, nibbling her biscuit, sipping her coffee, and trying to keep out of the way. Yearlings were housed in one stable, but the wash stalls in all four barns were being used. Horses were led back and forth, shampooed, dried, then brushed until their coats gleamed. Hooves were trimmed and polished, manes were shortened and ears trimmed. Even their teeth were brushed, then examined by the veterinarian, Gail. She could hear the mood of expectation in the voices of the stable workers as they prepared their animals. The horses seemed to pick up on the excitement of the day, too, moving restlessly in their stalls, ears forward and heads high.

Teddy nearly spilled her coffee when needle-like claws pierced her jeans and traveled up her leg and back. She was glad for the thick jean jacket she wore over her T-shirt when the orange furball came to perch on her shoulder. "What the heck? Why are you up here at the stables?"

The kitten extended a paw toward the biscuit Teddy held near her mouth.

"Hungry, huh?" She laughed and took another bite of her biscuit, careful to leave a last bit in the napkin, which she held up for the kitten to devour. "You'd better stay up here so you don't get stepped on."

Britt came out of the office, ducking into several stalls, then reappearing as she worked her way toward where Teddy stood. Britt smiled as she came to stand beside her. "Argh, matey. Where'd you get that fine-looking parrot on your shoulder?"

Teddy smiled at Britt's high spirits. She was also happy to see Britt wearing the prosthetic arm, having managed to attach it without her help. "He sort of found me. I was just standing here, staying out of the way, and the little bugger climbed up my back to perch there."

"What'd I tell you? Perfect match. He's definitely claimed you as his."

"We'll see." Teddy wasn't ready to admit she was smitten with the little feline. "You didn't tell me what a huge deal this would be."

Britt shrugged. "Honestly, I haven't been around for the past four years and forgot how excited everyone gets."

"So, these guys come and tell you how much your horses are worth?"

"No. They're experts who will score each horse according to their look, confirmation, and ability to move. Their individual scores are averaged for a final score. The Keeneland September Yearling Sale actually consists of two weeks of auctions. A horse's score indicates which of those auctions he or she qualifies to enter. When they're shipped to Keeneland, the horses are turned over to a consigner—a sort of broker, who enters your yearling in the auction where it has the best chance to bring a top price. They generally have scoped out which buyers are planning to show up at which auctions and what other horses will be offered in that lot. And they also handle the financial transaction."

"But you said you were going next week. What do you do there?"

"Watch, basically. We want to see what other farms bred and their results."

Teddy had been hinting for weeks that she wanted to go, but Britt had yet to invite her. "It sounds exciting. I've never been to a horse auction."

Britt looked at the time on her phone. "Thirty minutes, folks. Let's settle them down."

The chatter immediately quieted, and after a moment, soft classical music flooded the barn. Grooms traded brushes for soft cloths they stroked over the gleaming hides of the young horses while they murmured to their charges.

"They'll also judge each horse's temperament. A nervous, fretting horse loses points because you don't want one that will use up all their energy fussing around before they even get on the racetrack," Britt said.

Teddy sighed inwardly. Britt had again ignored her hint for an invitation to go with her to the September Yearling Sale. The auction Britt had invited Teddy to attend earlier to buy the Tapit filly had never happened because Britt was able to make a deal with the cash-strapped owner beforehand. Teddy wasn't giving up. "How long will you be in Lexington?"

"Three days. Pop and I'll get hotel rooms near Keeneland. So, you can go home a few days. I'm sure you're ready to sleep in your own bed a while."

"What about Mama Cat and the kittens? Who'll feed them?" She and Britt had added a visit to the hay barn to their nightly porch-sitting routine.

"Lynn's taking both of the gray kittens home with her, and Gail plans to pick up Mama Cat to be neutered next week. Lynn will let her recuperate at the house while Pop's gone, so she'll be at home there when he returns. He might resist letting her in the house the first time if he's there, but he's too big of a softie to throw her out if she's ensconced." Britt pointed to the ginger kitten, who'd finished eating and was trying to use his claws to hook the dog-tags chain that peeked out from under Teddy's collar.

The tiny claws missed the chain and grabbed skin. "Ow, you little brat."

Britt laughed. "That's what you should name him."

"I just might." Teddy gave Britt a sideways glance.

"You could take him with you next week, but you probably should wait until you're going to be home during the day to make sure he doesn't shred your apartment."

"Who said I wouldn't be home. There's no reason for me to stay here if you're gone."

The metal hook on Britt's arm clicked open and closed again when she shrugged. "Well, you've been hinting hard enough for the past week. I thought you might like to go to the auctions with us."

Teddy playfully punched Britt's shoulder. "You're just a big brat. Were you hoping I'd beg? I was about to, you know."

"Damn. I should have held out a bit longer."

Jill walked up behind them, carrying the halters of two mares she'd just turned out into the paddocks. "They're here. I saw the van pull up and E.B. heading over to greet them."

Britt rubbed her hand on her jeans. "That's my cue. I've been elected stage manager of sorts. Come with me if you want to watch." Jill reached for the kitten. "How about I take him to the other barn to get him out of the way?"

"That'd be great. Thank you." Teddy pulled the kitten from her shoulder, despite his claws digging into her jacket in protest. She held him up to look into his green eyes. "Go with Jill. You can play in her barn while I'm busy."

"Thanks, Jill," Britt said.

"You bet, pal." Jill winked at Britt, who seemed to ignore her, except for the blush that tinted her neck and cheeks.

Britt strode down the long center aisle of the stable. "Halters on, people. Get ready to lead them out."

CHAPTER ELEVEN

The day was a tedious process of leading the yearlings in a line for an initial look, then walking each of the twenty-seven individually back and forth, toward and away from the four judges, and finally holding the yearling at a standstill so the judges could examine the yearling's confirmation—musculature and bone structure. A judge or two almost always requested for the horse to be walked a certain way or turned left or right. The grooms, the audience and, most of all, the young horses needed a lot of patience.

The inspectors took an extra-long look at Home from War, the yearling E.B. expected to bring big dollars at auction. Thankfully, the sometime-temperamental colt stayed alert but calm throughout the process.

At the end of the long day, everyone went home exhausted. Dinner consisted of leftover roast and lamb, with mashed potatoes and peas. Simple and quick. Teddy took her after-dinner coffee to the porch as usual, but Britt followed Pop into his office to go over the scores of their yearlings. Before long, the old man began to yawn. For the first time since she'd returned, she noticed the extra lines in his face and the blue of his eyes that had paled with age.

"You should turn in, Pop. We were up extra early this morning."

"We're only halfway through the scores." His protest lost wind as he rubbed his bloodshot eyes.

"It's nothing we can't go over tomorrow," Britt said, standing so he would.

Pop pushed up out of his chair. "Okay. You're right. Bed sounds really good about now." He squinted at her. "You should go up to bed, too. I know you're younger, but you're still healing and need your rest."

"I will in a bit. I just have a few things to check on."

Pop raised an eyebrow at her. "You mean somebody to check on."

She shook her head but didn't bother to deny his insinuation. "Get your mind out of the gutter, old man. We don't even really know anything about her." Britt hesitated to share but trusted Pop's discretion. "She has nightmares about something. Maybe from when she deployed years back. I don't know."

"Huh. You sound like you have an idea."

"When we went to her office last week, I saw a photo of someone on her desk. She went to get something and caught me looking at it when she came back. Her whole mood changed. It was obvious she wouldn't talk about the woman in the picture."

"Did you ask?"

"No. I didn't want to invade her privacy. She would have told me if she wanted me to know."

"Google her."

Wait. Say what? Google who?

"Don't look at me like that," Pop said, shaking his finger at her. "I know what it means, and I know how to do it. Lynn's niece taught me. You wouldn't believe the track gossip you can find on the computer. No more paying the big ears in the backstretch barns for information."

"You googled Teddy?"

"Of course not. But you should. Maybe she has some of those social-media pages."

"You know about social media?"

"How do you think I kept up with you over in that godforsaken Afghanistan?"

This wasn't a conversation she'd ever expected to have with her grandfather. "I'm not on social media. It's filled with nothing but fake news and cute animal videos."

"I know you're not, but your unit is. And a lot of families use Facebook to stay in touch with children or cousins who've moved away."

She did know that, but she never looked at the Facebook or Instagram pages. Before deployment, all soldiers and their families had to watch videos about what could and could not be posted on social media. The video emphasized only appropriate posts and nothing that would reveal troop locations or schedules.

"I do. But I'm not going to google anybody. It's an invasion of privacy."

"Do you think Teddy would put anything private out there where anybody could read it?"

"No."

"I'm just saying. You're more like your old self when she's around, so I think you should get your head out of the sand." Pop waved her off. "Or you two can just keep shying away from the starting gate until she's gone. I'm heading to bed."

She stared after him. Is that what they were doing?

Britt stepped out onto the porch with her cup of coffee and sat in the rocking chair next to Teddy.

"So, did today go well? Is E.B. pleased with the scores?"

Britt nodded. "Very pleased."

"I didn't hear his television go on."

"He turned in early. He was already down at the barns when I got up at five this morning. I'm not sure he even went to bed last night."

"His energy amazes me."

Britt snorted. "That old man will still be going when you and I are gumming our food."

Teddy chuckled. "It's sweet, the bond between the two of you."

Britt rocked and thought of how she could put into words what her grandfather meant to her. "I was never the debutante my mother wanted, not that she didn't try. She'd dress me up in frills when I was little, then find me in the barn with mud splattered up to my shoulders. I never played with the dolls she bought me but slept with the GI Joe Pop gave me one Christmas. He and Mother never got along. Pop always complained that Dad should stand up for me more against her. He said I should be allowed to be who I am, not forced into what my mother wanted me to be." Britt ran her hand through her short hair. Her mother had hated when she'd cut it. "Should we walk down and feed the cats?"

Teddy smiled. "I was just about to give up on you and go by myself. I saved them some of the roast-beef and lamb scraps." She looked up at Britt. "I didn't know how long you and E.B. would be holed up in his office."

"I would have understood, but thanks for waiting." Britt looked forward to their walk each night. They rarely took the golf cart anymore, preferring to stroll and talk.

Teddy grabbed the foil-wrapped scraps sitting by her rocker, and they headed down the steps. "What happens now? With the yearlings, I mean."

"We'll start shipping groups of them to Keeneland, where they'll be stabled until next week's auctions. It'll give them an opportunity to adjust to all the activity, and the consigner the opportunity to judge the interest in each horse and decide which auction would bring the best price."

They walked in silence for a while, shoulders nearly bumping. Britt was only an inch or two taller than Teddy. She shoved her hand into her pocket to rein in her need to entwine her fingers with Teddy's. What if she did? The fact that desirable Teddy always walked on Britt's right side seemed like an invitation to do just that. Otherwise, she expected therapist Teddy would walk on her left side, guarding her from further injury. Or maybe she just wanted to think that. The near darkness of the crescent moon seemed to open the gate to the attraction, speculation, and desire between them. Maybe it was just her, but Teddy seemed to edge closer with each step they took.

"Can I ask another question?"

"Sure." Britt tensed in anticipation that maybe, just maybe Teddy was going to admit that what was growing between them was more than friendship. Maybe Teddy would do what Britt wasn't brave enough to—

"Before we met, I saw a video clip where you and your father were interviewed together while he was still in the service. You appeared to have a close relationship. But when he showed up at the hospital last week, you barely looked at him or spoke to him."

What? Britt stopped in front of the hay barn, her brain stumbling over the bucket of ice water Teddy had tossed into her path.

"You want to talk about my father?" Britt gave the door to the hay barn a rough shove, much harder than necessary. "My fucking father?" Maybe it was the PTSD. Maybe it was his intrusion once again into her life. But her anger rose unexpected and quick, hot and cutting.

"I'm sorry. I didn't mean to pry." Teddy took a step back, darting her glance from the ground to Britt and into the dark barn. "I just…I thought we…I care about you and thought maybe it would help if you could talk about it."

Britt inwardly flinched at the sadness—or maybe loneliness—in Teddy's tone and struggled to regain control of her emotions. "I'm sorry." She opened the other half of the barn door and let the floodlight at the entrance pour into the barn's interior. Then she gave in to her need to take Teddy's hand and tug her deeper into the barn. "Let's feed the cats."

She let go of Teddy's hand while they set the food out, but she reclaimed it as they settled on the short bench Britt had brought to the barn when the cat feedings became routine. Teddy didn't question the dim lighting as they watched the little cat family dine.

"Your question caught me off guard. I apologize for my anger," Britt said, realizing that she wanted to tell Teddy everything. The weight of what had happened still crushed her. Surely the patient-therapist part of their relationship would guarantee that no one could order Teddy to reveal anything Britt told her. But the army was famous for making rules, then circumventing them whenever it suited the corps.

Teddy pressed against Britt's side, squeezing her hand. "It's okay if you don't want to…if you can't tell me."

Britt lifted their hands and pressed the back of Teddy's to her cheek. It was warm and smooth. "I want to." The night felt like a dark, safe cocoon, and Teddy was her shield maiden against the emotions that kept trying to tear her apart. She would try.

"We used to be close. Pop has always been my safe haven. But Dad, he was my hero. He taught me to always do the right thing, no matter what it cost personally. And that can be really hard."

"Yes, it can." Teddy's quiet words held more unsaid, but Britt needed to finish.

"He forgave my mother an affair because he said he drove her to it by volunteering for long deployments to boost his career and not making more of an effort to adjust emotionally when he returned home to his family. I was angry with her, but Dad told me forgiving her was the right thing to do."

Teddy offered no opinion.

"When I was twelve, my parents let me adopt a dog from the shelter. She was just a mutt, but the smartest dog I've ever known. We were inseparable. She ate with me, slept with me, and went everywhere with me. She walked me to the school-bus stop every morning and met me there when the bus returned that afternoon. But she got sick, and the veterinarian told us it was incurable lymphoma. He gave us medicine, and she seemed to get better for a while. But he warned us that the medicine would work for only so long, and she would get very sick again.

"Dad said it would be my decision to make, but he had important deployment meetings the day it became suddenly obvious she was in constant pain. Still, when I called him, he immediately came home to load her into the car. I sobbed my heart out while the vet gave her that final shot. As much as that hurt, I was proud I had done the right thing. I knew Dad was proud, too."

Teddy's eyes filled with tears. "Oh, Britt. He sounds like a wonderful father. What has happened to change that in your eyes?"

Britt turned to Teddy, their faces inches apart. "He sold his soul and became a politician. Doing the right thing apparently means something different in Washington."

Teddy cupped Britt's cheek with the hand she wasn't holding, her eyes searching Britt's. "Surely, you must be wrong. The man who raised you must still be inside him, no matter what he's done to disillusion you."

Teddy's breath on her face was warm and sweet. She only had to lean in an inch, maybe two to taste, to caress those full lips. "Don't waste your time thinking about my father. Think about this." And Britt kissed her.

CHAPTER TWELVE

Britt's lips were gentle and tentative at first, and Teddy closed her eyes to savor them. She slid her hand from Britt's cheek to her lap and pulled her closer, opening to her and dancing her tongue against Britt's. God, she tasted like warm, rich coffee. Teddy heated as she drank Britt in.

She wanted to be surprised, but even she didn't believe the lie she'd told herself—that their flirting was just platonic banter. She'd wanted this. Every time she'd allowed Britt into her personal space, every time she'd stepped into Britt's, she'd been aware of the permission she was offering. But she'd ignored that inner voice, just like she was ignoring the alarms going off in her head now. *She's a patient. She's critical to the prosthesis project. She's fragile from recent deployment.*

Teddy gasped, jerking her mouth from Britt's.

"I'm sorry. I'm sorry." Regret flashed in Britt's eyes, but Teddy held tight when Britt tried to withdraw from their still-clasped hands.

"No, wait. Ow, ow. There are needles in my back. Ow." Teddy wasn't wearing the thick jean jacket from earlier in the day, and her soft sweatshirt wasn't much protection against the sharp claws of the ginger kitten climbing her back. He was growing fast and wasn't the tiny tyke he'd been the first time he clawed his way up her pants leg. His hind claws dug in as he propelled himself up to perch on her shoulder. "Brat," she said.

Britt chuckled. "You and I, little boy, need to talk about your timing."

The kitten swiped a paw at Britt, and Teddy laughed, too. "I think he's jealous." She gazed into Britt's eyes, suddenly feeling shy. They both looked away, then shared sideways glances and small smiles.

Teddy's ears burned, but she took some satisfaction that Britt's also were practically a red beacon in the semi-light. God, they were grown women who were acting like schoolgirls crushing on each other. She needed to do something to keep busy, or her lips would be right back on Britt's, and if that happened, she'd be crawling into Britt's lap and undressing her. Teddy dragged the resisting kitten from his perch, then gave him a good rub to apologize for the relocation. Maybe she ought to name him Velcro. She stood and set him on the floor. "We should head back."

Britt accepted the hand Teddy offered to pull her to her feet. "I am pretty tired."

Teddy closed the barn door as they left because neither wanted to let go of their entwined hands. The night was silent as they walked, but Teddy's brain wasn't. She pushed all thoughts aside... except for the kiss. She released Britt's hand and wrapped her arm around Britt's waist, pulling her even closer as they walked. Britt didn't look at her but smiled and mirrored her action.

They found themselves on the porch, at the door all too soon, and Teddy turned to block Britt's path. God, she wanted one more taste. She wanted the warmth that blossomed in her belly. She wanted to ignore all the reasons this was a very bad idea. And she did just that, pulling Britt's head down for another scorching kiss that made her shiver.

"Are you cold?" Britt whispered against Teddy's lips.

"Just the opposite," Teddy whispered back. She stepped back and opened the door.

In silent agreement, they parted. Teddy led the way through the kitchen and up the stairs. At the top, Britt caught her hand again and pulled her close. This kiss was light and gentle—a brush of lips, a pause, and another light touch—assurance there was no regret. It wasn't late, but the day had started very early. Tomorrow would also dawn early, as usual.

"Good night, Teddy."

Teddy touched Britt's cheek, then backed away. She wasn't ready for more and thought she sensed the same in Britt.

"Good night, Britt."

❖

The day dawned gray and rainy.

E.B. was in the kitchen at six as usual, but he frowned every time he cast a look outside. Britt was conspicuously absent as Teddy poured coffee for herself and topped off E.B.'s mug. She was about to ask if she should go up and see if Britt had overslept, when boots stomping across the porch drew her attention. Britt stood in the open doorway, toeing off Wellington boots caked with mud.

"I told Ernie we'd wait a day to start transporting the yearlings. This rain is supposed to move out by tomorrow." Her brow drawn into a scowl, she offered only a hint of a smile when she looked up at Teddy. "Damned weather. I woke up with a headache." She rubbed the heel of her hand against her forehead. "It's probably sinus."

Teddy handed her a mug of coffee. "Sit and eat."

E.B. slid a plate of soft-fried eggs with biscuits and sausage gravy in front of Britt, and Teddy was surprised to see Britt sit without protest. Teddy accepted her own plate from E.B., and they joined Britt at the table.

"We can look over the rest of those scores this afternoon, after you get rid of that headache," E.B. said to Britt. "I know you've got your therapy this morning, and I can use the time to catch up on track gossip."

"Okay," Britt said, not looking up from the food she was moving around on her plate.

Teddy watched as Britt shoved a forkful of biscuit and gravy into her mouth, then held her coffee mug up to inhale the steam. Her face was flushed, and her shoulders slumped. Teddy also noticed this was the first morning since she got the new harness that she'd come to breakfast with an empty sleeve rather than wearing the prosthetic arm.

"Have you taken anything for your headache?" Teddy asked.

"I got up about two o'clock and took some Tylenol, but I think it's wearing off. Maybe I need a decongestant."

"Are your sinuses stuffy?"

"Not really." Britt's flushed face paled, and she slid her chair back, then dashed to the half-bath off the kitchen.

E.B. looked at Teddy as they listened to Britt retch behind the hastily closed door. "I'll take care of the dishes," he said. "You see if you can get her upstairs."

"Okay. I want to check her arm. Infections can develop and go sour quickly. She finished her antibiotic more than a week ago. Maybe we need a second round."

"Let me know if I can do anything."

Teddy smiled at the worry in his eyes. "I will. These small setbacks aren't uncommon. I'll get a doctor out here if I think she needs one." Teddy stood and put her plate in the sink when she heard the toilet flush. "Duty calls."

"There is a slight redness and increased swelling of her residual limb, but not more than I'd expect, considering the length of time she wore the prosthesis yesterday." Teddy adjusted her laptop to better center her image on the video conference call with Tom and Will. "She was exposed to an unusual number of people during the yearling inspection yesterday and could have easily picked up something from one of them. I'm crossing my fingers it's just a twenty-four-hour virus."

"Just to be safe, I'd like another round of antibiotic prescribed," Will said. "An infection in that residual limb could set the project back months."

"Do you have any meds you might need there?" Tom asked.

"All I've got in my kit is penicillin, which she's allergic to. But I have plenty of nausea meds and several bags of saline if she becomes dehydrated."

"I'll get an antibiotic delivered out there today," Tom said, typing on his keyboard.

"Capsules for when her stomach settles, but can you send me a cocktail of antibiotic and fever-reducer, too, in case I need to get it into her through an IV?"

Tom tapped out the order on his keyboard. "Done. I'll send it as soon as the pharmacy has it filled."

"Otherwise, is her rehab on schedule?" Will asked.

"She's been much more receptive since progressing to a functioning prosthesis. Britt adapts very quickly. It's getting hard to keep her from jumping ahead in the rehab schedule."

"Has she signed the consent forms for the project?" Will's face grew larger, his eyes intense as he leaned toward the webcam.

Teddy shifted uncomfortably. "I haven't pressed her yet. Britt's not someone you can push. I'll ask when the time is right."

Tom nodded. "I trust you to know when." He looked off camera when an indistinguishable male voice sounded. "I've got a meeting. Good luck, Teddy. I'll find someone to bring that antibiotic out to you today."

"Thanks."

"I'm out, too," Will said. "Email me any updates, but feel free to call my cell if our patient gets worse."

"I will. Thank you." Teddy signed off and looked around the room they'd turned into a rehab station. She knew she sounded confident and on top of everything while on the conference call, but it had been an act for her commanding officer.

Britt's fever was higher than she'd like, even after she'd managed to finally keep a couple of acetaminophen tablets down long enough for them to dissolve. Whether they'd stayed in her stomach long enough to absorb was another question.

Then there was the kiss. Teddy stared at the treatment table under the window where Britt usually reclined while having her scar treated. Teddy could see the brilliant blue of Britt's eyes in the sunlight as if she were lying on that table right now. Teddy's gut clenched at the image, and she closed her eyes to steady herself. It wasn't like she hadn't kissed, even slept with other women since Shannon. Only a few. A one-night stand. Another grieving widow who understood what she felt. And one attempt at actually dating that ended badly. Britt's kiss, though, had built a fire in her the others hadn't. Teddy mentally shook herself. She needed to get out of her own head.

Teddy rose and slipped down the hallway to the bedroom where Britt, eyes closed and face flushed with fever, was reclined on a pile of pillows and tucked under a thick Sherpa comforter. The small trash can next to the bed stank of vomit. Britt had been sick again while Teddy had been on the conference call. She tied off the can's liner and lifted it out, then dropped in a fresh one.

"Sorry," Britt said without opening her eyes.

Teddy placed the vomit bag in the hallway to take downstairs later for disposal, then returned to Britt's bedside. "Nothing to be sorry about. Your aim was very accurate, so the clean-up was easy. I could tell you some real war stories about projectile vomiting, but not while your stomach is still wobbly." Teddy laid her palm on Britt's forehead. Hot and clammy. She stuck the digital thermometer in her ear. One hundred and one degrees. Britt's lips were dry and chapped. She picked up the glass of water on the nightstand. "Can you drink a few sips of this? I'm afraid you're getting dehydrated."

Britt shook her head slightly. "Barely hanging on here." She visibly shivered.

Teddy checked her watch. "Tom is sending a couple of prescriptions out to us, but I'm going to start an IV now and give you something more for nausea."

"No IV. I need the one hand I have." Britt barely uttered the words before she rolled to her side and dry-heaved over the trash can.

Teddy calmly walked into the bathroom, wet a clean washcloth, and returned to Britt's bedside. She laid the cold cloth across Britt's nape, but Britt grabbed it and wiped her face before rolling back to her previous position on the pillows. Her hand shook slightly as she positioned the cloth across her forehead, above her closed eyes.

"If you won't let me put an IV in, then I have some suppositories in my med kit."

Britt cracked open one eye, the single brow lifting in challenge.

Teddy didn't look away or back down. "Your choice."

Finally, Britt sighed. "I'm too sick to fight you." She offered her arm. "Do your worst."

Teddy laid out the things she needed from her med kit. Britt's four-poster bed was ideal for hanging the first bag of saline, and she made quick work of inserting the IV, then shooting a dose of anti-nausea medicine into the IV portal. Minutes later, Britt's face relaxed, and she drifted off to sleep. Teddy retreated to the wingback chair on the other side of the nightstand, pulled the ottoman close, and propped her laptop on her knees to chart the medicine she'd just administered.

"No! Down. Avery, get down!"

Teddy woke with a start, toppling her laptop to the floor. Britt was thrashing in the bed, tangled in the covers. The IV line whipped back and forth, jerking the bag loose from where it hung on the bedpost. Teddy dove and caught it before it hit the floor, then pinned Britt on the bed to stop her flailing. "Britt, Britt. It's okay. You're safe."

"Fuck. Avery. No, no, no. You didn't have to do this." Britt jerked and bowed her back. "Oh, God. Oh fuck. It hurts. Her first. No, no." Britt's pleading turned to sobs. "...her...first."

"Sh-h-h. You're safe, Britt. You're home. You're at Pop's house in Kentucky. Safe. Home." Teddy held tight and crooned words she hoped would soothe Britt's fever-fueled nightmare.

"No. Avery. Don't. Get down. My fault. My fault." Britt began to quiet, her sobs and plaintive pleading tearing at Teddy's heart. Her shouts were mumblings now, and her movements lessened to an occasional jerk of her fingers or shoulders.

Teddy touched Britt's cheek. Shit. She was burning up. She needed to cool her down. Teddy stood to hang the IV bag, then hesitated. She bent to brush her lips against Britt's fevered forehead. "Be right back, baby."

Teddy nearly barreled into Sen. Brock Story when she rounded the corner to enter the kitchen. He caught her by the arms. "What's wrong. Where's Britt?"

It took a moment for Teddy to refocus from her imperative mission—ice packs. "She's upstairs. Her fever is rising because I haven't been able to keep any Tylenol in her. I need to make some ice packs." She looked to Lynn. "Colonel Winstead is sending some medications for her. Can you let me know the minute they arrive?"

Senator Story held up a small paper bag. "I have the medicine. I'd dropped by the hospital and had planned to come out here before heading back to DC, so Tom gave me her meds."

Teddy took a deep breath in relief. "Thank you." She took the bag and peered inside to confirm Colonel Winstead had included everything she'd asked for. "I think we still need to try to cool her down."

"Large ice packs will be out in the stables. I'll go get some," Senator Story said.

He was charging outside before Teddy could answer. "Right."

Lynn shrugged. "Whatever's keeping those two mad doesn't matter right now. His moon hangs on that girl upstairs. It always will. I reckon they'll eventually work it out." She pointed to a grocery bag on the kitchen table. "He brought enough of her favorite crackers and ginger ale to choke a horse because he called E.B. earlier and found out she had the stomach flu."

Teddy smiled, but she didn't have time to linger. "I need to get this upstairs. Can you send him up as soon as he returns with the ice packs?"

"You've got it."

Teddy sprinted up the stairs, relieved to see Britt hadn't yanked her IV bag down again. It was getting low, but Tom had also sent a couple of extra bags of saline. She drew the medications quickly and injected them into the IV port. The anti-inflammatory was paired with a low dose of muscle relaxer to help with the aching Teddy knew the fever produced. After a few minutes, Britt visibly relaxed into a less-restless sleep.

"I've got the ice packs," Senator Story said quietly from the door.

Teddy waved him in as she pulled the covers back. Britt was wearing sweatpants and a T-shirt, the left sleeve leaving the end of her residual limb exposed. She was aware of him staring at Britt's arm.

The packs were like contained ice trays encased in cloth covers with Velcro straps, handy for wrapping around a horse's knee or fetlock. She hesitated. "They use these on horses? How clean are they?"

Senator Story let out a snort. "Cleaner than they'd be if they were in the house for human use." He met Teddy's eyes. "They're washed after every use, the covers laundered and even replaced if they contact an open wound. Dad's high-dollar horses get nothing but the best."

Teddy let the note of irritation in his voice pass, busying herself with placing the eighteen-inch-long packs against Britt's sides and draping one over her head like a barrister's wig. "That and the medicine should get her fever down pretty fast." She tucked the covers around Britt again, rechecked the IV, and stepped back.

She gestured to the chair she'd occupied before. "Would you like to sit with her for a bit?"

Senator Story glanced at her as if to confirm permission, then ignored the comfortable wingback chair. Instead, he dragged a straight-back wooden desk chair into the space she vacated. He sat, and his shoulders slumped as he rested his hand on the bed where her left hand should have been.

"If you can stay for a few minutes, I'd like to freshen up and grab a sandwich downstairs." She really did need to pee, and her stomach growled at the thought of one of Lynn's thick sandwiches. But mostly, she sensed he needed some time alone with his daughter.

"Take your time," he said, bending forward to brush a strand of sweat-soaked hair from Britt's forehead. "I'm not going anywhere until I know she's okay."

CHAPTER THIRTEEN

Britt felt weak…and wet, as if she'd been drowning and fighting, fighting, fighting to reach the surface and finally crawled onto a sun-baked beach. Her muscles were sore, like when you wake the day after stacking hay bales for the first time. Her eyes were crusty, and she rubbed them carefully to clear her vision. She was in a room of shadows—the closest was the shape of a man straddling a backward chair, his head bowed to rest on his arms crossed atop the chair's back. Her throat was sore and dry, but better after a few swallows to wet it.

"Dad?"

His head rose, and the figure in the wingback chair nearby sat forward.

"Britt?" He stood and moved the chair out of the way so he could sit on the edge of the bed. "How are you feeling, kiddo?"

"Not ready." She stopped and tried to clear her throat.

Teddy rounded the bed and thrust a glass of water with a straw near her mouth. "Small sips," Teddy said quietly.

Ignoring the advice, Britt sucked greedily on the straw, then dropped back onto her pillows. "Not ready to report for duty, sir."

Her father chuckled. "I think you'll be listed on sick call for a couple of days, soldier. So relax and repair."

An inadvertent move sent a blaze of fire through her residual limb. Britt instantly found Teddy's stare. "My arm?"

"A bit swollen and probably tender from wearing the prosthesis too long yesterday, but it's not why you're sick. You simply picked up a virus, probably from somebody in the crowd of people here yesterday."

Britt was relieved. Even though she hadn't signed up for Teddy's program yet, she disliked setbacks. She pulled her damp T-shirt away from her body. "I could use a dry shirt. I think I've sweated through this one." She looked to Teddy, who was sitting on the other side of her bed and checking her IV. "Can we take that out now?"

"Any nausea?" Teddy stuck the digital thermometer in Britt's ear and waited for it to beep.

"No. Throat's sore, and I'm still really tired. Have I been out long?"

"About eight hours. I gave you a second dose of medicine two hours ago and this bag is almost finished, so I think we can get rid of the IV. Then we'll get you in some dry sweats and change the sheets on the bed, so you'll be more comfortable." Teddy rummaged through her med kit and set out the bandage she'd need to tape in place when she withdrew the needle. "But if you can't hold down oral meds, we'll have to restart it."

"Okay." She'd fight that battle later. "What are you doing here, Dad?" Despite the rift between them, his presence comforted the daughter side of her. He was the parent who read her bedtime stories, attended her sporting events, and brought her treats when she wasn't feeling well.

"I'd stopped by the VA on my way back to DC to meet with General Schrader about some legislation we're trying to push through and ran into Tom Winstead. He had your meds in his hand, complaining about not having support troops at the VA, and digging money out of his wallet to bribe a civilian nurse to drive out here and deliver them." He shrugged. "Where else would I be after learning my favorite daughter was sick?"

Britt offered a weak smile, her throat tightening at the familiar love—and the unfamiliar touch of sadness—in his eyes. Although she had a major problem with the senator, she didn't want to be at odds with her father. "I'm your only daughter." It was the expected reply to their familiar jest. "But thanks."

"So, fresh clothes?" Teddy stood by Britt's dresser.

Britt pushed the covers back and sat up to swing her feet to the floor. She paused to wait out a wave of dizziness and gather her strength. Her father was at her side the instant she tried to stand. He steadied her with an arm around her waist and his strong physique pressed against her side.

"Slow down, minnow," he said. "Wait until you get your sea legs back."

She gave him a mock glare and replied with the rote retort. "I'm no freaking navy minnow, sir. I'm all army. Hoo-ah."

"Right you are, soldier. Hoo-ah." He stepped back but stayed close enough to catch her if she faltered.

Britt selected her underwear but let Teddy dig around in the lower drawers for the soft flannel pajama pants and long-sleeved T-shirt she wore only in the dead of winter. Her head still ached with a dull throb and felt like it would topple her over if she bent down.

Teddy escorted her to the bathroom door, then handed her the clothing. "I'm going to change your sheets while you freshen up and change. No shower until tomorrow. I don't want you to get chilled again."

"Okay." Britt already wanted to crawl back in bed and snuggle under the warm blanket, so she didn't intend to argue. But she was dying to pee after two IV bags and wasn't going to miss the chance to scrub the acrid taste of raw stomach juices from her teeth. When she emerged from the bathroom, a tray of nourishment was on her nightstand, and her father was helping Teddy change her bedding. She sat in the wingback chair and accepted the tray Teddy slid onto her lap. She wasn't really hungry, but the mug of Lynn's chicken noodle soup, buttery Club crackers, and glass of ginger ale were a little tempting. She nibbled a cracker, then dipped it in the soup to finish it off.

Pop appeared in the doorway. "How's my granddaughter?"

Teddy smiled as she fluffed the last pillow and turned to sit on the side of the bed. "Much better. Still running a bit of fever, but this virus should have run its course after a couple of days."

"Good. Now, how's my partner?" This question was pointed directly at Britt.

"Done in for today." Britt knew Pop would want total honesty. "But probably well enough to finish going over those scores with you tomorrow morning."

Pop nodded. "Good enough. We've got time before we need to head to Keeneland. Don't try to overdo things too soon. I need my partner well for the yearling sale."

"You've got it, Pop." Britt sipped the soup. She'd managed about half the mug, but she felt like if she didn't get back in the bed now, somebody might have to carry her. She motioned for Teddy to take the tray.

Her father was instantly at her side, hesitating in a moment of confusion when he held out his hand, then realized he was reaching for her left arm. Before he could switch, Britt grasped his forearm with her right hand and levered herself to stand. His ears and neck reddened at the faux pas.

"It's okay, Dad. I'm ambidextrous now. Anything I can do with my right hand, I can do with my right hand."

Teddy shook her head, looking amused at Britt's joke. "Back in the bed with you. You're getting delirious again."

Her dad, however, wasn't in tune with their humor. "Britt. If I could change what happened..."

Britt stiffened, her anger rising as hot and as fresh as the day she'd confronted him in the hospital in Germany. "Don't. It's too late to change what's already happened, but it's still happening at every base over there. Hell, every base here in the US. The question remains as to whether you'll do the right thing to stop it."

Brock frowned, the red creeping up his neck, angry rather than embarrassed. When he opened his mouth to speak, Pop clamped a large hand on his son's shoulder.

"Dinner's ready downstairs. Let's go eat and give Britt a chance to rest."

With one last scowl at Britt, her father followed Pop down the stairs. Teddy hung back, setting the food tray on the nightstand. "I'll take the soup mug but leave the ginger ale and crackers." She hovered over Britt, tucking her blankets in and fluffing her pillow, then stopped when Britt grabbed her hand.

"Sorry you had to see me at my worst. I hate throwing up." She leaned into Teddy's hand when Teddy cupped her cheek. "I know these viruses can be very contagious, and I hope you don't get whatever I had."

Teddy pressed forward and brushed her lips against Britt's. "I'm sure that since we shared spit last night, I would already have had symptoms if it'd gotten past my immune system."

"Shared spit?" Britt smiled, her mouth still inches from Teddy's. She was exhausted and aching, but she wanted the taste of Teddy's tongue against hers more than she wanted breath right now. "Well, since you're immune, let's share a little more." She pulled Teddy down and opened to her. Their tongues danced for a moment, but then Britt pulled back. She didn't have the breath or stamina to keep going. "Mmm. I approve of your treatment techniques, but I'm going to nap while you go eat."

Teddy, flushed and smiling, backed away. "Sweet dreams."

Britt's dreams were not sweet.

Teddy had woken Britt after dinner to take more medicine and eat a handful of crackers. Her stomach seemed to be settling, but the low-grade fever persisted. Her symptoms were typical of a stomach virus, so Teddy wasn't worried. In fact, she was surprised Britt's high fever had broken so quickly. E.B. and Senator Story, however, said she'd always been that way, even as a child. They insisted Britt could sweat out a fever and throw off a virus faster than anyone they knew. Still, she wanted to keep a close watch in case Britt's fever began to rise again, so she returned to her nest in the wingback chair after showering and putting on her pajamas. She donned her headphones and streamed a movie she'd been wanting to see on her laptop. She was halfway through the movie when movement on the bed caught her eye.

Teddy snatched her headphones off as she set the laptop on the ottoman and launched herself from the chair to Britt's bedside without conscious thought.

"Get down. Avery. Stop. Avery. No." Britt shouted and thrashed under the covers.

Teddy tried to pin her to the bed like she had before, but Britt was stronger now that her fever was down. Teddy quickly found herself bucked off and sprawling on the floor. "Son of a bitch." She jumped up and rounded the bed to try from the other side. If she could pin Britt's arm, maybe she could get her to calm.

"Bastard. Bad command. No, no. He killed her. Should have done more. Something. I should have—" Britt's words dissolved into sob-like gasps, and her arm came from under the covers, her elbow headed straight for Teddy's face.

Teddy ducked. As a medic, she'd developed an instinct for dodging elbows and fists when wounded soldiers suddenly regained consciousness and flailed in panic. She grabbed Britt's arm and pinned Britt's right side with her full body. Britt shook all over, but her skin didn't feel fevered. "It's okay. Britt, it's okay. You're home. You're safe."

Teddy could tell the moment Britt came awake. She went completely still except for the heaving of her chest. Teddy looked up into alarmed blue eyes. "Hey there. I promise I'm not molesting you in your sleep. I was just trying to keep you from tumbling out of the bed."

Britt stared for a few seconds, then averted her eyes. Teddy eased off her but remained lying on her side, propped on one arm, next to Britt.

"Want to talk about the nightmare?"

Britt shook her head, still refusing to meet Teddy's eyes.

Teddy stroked her cheek. "It's okay, honey. I have my own. Not as bad as I used to. They do improve over time, but it sometimes helps to talk." Not that she'd ever discussed hers with anyone.

Britt shook her head again. "Can't."

Teddy noted that Britt's skin was still cool and her face less flushed. "Could be all the medicine I've pumped into you today, ya know? Making you dream."

Britt shrugged, remaining basically nonverbal but using the sheet to wipe sweat and some tears from her face.

Teddy decided a diversion would let Britt keep her dignity and privacy intact. "How about I bring my laptop over here, and I can stream something we can watch together?"

Britt chewed her lip, then nodded. "Yeah. Okay."

Teddy smiled at her. "I'm going to grab some more pillows off my bed since you're hogging all the ones here. It'll just take a minute."

Fifteen minutes later, they were eating crackers and drinking ginger ale in bed, watching *Secretariat*. Britt added commentary in appropriate places, pointing out where the movie departed from real life at the track.

By the movie's end, Britt had relaxed and her breathing deepened. Her head had dropped onto Teddy's shoulder, and, somehow during the movie, their hands had become entwined. Teddy closed the laptop and slid it onto the nightstand on her side of the bed. The reading lamp by Teddy's chair still burned, but Teddy rested her chin on the top of Britt's head and closed her eyes. Although she lay on top of the covers and Britt underneath, the solid length of Britt's body next to hers to brought a peace she hadn't experienced in years. Safe. Warm. Not alone.

Teddy woke to the shower running in the bathroom connected to the bedroom and Britt's side of the bed unoccupied. She rubbed her eyes and stretched. Someone had draped a soft blanket over her during the night. The shower shut off, so Teddy rose to fold the blanket, clean up the trash from their cracker and ginger-ale feast the night before, and gather her things to return to her own bedroom. She was headed to the door when Britt emerged from the bathroom, hair wet and dressed in athletic pants and a white thermal Henley.

"Hey, you feeling better this morning?" Without thinking, Teddy went to Britt and began rolling up her left sleeve so it cuffed at the end of her residual limb. She inspected Britt's arm. "This is good. The redness from yesterday is gone. How's it feel?"

"I do feel better. Well enough to try some scrambled eggs and toast. And my arm feels good. Not sore at all."

"That's wonderful." Teddy laid her palm against Britt's cheek, then her forehead. "No fever."

"Oh? I didn't know you had a thermometer built into your hand." Britt's tone was teasing.

"Why, yes. Yes, I do. It's another innovation the army's testing." She stuck her tongue out at Britt. "Brat."

They stared at each other, grinning like idiots for no reason. At least no reason they cared to examine.

"Breakfast in fifteen minutes." E.B.'s bellow from the kitchen made them both jump, and they laughed.

Teddy backed out of the room. "I've got to hurry. Fast, fast, fast." She bumped into the door frame and corrected her path to step backward into the hallway. "Shower. Now." If she stayed in the room another minute, staring into Britt's blue eyes peeking at her from under wet, tousled hair, she was going to kiss her and forget that E.B. or Senator Story—if he was still here—could walk in on them at any minute. She wasn't that worried about E.B., but the senator was another matter.

Britt was relieved her stomach didn't rebel at the smells of breakfast when she paused in the doorway of the kitchen. She was hungry, but the memory of yesterday's virus was still vivid enough to make her cautious. "Just some scrambled eggs and toast for me, Pop." She hesitated when she realized he was stirring a pot of fresh grits. Real, high-quality grits. "And maybe some grits."

"Got ya covered, kiddo. We'll start you out easy and see how it goes."

"Thanks." She turned to scan the living room, then back to peer through the windows on the other side of the kitchen table. Nobody was on the porch, but a lone rider loped a tall, black Thoroughbred up from the sandy tractor paths that ran between the paddocks and hay barns. "He's still here."

"Yep. He still comes back from time to time. Can't stay away from the horses, especially when he's got something on his mind."

"Like what?"

"He doesn't usually say. Just shows up for a day or two and rides the farm until he works it out." Pop squinted one eye at her. "You gonna make a fuss about him being here now that you're up and around?"

She clenched her jaw and considered the question. "Not if Dad walks into this kitchen. But the minute he turns into the senator, I'm taking my breakfast to the office."

"Fair enough. You up to looking at the rest of those scores?"

"Yeah. I think Teddy was right about it being one of those twenty-four-hour bugs." She accepted the plate he handed her and took it to the table.

"I'm always right," Teddy said, heading straight for the coffee station. "But what am I right about this time?"

"The up-chuck virus." Pop held out a plate to Teddy. "You almost missed breakfast, missy."

"Don't remind me of yesterday unless you want a repeat." Britt's mood had gone from sunny and clear upstairs, to dark and brooding downstairs. Not even the sunshine that seemed to follow Teddy into the room could brighten Britt's mood.

"Sorry. I was up late taking care of a certain patient." Teddy, obviously failing to pick up on Britt's change of mood, remained cheerful. She took her plate and sat next to Britt. "Thanks, by the way, for the blanket."

"Blanket?"

"The one I woke up under this morning," Teddy said, giving Pop a don't-be-coy look.

Pop shook his head. "Must have been Brock when he went up to bed."

"The senator's still here?" Teddy spoke carefully, but her alarm was written all over her face. She looked at Britt, lowering her voice to a loud whisper. "He saw us on your bed together."

Pop's forehead wrinkled like a slept-in shirt as his eyebrows rose. "I hope you girls had your clothes on."

Despite her mood, Britt shook her head and chuckled as Teddy's expression turned from alarmed to mortified.

"Uh, Pop might be old, but his hearing is as good as a twenty-year-old's," Britt said. "And yes, we were in our pajamas. I was under the covers, and Teddy was on top."

"Of the covers. I was on top of the covers," Teddy frantically clarified.

"We fell asleep watching a movie on her laptop." Britt ignored Teddy's figurative hand-wringing.

"He's coming," Teddy said, her face now a mask and her posture military stiff in her chair.

Britt, sitting with her back to the windows, refused to look over her shoulder or turn around. "Does he have his phone out, texting or talking to someone?"

Teddy glanced out the window. "Uh, no. He's just smiling and walking this way. He's waving at Jill."

Britt let out a long breath. "That's Dad, not the senator. You can relax." She mixed the buttery grits on her plate with the scrambled eggs and scooped up a big forkful. "When that phone comes out, he turns into the senator. Unless that happens, then no drama." She bumped her knee against Teddy's under the table. "Eat before your breakfast gets cold."

Teddy appeared to relax, then tucked into her breakfast. "If I stay here much longer, I'm going to have to start running again."

"Breakfast is the most important meal of the day," her dad said, closing the door behind him.

"Boots, damn it." Pop pointed to the wet dirt clinging to his son's barn boots. "Outside on the porch. Then you sweep up that dirt you tracked in, or I'll tell Lynn who did it."

Britt had to smile as her dad scampered out the door to take off his boots, then dutifully took the broom and dustpan that Pop handed him and began sweeping up the mud he'd tracked in.

Teddy chuckled. "It's clear who runs the show in this house."

Pop widened his eyes in mock fear. "That woman was a drill sergeant for fifteen years. She can make your life miserable if you don't toe the line."

Her father reentered the kitchen in socked feet. "As any good drill sergeant should," he said. He went to the coffee station for his own mug of coffee, then heaped a plate with food from the stove before joining them. "Is that Mysty I saw in the paddock?" He looked at Britt as he reached for the butter.

"Yeah. Her breeding didn't take this year. We might be looking to rehome her."

"Why? I haven't seen you bond with a horse like you did with her since your first pony."

Britt shoved a forkful of food into her mouth and chewed. She didn't have a real answer. Maybe because, like Mysty, she'd lost control of her life and career?

"She's not going anywhere," Pop said. "Plenty of jobs for her around the farm. She can mind weanlings. She was a pretty good mama to the one baby she had. She might even work out as a surrogate if needed."

It was fairly rare, but they occasionally lost a mare when birthing or the mare rejected the foal for whatever reason, and the orphan would be introduced to a surrogate mare with a tendency to nurture so strong that she'd accept and raise a strange baby.

"Jill wants to breed her again," Britt said. Horse talk was safe ground for all of them.

"Up to you," Pop said. "You pay the breeding fee, and it's your foal if she has one."

"I'll think about it. Don't know how long I'll be around. I'm currently still a prisoner of the army." Britt rose and topped off her coffee.

"You're not a prisoner, Britt," her father said. "I had to use every persuasive tactic at my disposal to convince that surgeon to rearrange his schedule and then get the general to fly the guy to Germany. The US Army has made a huge investment in you, and it's your duty to repay that by finishing your mission. The horses will always be here later."

"Persuasive? Is that what you call it, Dad, when you back people into a corner with your money and influence to serve your own needs? I call it abuse of power. I don't know what you used to lean on the surgeon, but you know damn well the general wouldn't refuse you because you chair the committee that allocates military money." She stood and threw her napkin onto her plate of unfinished breakfast.

"Sit down, Britt."

"You don't get to give me orders in this house, Senator." Britt pointed to E.B. "The general at this post commands by respect. He doesn't have to resort to collusion. You and I both know getting me some fancy bionic arm isn't your real goal." Britt strode toward the stairs. "I'll wait for you upstairs," she said to Teddy, sliding her accusation onto her father's plate and leaving him to chew on it alone.

❖

Teddy peeked over the top of her mug at Senator Story. He shook his head once, then began to methodically consume his breakfast as if nothing had been said. But E.B. wasn't going to let it pass.

He put down his coffee mug and leveled a hard stare at his son. "You got something to do with holding up her papers?"

Senator Story put his fork down and faced his father. "Some things are more important than her immediate discharge from the army. She's getting the red-carpet treatment. They're letting her recover here. Do you think they send every soldier their personal live-in therapist?"

E.B. leaned across the table, pushing his face into his son's personal space. "There is nothing more important than my granddaughter, your daughter. And I don't care if the God-damned army builds a hospital across the street just for her. She wants out." E.B. poked his finger against his son's chest. "You're a big-shot senator. Make it happen."

E.B. stood and addressed Teddy. "Please tell Britt that I'll be in the study when you're done with her therapy. And leave the dishes for Lynn." Then he stalked out of the kitchen.

Senator Story sighed and glanced up when Teddy began clearing the dishes left by E.B. and Britt. His phone pinged, and he drew it from his pocket, read a text, and typed a quick reply. "I've got to go to Frankfort to meet with the governor before heading back to DC, but I'll be in Lexington again in a couple of weeks to connect with some supporters attending the yearling sale."

"Have a good trip. I'm just clearing the table before going upstairs. Britt's waiting for her morning therapy."

He shoved his last bite into this mouth and gathered his dishes to add them to the others in the sink. "I'm happy to see you've established a close rapport with my daughter."

Teddy's face heated. She didn't want to think about him seeing them in the bed, however innocent, but with hands entwined and bodies touching. "I've come to admire her a great deal. And, despite my initial reservations about this assignment, I'm enjoying my time here at Story Hill Farm."

"Good. That's good." He propped himself against the counter. His eyes were the same intense blue as Britt's, but calculating where Britt's were open, honest. "What has she told you about Afghanistan?"

Britt had confided nothing, and Teddy wouldn't tell him anything either. She desperately wanted Britt to participate in their advanced prosthetics program, even though she hadn't let herself examine why this mission had become so important to her, why it was more than an ordered one. But she didn't like seeing Britt manipulated for political reasons, especially by her own father. "I'm sorry, sir, but the privacy of anything discussed between myself and my patient is protected by law. I know you're her father, but E.B. Story is the only person authorized in her file to have access to her medical information."

Senator Story cocked his head and spoke as if addressing a child. "The government has access to anything they want, Lieutenant. No information is safe when Washington wants it." His phone vibrated from where he'd laid it on the counter, and he picked it up to read the text. "I've got to go. Tell my father I'll see them at the yearling sale in a few weeks." Then he looked her over, his expression reminding her of the way Britt would estimate the value of a racehorse. "And stay close to Britt any way you need to. Your influence will be helpful."

He spoke as though ordering rather than requesting she relay his message. Teddy was beginning to understand how Britt had come to see her father and the senator as two different people. She resisted barking a "Sir, yes sir" and snapping a smart salute. Instead, she dipped her chin to acknowledge the message. "Have a nice day, Senator," she said over her shoulder as she left him standing alone with his phone buzzing in his hand.

CHAPTER FOURTEEN

Teddy had never seen so many beautiful horses in one place before. And she was sure she'd never seen Britt look so attractive. She was the picture of country elegance dressed in jeans, a crisp white shirt, a tweed blazer, English boots, and a gold watch and necklace.

The day was overcast and a little chilly, so Teddy had worn jeans, a turtle-necked sweater, and a down vest. She'd also opted for paddock boots since they'd be walking around the barns, and any rain would likely turn those paths muddy.

They'd checked in on almost every one of the Story yearlings, saving the top horse for last. It wasn't hard to find him, because a crowd seemed to form every time Home from War was taken from his stall for exercise or a bath.

Teddy and Britt rounded the small crowd to see the colt peacefully grazing on a loose lead while his groom used a fly whisk to shoo away the occasional pest.

"Wow. He looks really calm. Are you sure this is my horse?"

The groom broke into a broad smile at Britt's question.

"Home from war, both of you," he said, stepping forward and pulling Britt into a tight hug even though she was six inches taller than him. "And who is this?" He turned to Teddy.

"Roberto, this is Teddy Alexander. Teddy, this is Roberto. He's the best groom on the backstretch."

"She does not lie," Roberto said, taking Teddy's hand and bowing as he touched his lips to it. "I am the best with horses, but I would rather have her luck in finding the prettiest ladies."

"You, sir, are a charmer," Teddy said, chuckling at the blush flooding Britt's cheeks. "So, she brings a lot of ladies around to impress them with her horses?" She smiled at Britt to assure her she was teasing.

Roberto wagged his finger at Teddy. "Oh, no. Not so many, but always very pretty."

"You look good, Roberto." Britt patted the man's small pouch of a stomach. "Appears that Melina has been feeding you well. I hope she's also doing okay."

"Bossy as ever, and enjoying our two grandchildren."

"Grandchildren. Congratulations. The years go by fast, don't they?"

"And look at you, chica. All dressed up like the lady of the manor." He held up a finger. "That's right. You aren't that kid tagging along after me any longer. You are back to stay, aren't you? The old man has been talking about you taking over for a couple of years now."

Teddy wanted to laugh at Roberto referring to E.B. as an old man. She figured them to be about the same age.

"I don't know yet." Britt's smile dimmed. "I still have some things to work out."

Roberto frowned and, without a hint of self-consciousness, took the hook mechanism of Britt's prosthetic arm in his hand. "We heard that you had a wing clipped in that terrible place. But you'll be fine, yes?"

Britt nodded. "Yes. I will."

Teddy was surprised when Britt reached out, took her hand, and didn't let go.

"Teddy is helping me. Among other things, she's my physical therapist. I'm going to be fine."

"Good, good."

"Now tell me about my horse. I can hardly tell he's the same colt. At the farm, he was restless and jittery."

"He was a handful when he arrived, but his curiosity at all of the activity around the barns distracted him almost immediately. This colt is a showman, he is. He loves to prance around the barns for an audience, do silly mischievous things at bath time, and pose for pictures. He only gets testy when nobody's around for him to impress. So, I parade him a lot. He likes it. The buyers like it."

Britt ran her hand over the colt, up and down his legs while Roberto talked. When she straightened again, Roberto edged close, and Teddy leaned in to hear, too, as he lowered his voice.

"Lots of interest in this one, chica. He's going to bring top dollar. You mark my word."

Teddy could see the excitement in their eyes and felt the undercurrent of anticipation as they shared a look. They weren't building up to a race, but the auction felt no less exhilarating.

"That's what we're counting on," Britt said. "And thanks for the extra time you spend with him. I didn't even have to argue with Ross when I asked that you be assigned to him, which means he's expecting a good sale with a big commission. If he goes at the price we hope tomorrow, there'll be something extra for you, too."

Roberto shrugged. "I don't need to be paid extra for doing my job."

"Those grandchildren are going to need a college fund," Teddy said.

Roberto laughed. "Smart and pretty." He nudged Britt with his elbow. "You have an eye, my friend, for fast horses and excellent women."

While activity was a constant buzz around the long, shed-row barns, the auction house was like driving through hill country.

Bidders and curious watchers sat alone, or in pairs, or small groups. Conversations were so muted and private the flipping of pages in the auction catalogue was audible. The hum of the semicircular auditorium would slowly gain volume and momentum, like a truck trudging uphill, in anticipation of the next yearling. Then a horse was led in, and the abrupt introduction was like bursting onto the hilltop. The ensuing auctioneer's singsong chant was a downhill race, picking up momentum until the final bid was marked by the thump of the gavel, the horse was led out, and everything dropped back to the low hum.

It was crazy, and Teddy found it a little hard to follow the fast pace of the bidding and odd rat-a-tat bark of the auctioneer. No bidding paddles were distributed like at the estate auctions she'd attended a few times with friends. The faces in the crowd apparently were familiar to the three men who stood outside the ring, scanning for the next person to up the bid.

A bay colt, sleek and groomed to perfection, was led into the ring, and the announcer began to recite his pedigree and the racing record of the colt's parents and prominent siblings. Then the auctioneer announced a minimum, and the bidding began.

Most bids were too quick for Teddy to detect, but she did catch a raised finger, a nod, even several fingers displayed against the shoulder of one bidder who wanted to jump ahead. Teddy became so caught up in it, she almost wanted to bid herself.

Britt put her hand on Teddy's arm when she began to squirm in her seat. "Don't scratch your nose," she warned her, then chuckled. "You could end up owing a million dollars for a horse you didn't mean to buy."

When the colt's price did, in fact, surpass the million-dollar mark, the bidding climbed in increments of a hundred-thousand dollars.

Teddy pressed her shoulder against Britt's and whispered. "I would never guess these people had that much money to spend." Most of the crowd were men, dressed in khakis, open-collared shirts, and wind-breaker jackets. She'd expected Arab sheiks, flashy billionaires in designer suits, even a few women in designer outfits that screamed wealth.

"Even though the core of the racing community still is gentry with bloodlines that go back as far as their horses, consortiums or equity groups, not individuals, own a lot of racehorses today," Britt said. "So, most of the people you see bidding are trainers or purchasing agents for the real owners."

Teddy took in Britt's blazer and polished boots. "You look nice today. More dressed up than I've seen you before."

"Thank you." Britt turned her head and smiled, her lips inches from Teddy's. "I'm a seller, not a buyer at this auction. I need to look like my horses are good enough that I can afford nice clothes."

"Ah. I see."

"Sold. Hip number zero-five-six for one-point-six million," the auctioneer announced.

Britt shifted in her seat but maintained her relaxed slouch. "Next is one of ours," she said quietly, as a chestnut filly was led into the ring.

"Hip number six-one. This filly has a blue-ribbon pedigree, folks...sired by Tapit, out of Cat Lady, she's a full sister to Kat's Song, a two-point-three-million stakes winner. Bred by Story Hill Farm. Bidding starts at three-hundred-thousand. Thank you. Do I hear three-ten? Three-ten. How about three-twenty. We've got three-twenty."

Britt's face was calm, but they were positioned to observe most of the seating, and her eyes flicked sharply back and forth over the crowd. Teddy could hardly breathe when the bidding topped nine-hundred-thousand. She gripped Britt's forearm as the numbers climbed higher.

"Nine-fifty. Can I get nine-seventy. Nine-seventy. What? One million. We have one million." A hand raised in the far corner. "One-point-one. Do I have one-point-two?" A nod confirmed the bid, but the far-corner bidder immediately held up three fingers. "One-point-three. Can I get one-point-four?" A new bidder held up her open hand. "One-point-five? Yes, that's one-point-five, folks. Can I get one-point-six?" The other two bidders both shook their heads. Either the price was too steep or the woman who had waited to jump in with a high bid was too daunting.

The auctioneer slammed his gavel down. "Sold. One-point-five-million for hip number six-one, the filly by Tapit, out of Cat Lady." The slender, older woman turned to Britt, nodded and smiled, apparently pleased with her purchase.

"Good price." Britt let out a breath, returning the nod and smile. "The auctions are bringing top dollar this year. That's a good sign the economy is improving."

"How do they know where to start the bidding?" The process fascinated Teddy.

"A combination of things set it—the horse's score from the inspection, the pedigree, and the owner. The stud fee alone for Tapit was three-hundred-thousand, so it was expected that would be the minimum acceptable bid."

"Wow. Three-hundred-thousand for his little swimmers?"

"Yep." Britt checked her auction booklet. "That's the last of ours scheduled for today's auctions." She checked the time on her phone. "So, how much of Kentucky have you seen?"

Teddy was intrigued. "Not much outside the hospital and the few restaurants between there and my studio apartment. Tom—Colonel Winstead—and I transferred here only four months ago, and we've spent about two months of that time traveling to gather research, drum up financial support, form a team, and recruit participants for the prosthetics project."

Britt stood and held out her hand to pull Teddy up, too. "I'm shocked, Lieutenant Alexander. Too many military personnel isolate themselves. The most critical element to gaining public support for military funding is for us to infiltrate and engage the community we serve. And, it's an officer's duty to lead by example."

"An officer's duty?" Teddy was skeptical. She wasn't familiar with any military directive like that.

"Yes. To infiltrate and engage." Britt held tight to her hand as she led her out of the auction building. "It's the wrong time of year for the Derby, but I think I can create some semblance of the experience if you're up for a little adventure."

Teddy stopped, her hand pulling loose from Britt's grip. She couldn't put words to the feeling that exploded and filled her. It was... it was completely unexpected. It was...it was an emotional orgasm. Yes. An emotional orgasm after what she hadn't realized was a long, long, long drought. Britt was offering fun. Pure, unadulterated fun. It wasn't like Teddy had been miserable for years. She had a good relationship with her parents, even if they saw each other only a couple of times a year. And she had Shannon's family, who still treated her like a daughter. She had friends, and her military family. Her job was interesting and fulfilling. But somewhere along the way, she'd forgotten to have fun. She suddenly felt like that kid who was just told she's going to Disney World for her first time ever.

Britt looked uncertain at Teddy's hesitation, the grasper on her prosthetic arm clicking as she unconsciously shifted her shoulders uneasily. "Unless you already had plans. I mean, it's no big deal."

Unable to contain herself, Teddy gave a little hop. "I'll need a big hat, right? All the ladies wear those big hats. I've seen them on television."

Britt laughed, her face and posture instantly relaxing. "Don't worry. I've got you covered."

Teddy slipped her car keys into the pocket of Britt's blazer and took possession of Britt's hand again. This time, she led their way to the parking lot. Louisville, where Churchill Downs is located, was an hour and twenty minutes away. There was no time to waste. "You drive. I'm too excited. Come on, come on!"

"Come on, baby, come on."

The announcer's deep voice called the lineup as the horses rounded the far turn and headed down the homestretch. "Coming out of the far turn, it's Goulding on the inside, with Dancing Destroyer keeping pace a nose behind. Closing at third is Jilted Bride with Turtle Trax fourth, followed by Sense a Million, Misty Blue…"

"Come on, Misty Blue. Misty Blue. Misty Blue. Misty Blue." Teddy chanted the name of the horse she'd placed a twenty-dollar bet on—at Britt's recommendation—despite the filly's eight-to-one odds.

"…with Auction Fever and Boomtown trailing the pack." The announcer's voice rose an octave. "Misty Blue, running sixth, is making a move, coming up fast on the outside."

"Come on, come on. Misty Blue. Misty Blue. Misty Blue." Teddy chanted louder, as if her cheers could propel the horse and jockey faster.

"Dancing Destroyer has the lead and is pulling away. Jilted Bride is second, and Goulding has dropped to third. Misty Blue is still surging on the outside. Misty Blue is third. Misty Blue is second and challenging Dancing Destroyer."

"Misty Blue. Misty Blue. Misty Blue." Teddy was screaming now, joined by Britt's low, tight "Come on, come on, come on."

Teddy jumped up to stand on the metal stadium bench and waved the wide-brimmed straw hat, its band a rainbow of color, that Britt had provided as promised. She had made Britt stop by her apartment so she could change into something less casual, including knee-length fashion boots that she used now to stomp noisily on the metal bench.

"It's Misty Blue by a head at the finish line," the announcer shouted. "Dancing Destroyer is second, Jilted Bride third, and Goulding in fourth place."

"I won!" Teddy grabbed Britt's face with both hands and kissed her without thinking. Well, it was probably the Kentucky straight bourbon she'd tasted multiple times and in multiple cocktails during their afternoon distillery tour thinking for her. But she was so excited, and Britt was so attractive. So present. Here. With her. Now.

They grinned at each other when Teddy broke off the kiss and stepped back. Teddy held up her betting ticket.

"Twenty dollars at eight to one is…oh, I can't think."

"A hundred and eighty dollars. You should have bet a hundred." Britt put her arm around Teddy's shoulders to turn her toward the window to cash out her winnings.

"Says the woman who sold a horse for one-point-five-million dollars this afternoon." Teddy missed Britt's warmth when she dropped her arm from Teddy's shoulders, so she hooked her arm in Britt's and pressed close as they walked to the cash window. To steady herself. Because she'd had too much bourbon. And because Britt was driving and had only sipped a little.

They cashed in her ticket, and Teddy protested when Britt steered her toward the parking lot.

"I want to bet some more."

"There's only one more race tonight, and we have reservations for dinner."

"Okay." Teddy was always interested in food. "But I want a mint julep before we leave here. I can't tell people I went to Churchill Downs and didn't drink a mint julep."

"You won't like it."

"You don't know that. I might."

Britt shook her head. "I'm afraid the track restaurants, thus the bars here, are closed. Most aren't open this late in the racing season anyway. But if you're determined to try one, I'm sure we can get one at The Brown."

"What's The Brown?"

"It's where we're going for dinner."

"Okay." Teddy was happy with that prospect. The mention of dinner again was really making her hungry.

"Wow."

Britt was pleased that Teddy seemed amazed by the ornate interior of The Brown Hotel. The historic building was still impressive to her, even though she'd been here many times to dine in the restaurant with her parents or grandparents over the years. It was a step back in time, with floor-to-ceiling opulent Baroque design and furnishings.

Teddy's face was a beautiful study in rapturous wonder as she took in the lavish furnishings. Her eyes were a wide and smoky green. Her blond hair shimmered like the hundreds of crystal teardrops on the chandeliers lighting the lobby. Teddy had changed into a burgundy silk shirt that draped her shoulders like a caress and tucked into cream-colored trousers that hugged her hips and legs. The thin belt at her slim waist matched the knee-high boots with fashionable but solid two-inch heels. Britt always thought spike-style high heels looked silly on boots and the women who wore them. She had to stop staring. Britt followed Teddy's gaze to the carved panels that made up the ceiling.

"If you grew up a military brat, surely you've seen more ornate architecture than this hotel."

"My dad was in a combat-engineer unit. He deployed a lot, but not to places where we could live with him. My grandfather was navy, and mom grew up with her father being out to sea for months out of every year, so I guess Dad being gone a lot didn't seem unusual to her." Teddy shrugged. "Grandpa was a jet mechanic on aircraft carriers, so he was mostly stationed out of Virginia, while Dad was frequently stationed out of North Carolina. We lived with Grandma, or she lived with us while Grandpa or Dad was deployed. So, no, I didn't get to see the world."

"The restaurant is over there," Britt said, pointing. "We're just in time for our reservation."

Teddy didn't seem to mind, and Britt couldn't seem to stop the brief touches, like placing her hand on the small of Teddy's back to guide her into the restaurant. They had so many reasons to stay out of each other's personal space, but damn, if she wasn't irresistibly drawn to Teddy like a flower turns to face the sun. Maybe this was just part of her healing. They were adults. They both knew the consequences if they were indiscreet. It wasn't that Britt outranked Teddy, but their patient-therapist relationship made any intimacy a professional taboo. Teddy's career could be sunk, and Britt would be held accountable for adversely influencing an officer below her rank.

Britt looked up from spreading her napkin in her lap to find Teddy watching her. When their eyes caught and held, so much more than words passed between them. Yes. They were on the same page. Desire crackled between them like static electricity.

"Hello?"

Britt blinked, suddenly realizing the young man standing next to their table had been speaking to them. "Sorry. What were you saying?"

His smile showed dimples and straight, white teeth that were surely the work of a skilled orthodontist. "I'm so sorry to interrupt. You seemed to be having a moment, and I just barged right in. Would you like me to come back in a few minutes?"

Teddy's face flushed red, but she reached out to grasp his forearm. "No. Please. Could I have a mint julep?"

"You sure can." He laid two menus on the table and handed Britt a slim bourbon and wine menu. "Something for you?"

Britt laid it down without opening it. "Please make her mint julep with Jefferson's Reserve rather than Jim Beam. And I'll have a Kentucky Mule."

"Would you also like that with Jefferson's Reserve?" He filled their water glasses as they placed their drink order.

"No. Evan Williams is fine in the Mule."

He smiled. "I'll be right back with your cocktails, ladies."

Teddy smiled. "So, I gather that bourbon is a big deal in Kentucky."

Britt nodded. "It is. They say true sons," she dipped her head in a small bow, "and daughters of Kentucky taste a bit of Beam before ever latching onto their dear mother's teat."

Teddy smirked at Britt and opened her menu. "Yeah, right." She perused it for a moment but looked up again. "Do women even have teats?"

Britt chuckled. "Technically, they do. If you go by the strict definition of the word. But I wouldn't advise using that word in a moment of intimacy. I think it's safe to say most people associate it with animals. Not people." Britt opened her own menu, then closed it.

"You're not hungry?" Teddy asked.

"I'm going to leave it up to the chef. They don't appear too busy tonight, and some chefs will go off menu and cook something special when given the chance."

"I like it." Teddy closed her menu, too, and studied Britt. "Me, too."

"Yeah?"

"Yes."

"Okay, then." Britt raised her hand to let their waiter know they were ready, but he was already on his way to their table, clearly having been observing them.

"What may I serve you, ladies?"

"We're going to let the chef decide," Britt said.

He clapped his hands together with a gay flair. "Excellent choice! Chef Rick will be so pleased with the opportunity."

Britt held up her finger to pause his enthusiasm. "Only three… okay, four courses…and we have to meet someone out front by ten o'clock sharp."

"That should not be a problem." His hands performed another small flutter of applause. "You are going to make his night."

Teddy's mouth dropped open. "What's at ten o'clock? Don't we need to drive back to Lexington?"

Britt took a long sip of her drink to stall. She hoped she hadn't overstepped. "Well." She cleared her throat. "The hotel is famous, food-network famous, for its signature breakfast dish, The Hot Brown. It'd be like going to the Derby and not trying a mint julep if you didn't stay long enough to have a Hot Brown. So, I booked a couple of rooms for us to stay here tonight. The auction doesn't start until noon. I mean, I'll need to be at Keeneland by ten or so to check on our horses, but we'll have plenty of time for breakfast before we drive back."

Oh my God. She was rambling. She'd been nervous before, but she'd never rambled like an idiot. Well, she was now. She should just shut up. Heat crawled up her neck and burned her ears. But the runaway horse that was her mouth had mercifully stopped, and Teddy smiled. Or maybe it was the mint julep smiling.

Teddy didn't speak for a heartbeat. More like ten heartbeats, because Britt's was galloping. Then she tilted her head, and one eyebrow moved elegantly upward. "You booked *rooms*?"

Britt nodded. Her ears went from hot to scorching, if that was possible. She was sure she'd have blisters later. "But if you prefer to return tonight, I can cancel the reservation. If we have time before you're reassigned, I'd like to show you Mammoth Cave. We could detour back through Louisville to indulge in a Hot Brown before going on to the caves." There. That sounded reasonable. Her temperature was returning to normal, and her brain was rebooting.

Their waiter appeared, slipping appetizers and a second round of drinks onto the table without interrupting their conversation.

"I'd love to see Mammoth Cave. I've read about it but didn't really want to go by myself." She sipped her drink. "When I first met you, I would have never guessed you could be so adventurous, so much fun." Was it the alcohol that lowered Teddy's voice to a melodic, flirty tone? God bless Kentucky bourbon.

Britt bent forward, offering her last bite of crab appetizer on her fork because Teddy had inhaled her own. "I can be a lot of fun," she said, watching Teddy take the offered treat into her mouth and slowly slide it from the fork.

"And persuasive," Teddy added for her.

Persuasive? Is that what you call it, Dad, when you back people into a corner with your money and influence to serve your own needs? I call it abuse of power.

Britt's own word echoed in her head. "I've overstepped." She sat back in her chair, the flirtation lost.

Their waiter appeared, and they both stayed silent as he placed small bowls of bourbon peach sorbet before them. He seemed to read the shift in mood. "To cleanse the palate," he said, then melted away.

"In no way did I intend to pressure you," Britt said. "I know you got dragged into my father's agenda and ordered to rearrange your life for my rehabilitation. I know your prosthesis project is important to you. But you were not obligated to come with me today, and I'm sorry if I didn't make that clear. Today has absolutely no bearing on whether I participate in your project, which my father is also using to further his agenda. You owe me nothing. I expect nothing." Britt placed her napkin on the table. "In fact, we can leave right now and return to Lexington."

Teddy picked up her spoon. "Are you finished?"

"Finished?" Britt was confused. With her meal? Obviously not.

"With your speech?" Teddy spooned her first bite of sorbet into her mouth and closed her eyes as she savored it. "Nectar of the goddess. This is so good." She opened her eyes, and her slow, dimple-evoking smile captured Britt's gaze. "And, although indignant is a very sexy look on you, let me make this clear for *you*—my orders are to rehab you in preparation for a bionic prosthesis. I've done that. When we see Colonel Winstead tomorrow, that will be my report. So, me being here today..." she pointed to the table, "...has nothing to do with your rehab. I enjoy your company. I'm having fun. And I'm going to finish this fantastic meal you've promised me. I'm looking forward to the surprise you've arranged afterward and plan to sleep like a baby in a fancy hotel tonight." She aimed her spoon at Britt's sorbet. "Also, if you don't eat that before it melts, I'm going to."

Britt snatched up her spoon and used it to bat Teddy's away. "No way. This is my favorite dish next to The Hot Brown." She spooned a large scoop into her mouth, enjoying the smooth warmth of the bourbon and icy sweet of the peach. "And, just so you know, sassy is a very sexy look on *you.*"

"Really? Is that for us?" Teddy couldn't believe her eyes.

Their meal had been the best she'd ever eaten. The chef had personally emerged from the kitchen to light the flames of their dessert and thank them for allowing him to share with them the lamb dish he intended to become his signature entrée.

Now, they'd stepped out of the hotel to find an elegant white open carriage drawn by two matched grays.

A tall woman, wearing formal groom's livery and a short top hat, smiled. "Good evening, ladies. I'm Katelyn, your driver." She pointed to the two horses. "Your escorts tonight are Baron and Sterling." The horses bobbed their heads in turn at the sound of their names. Katelyn held out a hand to Teddy. "May I assist you?"

Teddy felt like a princess, accepting Katelyn's hand to steady herself as she stepped up into the carriage. She settled onto the soft leather seat and noted that, while Katelyn stood by in readiness, she gave Britt the opportunity to lever herself into the carriage without assistance. She thought the action unusually astute until Katelyn walked away from them for a last check of the horses and rigging. The average person wouldn't have noticed, but Teddy recognized the faint hitch in Katelyn's gait. She had a prosthetic leg.

Teddy smiled to herself. The world was such a small place. Britt settled beside her, and Teddy pulled Britt's hand into her lap and entwined their fingers. So much loss in so many lives. So much strength that carried them all forward. So much living still ahead. She didn't want to think of that now. She couldn't think of that roller coaster of elation and sadness now. Teddy lifted Britt's arm to drape it across her shoulders and snuggled against Britt's side.

Katelyn climbed into the driver's seat but twisted to face them. "Would you like the tour or to just ride?"

Teddy looked up at Britt. "The tour?"

Britt nodded. "Katelyn's the best tour guide in Louisville. Very entertaining."

"So, you take a lot of women on these rides?" Teddy asked.

"I do." Katelyn's response was quickly delivered with a hint of mischief.

"Good to know, Katelyn, but I think you knew the question was for Britt." Teddy looked from Katelyn to Britt. "I suspect collusion here."

Britt chuckled. "Katelyn's an old friend. We were roommates at West Point."

"If you prefer, I can just tell you stories about Britt as a college plebe."

"Don't forget that I haven't paid you yet." Britt's scowl and warning held a playful tone.

Teddy laughed. "That's very tempting, but I wouldn't want Baron and Sterling to be short of oats, so how about you give us the historic tour and save the other stories for another day over a few beers?"

Katelyn bowed her head in a courtly gesture. "I am at your command. A historic tour, it is." She turned to face forward. When she picked up the reins, the horses instantly raised their heads and stepped out at the soft click of her tongue.

CHAPTER FIFTEEN

The flick of Britt's tongue against the small fresh scar on the corner of her upper lip was driving Teddy to near madness. She recognized it simply as one of Britt's signs that she was nervous. But, damn, Teddy could imagine a lot of other things that her tongue could be doing.

The elevator door opened, but neither moved. When the doors started to close again, Britt stepped in to stop them. "This is our floor." Her voice low, she avoided Teddy's gaze as she held her arm out in a "you first" gesture.

Teddy slipped past her and turned to the right as Britt indicated. Her head buzzed—from the nightcap they'd paused in the bar to have, from the romantic dinner and carriage ride, and from the fact that Britt was walking so close right now Teddy could almost feel Britt's breath on her neck. She stopped at the door numbered five-zero-six and looked down at her key before turning around to face Britt. "This is my room."

Britt, her eyes impossibly blue, didn't step back. She also didn't close the breath of space between them. Her tongue worried that scar one more time. Did she know how it affected Teddy?

Teddy trailed a finger along Britt's jaw and down her neck to trace the *V* of her open collar. She tilted her head, her mouth hovering a nanosecond from devouring Britt's, then looked over Britt's shoulder to the door directly across the hall. "And there's your room."

Britt closed her eyes and dropped her chin to her chest. Her face was flushed as she dutifully stepped back and turned to cross the hall. The instant Britt slid her card key into the lock and opened the door, Teddy was at her back, pushing her inside as the door closed behind them. Britt spun in surprise, and Teddy used her body to pin her against the wall.

"I like your room number better. Seven's always been lucky for me."

Britt raised an eyebrow. "You could have asked to switch."

Teddy purposely parted her lips, drawing Britt's attention to her mouth. "I'd rather wrestle for it...naked."

Britt's mouth was on hers, that worrisome tongue dueling with hers before Teddy could mount her intended offensive. The last doubt gone, so were their clothes with battle-ready efficiency. Britt's prosthetic arm and harness, after more than a month of therapy sessions, was little more than another article of clothing to them. Only after Britt ripped the covers back and they tumbled onto the king-sized bed did they pause, breathless and staring into each other's eyes. Teddy lay on her back, Britt on her side with several pillows tucked under the armpit of her residual limb to free her right hand to explore.

"Are you sure?" Britt asked, her fingertips feathering across Teddy's cheek, then smoothing across her collarbone and down her arm.

"Yes."

Britt's kiss was softer, less desperate, but her hand wasted no time in finding Teddy's breasts. Britt was so responsive to her signals, lingering when Teddy's breath hitched at the feel of Britt's lips and light nips along her neck and shoulders, and sliding her hand downward when Teddy brought one knee up, opening herself in invitation.

Britt's long finger filled Teddy, her thumb lightly grazing Teddy's clit, stroking, stroking, stroking. Her teeth gently tugged at Teddy's nipples that were rock hard and seemed to pulse with every stroke between her legs. Then a second finger stretched her, finding that spot inside that swelled her clit more against Britt's thumb with each stroke, stroke, stroke. Britt's mouth was on her throat again, sucking where her pulse pounded, pounded, pounded. And it came so fast. So fast. She cried out and arched upward, bowed taut by the powerful spasm of pleasure that gripped and held her for long seconds. Seconds that seemed like minutes. She collapsed back onto the bed, limp and breathless, her heart pounding like a ceremonial drum.

"You are so incredibly beautiful," Britt whispered.

Light from the downtown streets filtered in through the window sheers, and the longing in Britt's eyes triggered an orgasm aftershock that made Teddy jerk and shiver. She drew Britt down onto her, skin to skin, warm breast to breast, and held her head as she kissed her long and deep. She shifted a thigh between Britt's legs, finding her warm and slick. Teddy broke the kiss, guiding Britt's head to her shoulder and cradling her there while she spoke.

"You are so strong and so noble. And you carry so much weight on your shoulders. Set all of that aside for tonight, and let me have you. Can you do that?" She rolled them over so Britt was under her. For a long moment, Britt wouldn't meet her gaze. "Britt, honey?" Had Teddy pushed too hard and ruined their night? Britt's eyes finally met hers, and she nodded.

"Okay. As long as you don't tell the army that I gave in so easily to your torture."

Teddy kissed Britt, pushing her tongue into Britt's mouth, teasing Britt's tongue with hers, then withdrew to nip at Britt's earlobe. "You say torture. I call it worship."

She took her time kissing her way down, learning Britt's body. The muscles she'd honed when conditioning for deployment were even more pronounced because of her weight loss since being injured. Most of Britt's scars were familiar to Teddy. Some that were normally covered by her clothes were not. Teddy paid special attention to Britt's response when she mouthed Britt's disfigured left breast. Too sensitive, or no sensation? No scarring, but Teddy's short nails raked across the muscle bands of Britt's lower belly and made her hips buck slightly, and her legs opened. Teddy looked up to find Britt watching her.

Britt's lips were parted, her chest rising and falling, rising and falling in quick breaths. "Your mouth. I want your mouth on me, and your fingers inside."

Teddy didn't hesitate. She shouldered between Britt's long legs and stroked through her sex from entrance to clit. She swirled her tongue around the turgid flesh and sucked at it twice before rolling her tongue, thrusting inside, then flattening her tongue again to lick upward. When she sucked this time, she gently raked her teeth against the hood of Britt's clit.

"Oh, God. Teddy." Britt's legs trembled.

Still sucking, Teddy plunged a finger inside Britt. Stroke, stroke, stroke. Suck, teeth, suck.

"Teddy. Baby. Oh, yeah." Britt groaned out her words.

Teddy withdrew and went back in with two fingers. Stroke, suck, teeth. Stroke, suck, teeth. Britt's quick breaths changed to audible pants. Britt needed only a nudge to fall over the edge. Teddy's heart soared at the beauty and trust and control—all swirling into a ball for her to unleash. She sucked harder, thrust deeper, and raked her nails across Britt's sensitive belly.

"Fu-u-uck." Britt arched off the bed and growled out the internal combustion.

Teddy moved upward, still keeping her fingers gloved in Britt's trembling body. She placed light kisses along Britt's taut belly, between her breasts where her heart still pounded, then on each nipple and along her neck. She paused to stare into Britt's glittering eyes before she reverently touched her lips to Britt's, caressing, parting, tasting, sharing.

They didn't need words.

Teddy woke with her tongue stuck to the roof of her mouth and her bladder screaming for relief. She half lay on top of Britt, her head pillowed on Britt's shoulder, her leg entwined with Britt's. The poor woman's entire right side must be completely numb. But as comfortable as her body felt nestled along Britt's warm length, her bladder continued to protest. She carefully extracted herself and made a quick trip to relieve the problem, then slipped back under the covers.

Britt hadn't moved. Her dark lashes, thick and long, lay against smooth cheeks. Overdue for a trim, her short, dark hair feathered around her ears and down her nape. She was beautiful in an androgynous way. Earlier, Teddy had imagined her as an Amazon warrior, strong and bold, but now she saw an Elven warrior, lithe and faster than light. So intelligent. And secretive.

Tonight was a victory. Teddy had wanted to cheer when Britt invited her to Louisville, for a clear—yet still honorable—seduction. Their attraction was undeniably strong. And they'd grown closer over the weeks. But the occasional kisses, long talks, and evening walks to the hay barn were baby steps in Britt opening up. The big door—why the army refused to release her, which Teddy believed was the root of her nightmares—remained closed.

But tonight had nothing to do with therapy. It had everything to do with Teddy's desperate need to help a friend she felt was mired in a personal trauma. She'd stopped thinking of Britt as a client weeks ago. She was a friend. One who needed help.

What secret did she carry for the army that tore so at her soul? The very thought woke every protective instinct Teddy possessed.

Britt stirred and started to roll onto her left side. Teddy slid in behind and took her weight easily when the discomfort of her too-recent injuries rocked Britt back. Britt was taller, but Teddy was more sturdily built. She wrapped her arms around Britt and rested her cheek against Britt's ear. Britt scooted back, tucking the angles of her body against Teddy's curves, then tugged Teddy's hand up to cup around her small breast. Was she awake? Britt's sigh, then her slow rhythmic breathing indicated any awareness was only momentary. So, Teddy closed her eyes, reveling in the softness of the breast resting in her hand, the bravery of the heart beating against hers, and the peace she hadn't felt for a long, long time.

❖

"Holy mother." Teddy was sure Britt's body pinning her against the shower wall was the only reason she was still standing. Her legs felt like those of a newborn colt, weak and wobbly. She wasn't sure how much of the steam was from the shower, or just from them. Wow.

"Are you...are you religious?" Britt panted out the words, apparently because she was suffering from the same tremors as Teddy. Her fingers were still buried inside Teddy, as deep as Teddy's fingers were inside Britt.

"No." Teddy slowly withdrew but couldn't resist the chance to stroke Britt's sensitive clit one more time. Britt jerked, pulling out of Teddy. "But if you keep sending me toward the light like that, you're going to make me a believer."

Britt shook her head. "That's bad, so bad."

"What? You didn't like my joke?"

They froze when a knock sounded at the door. Then Britt smiled. "I pre-ordered breakfast."

Teddy pushed her out of the shower. "Then you better dress fast and let them in."

Britt rubbed a towel over her head as she opened the bathroom and yelled at the door to the hallway. "Hold on a minute, please."

Teddy held up one of the hotel's thick terry-cloth robes for Britt to slide into before spinning Britt around and tying the sash herself. "I wouldn't want this coming loose and giving the bellhop an eyeful."

Britt grinned. "It might get us extra bacon."

"Ma'am? Did you order room service?" The disembodied voice leaned toward female but was husky enough to be gender neutral.

They looked at each other.

"Only if she's really cute and actually has an extra order of bacon on her cart," Teddy said, shoving Britt out of the bathroom and closing the door so she could dress.

The hotel's signature Hot Brown entre was as good as the hype, Teddy decided. She was skeptical when she eyed what appeared to be an open-faced turkey sandwich. For breakfast? Then she tasted it. What was in that sauce? Britt was lucky she ate quickly, or else Teddy would have shamelessly eaten hers too.

The fact they had no luggage didn't seem to bother the hotel staff. They had each been supplied with a shopping bag that held any toiletries they could possibly need and silk pajamas in the correct size—no doubt provided by Britt when she made the reservation—that they never got around to wearing. The baby-butch bellhop who delivered breakfast was cute enough, but didn't have an extra bacon order. So, no free peek, though Britt did tip her well for returning before they finished eating with two freshly pressed Oxford shirts—white for Britt and emerald for Teddy.

"I love those bathrobes. I'd stuff one of them in my bag if I didn't think they'd take you off to jail for the theft."

"Me?" Britt feigned surprise and pointed to her own chest.

"This is your room." Teddy also pointed to Britt's chest in confirmation.

"Oh, right. In that case, maybe you should just get one from the gift shop downstairs."

"They sell the exact same bathrobes in the gift shop?"

"Yep. I think a lot of guests like them." Britt shrugged. "Or you could stuff one in your bag. They wouldn't call the police. They'd just charge the cost to my credit card."

"Tempting, but I'll get a new one from the gift shop and charge it to my own card."

Britt snagged her shopping bag with her prosthetic hook and put her hand on the handle to open the door. "Are you ready?"

Teddy pulled her head down for one last lust-filled kiss. "Now I'm ready."

Britt blew out a breath. "Okay. I hope my luck stays this good all day."

When they reached the lobby, Teddy headed for the guest shop while Britt went to check them out and find the valet to bring Teddy's car around. They agreed to meet out front where they'd wait for the car.

The gift shop wasn't crowded so early in the morning. She and Britt were naturally early risers, so it was still only eight o'clock, even though they'd taken time for shower sex and a leisurely breakfast. She found her size quickly in the huge rack of robes bearing The Brown Hotel insignia and had her purchase rung up by a chatty older lady. All the hotel staff were genuinely friendly.

She scanned the huge lobby for Britt, just in case she was still checking out, before heading to their agreed rendezvous in front of the hotel. A man with a large suitcase shifted from one line at the front desk to a shorter line, and the very blood in Teddy's veins froze.

A tall blonde was revealed when the man moved aside. The wide shoulders, shoulder-length hair, and the slim hips cocked to the right were as familiar as if it'd been yesterday, not more than five years ago. The woman wore jeans and a hoodie, but a military duffel lay at her feet, lending further credence to the vision. "Shannon." Barely more than a breath, hearing her name come from her own lips startled Teddy nonetheless.

Then another person joined the line, tapping the blond woman on the shoulder to ask a question. Teddy held her breath as the vision turned, then deflated. The woman looked nothing like Shannon. And why should she? Shannon was gone. Had been gone for years. She stumbled to one of the many comfortable chairs in the lobby before her legs could collapse. How could she be so easily fooled? Why now?

She'd hadn't been a nun the entire time since Shannon was killed. She'd dated another widow the first time. They both were lonely and understood each other's pain. But there was no spark, and the distance between where they each lived and worked was an easy out for them. She'd had other anonymous, unfulfilling flings Teddy purposefully kept light and chose because the other person was unavailable—shipping out to a new base, deploying overseas in a few weeks. None of them mattered because none touched the places inside her that Shannon had.

She and Britt were just having fun. They both knew Britt intended to stay on the farm, and Teddy would likely be reassigned to Washington or North Carolina.

"Teddy? You okay? You're white as a ghost."

Teddy looked up into Britt's eyes, crystal blue pools swirling with worry. Bright sunlight slanted through a part in the curtains of a nearby window and seemed to seek out Britt, encircling her like an anointing beam.

"Are you feeling alright, ma'am?" Their attentive bellhop was breathless from sprinting across the lobby. "From across the lobby, you looked like you were about to pass out."

Definitely lesbian whether she knew it yet or not. A straight girl would have said "faint" instead of "pass out." Teddy sighed. "I got a little light-headed." She pointed to Britt. "I'm probably dehydrated from all the bourbon that woman made me drink last night."

Britt laughed, her relief palpable. "You're the one who kept saying 'one more mint julep, please.'" She took a money clip from her pocket and handed a twenty to the bellhop. Can you get us a Coke and a couple bottles of water from the snack shop and meet us out front, please?"

"Sure. I'll be just a minute."

"Thanks. And keep the change." Britt had to raise her voice because the young woman was already cutting a diagonal swath through the lobby traffic in her determined mission to the snack shop.

Teddy took the hand Britt offered to help her stand, but released it immediately when her legs proved steady again. They were soon on the road. The weather was wonderful, sunny and warm. Britt had put the top down, and Teddy was glad. The roadster was a small, intimate space with the top up. Too small for her, Britt, and the feelings growing between them.

A ball cap and dark sunglasses hid enough of her face for Teddy to steal glances at Britt's profile as she drove. Teddy wanted to drive. It was her car, and she felt like she needed to regain some control. But she could hardly insist after attributing her moment of flashback guilt to low blood sugar or dehydration. Still, why did Britt have to look so damn sexy driving Teddy's car?

That last thought opened the door to a barrage of mental images. Britt naked under the shower spray. Britt's head thrown back, mouth open in a silent scream as orgasm held her body in a taut arch. Britt hovering over her, voice husky, eyes a soft powder blue and full of affection.

Teddy had always been in love only with Shannon. Her family knew that. Shannon's family knew that. Their military unit had been like a third family, and they knew it. Hell, Shannon's casket was barely in the ground before the whole nation knew it.

Even though Shannon was killed several days before the Defense of Marriage Act was struck down, she was the first widow to be granted survivor benefits from a same-sex marriage after a very public lawsuit and campaign. Her military unit had stood strong with her. She and Shannon were good soldiers with exemplary records. More important, Col. Tom Winstead had gone to bat for her. The veterans in their rural community stood by her.

Surrounded by all that support, all those living reminders, Teddy had never been able to grasp the "death do us part" portion of their marriage vows. She'd never considered it. Until now. Until she realized sometime during the night that she wanted Britt's heart beating next to hers every night. She'd promised to love Shannon above all others...forever. But she was falling deeply in love with Britt.

And that scared her to death.

CHAPTER SIXTEEN

"Okay." Britt wanted to reach for Teddy's hand. No. She wanted to wrap Teddy in her arms and hold her for several long moments. "You remember that Home from War is going up for auction today, right?"

Teddy didn't meet her eyes. "Yeah. I hate to miss that, but I'd forgotten I have this conference call. I was thinking it was next week." She finally looked at Britt. "Good luck. I hope you and E.B. get the price you're hoping for."

"Okay." Lame. But Britt was at a loss for what to say. "I guess I'll see you later today for my appointment with Dr. Thomas."

"Four o'clock."

"Yeah."

Teddy hesitantly gave Britt's forearm a slight squeeze. She smiled, but her eyes were a bit sad. "See you then." She rounded the idling sports car and drove off without looking back.

Britt was a little surprised, yet half expecting Teddy's withdrawal. She just didn't know why. Britt had no doubt that Teddy had initiated their night together. Sure, Britt had set it up with the afternoon and evening of flirtation, and made an assumption when she reserved the rooms. But she was totally backing down until Teddy made it clear she was a more than willing participant. Everything had been fine until Britt had left her to check them out of the hotel and have the valet bring their car around. What had happened in those few moments?

"Where's Teddy going?"

Britt jerked and pressed her hand to her chest. "Christ. You shouldn't sneak up on people like that. Are you trying to give me a heart attack?"

Pop snorted. "I made enough noise to wake Lynn's old deaf and blind hound dog. You were just a million miles away, staring after that little sports car that I'm guessing was being driven by our hot blonde."

"*Our* hot blonde?"

"Far as I know, you haven't laid claim to her yet. So I figure she's still up for grabs." Pop wiggled his eyebrows at Britt.

"I'm not sure she's available for either one of us," Britt said, taking one last look at the parking lot exit as if Teddy might reappear, then scowled. "Especially not you, old man." She looked at her watch. "We'd better check on our horses. The auction will be starting in about an hour."

Britt paused with Pop at the top of the semicircular auditorium, surveying the open seats. Marianne Woodard, the woman who had bid big and won the Story Hill Farm filly in an earlier auction, waved at Pop.

"Come on," he said and headed toward Marianne.

Britt frowned. It was unusual for a seller to sit with a known buyer because it was a signal to other buyers there was probably an agreement already made and they were wasting their time. What was Pop up to?

Marianne and her son owned a training farm in South Carolina. They'd made a name for themselves in the stakes races, but word was that she'd put together a group of investors, intending to land a Triple Crown contender at her farm. In Britt's estimation, Home from War could be the horse Marianne wanted.

Whatever Pop had up his sleeve, Britt grudgingly approved. Marianne was widely respected for her knowledge and method of training. She'd be happy if all their yearlings went straight to Marianne's facility.

Pop sat on Marianne's right—the last seat in that row—because he was a little deaf in his right ear, leaving Britt to sit on Marianne's left, so that her prosthetic arm wasn't on their shared armrest. It always seemed to just work out that way, but Britt knew Pop was constantly conscious of her comfort around other people.

This auction was filled with colts the inspectors had scored high, and the bidding was fierce. Marianne seemed relaxed, taking her time as colt after colt was led out and the auctioneer began to work the bidders.

The auction handler led a black colt with a white star out while the announcer crooned his impressive bloodlines. Britt sat straighter in her seat, taking in the slope of his shoulder, his straight legs, long back, and muscled rump. He was slimmer than Home from War, who had a more powerful build. Still, she was intrigued. She'd spent most of her military career living in base housing, saving her money by living modestly and investing most of her salary. She'd hit it really big a while back when she invested in a new digital operating systems start-up and the stock went sky high. Not even Pop had any idea of her net worth, and she'd been toying with the idea of buying her own racehorse. She would, of course, place it with Marianne or her son for training.

She followed the bids but didn't make one. She'd wait until the interested parties narrowed down to two. It was getting close when some latecomers to the auction decided to crowd into the seats right behind them, and she almost missed who'd made the last bid. It didn't matter, though. The money had risen to more than she, as an individual, could invest. A California trainer who'd entered and won with more than a few horses at the Derby, Preakness and Belmont had snatched up the colt. But he'd also crippled or killed just as many horses with his aggressive methods.

Irritated, she turned to glare at the men who continued to talk too loud behind them. She wanted to growl, to order them out the second her brain identified them. Pop beat her to the punch.

"Brock. Outside if you want to jaw." The fact that Pop whispered took none of the command from his tone.

Brock sat back in his chair, thoroughly admonished by his father in front of a well-known big-time political donor and Gen. George Banks. Britt narrowed her eyes at her father. How dare he bring that bastard here?

"Hip number zero-zero-seven-seven. Bred by Story Hill Farm, he's already registered as Home from War. By War Front out of Unbridled Storm, a three-point-two million-dollar stakes winner by Tapit out of Lemons Forever, most recently named the 2017 Kentucky Broodmare of the Year." The announcer who introduced each horse as it was led into the ring rattled on about the colt's spectacular bloodlines and the winning race records in his family tree for what seemed like ten minutes. Finally, he cued the auctioneer.

"Bidding for this impressive colt begins at…" The auctioneer paused and checked his paperwork for the minimum set by the seller, then consulted with a man standing in the wings, who nodded. "Bidding begins at one million dollars. Do I have one million?"

Confirmation came before the figure was fully out of the auctioneer's mouth.

The bids climbed ever higher. When the number of bidders had winnowed down to three at eight million, Marianne lifted her hand and gave a terse nod for eight-point-five million. Three ground men worked as spotters for the auctioneer, and the one closest to Marianne had wisely kept an eye on her.

"I've got eight-five. How about nine? Nine million."

A bidder across the room nodded, but before the auctioneer could announce confirmation, Marianne nodded and flashed her open hand to her ground man. He immediately spoke over the other ground man, and the auctioneer responded.

"Ladies and gentlemen, I have nine-point-five million. Can I get ten?"

The third bidder shook his head. But the California trainer who'd won the black colt stared at Marianne, then turned to the auctioneer and gave a firm nod.

"Ten million has been bid for hip number double zero-seven-seven. Give me ten-point-five. Ten-point-five. Ten-five." The higher the number the faster the auctioneer's chant rang out.

Marianne nodded, but not as firmly as before. Britt saw Marianne's hand tighten on the armrest. She was about to hit her limit.

Britt placed her mouth almost in Marianne's ear. "Let me in your consortium for this colt, and I can chip in up to two million immediately. Three if you can front me a few days to move some assets around."

Marianne turned to stare at her, then started to turn to Pop until Britt grabbed her arm.

"He doesn't know. I've been investing on the quiet and got lucky."

"You're sure?"

"Absolutely."

"I've got ten-five. Gimme eleven. Eleven."

Marianne nodded.

"Eleven." The auctioneer, his cadence slowed as bidding became a duel between two top trainers, looked to the California trainer. "Eleven-five?"

The trainer stared back.

"Eleven-three. Can I get Eleven-three?" It was more of a statement than a question, but the trainer only stared. "Eleven-two." The trainer nodded.

"Eleven-two. Eleven-five. Can I get Eleven-five?"

General Banks stretched forward in his seat and whispered to Marianne. "Let me buy in. I can put up a million."

Britt shook her head. "Let him in, and I'm out."

Marianne shook her head.

"Eleven-two. I've got Eleven-two." He raised his gavel.

"Get it done, Marianne." Pop's gruff voice cut through their whispers.

"Twelve million." Dispensing with discreet nods, Marianne's calm alto rang out across the auditorium, followed by two full seconds of complete silence.

The auctioneer's gavel froze in mid-air, and then he pointed the gavel at Marianne. "Twelve million. The bid is twelve million. Do I have twelve-five?"

The California trainer shook his head and gestured with his hands to signify he was out completely. He'd already spent a lot on the black colt.

"The bid is twelve million." He and his three ground men scanned the audience one more time for any new bidder. Finding none, the auctioneer slammed his gavel down. "Sold. Twelve million for hip number zero-zero-seven-seven, Home from War."

They all rose from their seats and filed outside the auditorium.

Pop was practically vibrating with energy, and Marianne was all smiles. He shook her hand. "Congratulations. You've got yourself a prime colt in that one. The best I've ever bred."

"Thank you, E.B., for this opportunity. Story Hill Farm stock have always been sound investments for us. We've been waiting for this one, and the timing for both of us is just right." She turned to Britt. "Congratulations, Britt. You've just bought yourself half a racehorse."

"Thanks." Britt smiled, then frowned. "Wait. A couple million isn't half of twelve."

She looked to her father. If he'd wormed his way into her horse business with any of his dirty political money, she'd be done with all of them. Even Story Hill Farm. She glared at Pop. Would he have allowed this? Betrayed her, too?

"Hold your horses." Pop put his hands up to stop her. "When you were born, your grandmother came up with the idea that each year whatever yearling sold for the smallest amount, that money would go into an account in your name. Well, over the years, that money and investments from it have added up. I, of course, have the power of investment over the account until you withdraw the money. I'm happy to inform you that you've just invested in a racehorse."

"How much?"

"Five million." Marianne answered for him. "And I had five million. So, when the bidding went past ten million, I knew I'd have to drop out if it went past eleven. I could come up with six million for my half, but I didn't have two million more until you told me you did. I wanted to laugh because I knew you didn't know you already were going to own half the colt."

Britt didn't know what to say. Her throat tightened and tears threatened. She wished Dad, General Banks, and the other man weren't there. This should be a private moment between her, Pop, and Marianne. She wouldn't let them spoil it. She stepped forward and hugged Pop.

"Thank you." She kissed the stubble on his cheek and clung to him for a long minute. "You've always been here for me. You are truly my home."

Then she surprised herself and Marianne by giving her a quick hug before she stepped back. "There's no one I'd trust more than you or your son to train any horse I own." She glanced back at Pop. "But I guess Pop knows that."

Pop smiled and nodded.

"Well, you certainly won't have to worry about this colt, since we also have six million reasons to see him do well."

They all laughed, even the three men who had been ignored during the conversation. Then Marianne excused herself from the group.

"I have to go see about our colt."

"Wish I could have gotten in on that one," General Banks said as Marianne walked away. "Guess I'll have to settle for placing a few bets come race time."

"Excuse me." A man tapped Britt on the shoulder. "Are you Captain Britt Story?"

Britt turned to face the man. "Yes. I am."

"You've been served, Captain Story."

"What is this?"

The man was already walking away. This had to be something else her father had schemed. Britt tore open the envelope and began to read.

"What is it?" Pop asked, coming around her to look over her shoulder.

"It's a subpoena to appear before a Congressional hearing on the military's lack of response to female troops being assaulted by male members of their own units." She glared at General Banks. "Especially deployed troops."

"It's that pesky Elsbeth bitch." Brock waved his hand like shooing away gnats.

"I wouldn't take Senator Amanda Elsbeth lightly, Brock," the political donor said.

What was his name? Britt hadn't deemed him important enough to her world to remember.

"We will refuse to let you testify on the grounds of national security," General Banks said.

"This subpoena is for Britt Story, actually. Not Captain Britt Story." Britt didn't think it made a difference legally, but she was going to pretend it did.

General Banks' face reddened. "You are still in the army, soldier, and I'm ordering you not to appear before that hearing."

The donor turned to Brock. "I thought you were taking care of this."

"I am. Everybody calm down." Brock paced away from the group, then back.

The donor shook his head. "We won't back the general if he's going to bring this same sexual-harassment baggage with him that's plagued every candidate we've tried to float since that 'Me Too' crap started."

General Banks sputtered. "I have an exemplary record. I have always been absolutely faithful to my lovely wife. My father was an alcoholic who made my childhood miserable, so I've never had more than two beers in a twenty-four-hour period. I have no skeletons in my closet."

"I'm done here," Britt said. "I'm going to see my colt." She turned to her grandfather, who'd been standing by silently as the others revealed glimpses of the secret Britt had been carrying. "Coming with me, Pop? I'll need a ride later."

"I'm sure we can find better company down at the barns," he said.

CHAPTER SEVENTEEN

D r. Will Thomas, Col. Tom Winstead, and Teddy looked up when Britt knocked and entered the large lab room. Relief and uncertainty flashed across Teddy's face, but she came forward to meet Britt halfway.

"I was beginning to think you'd decided to not show up." Teddy whispered so the men, who were hunkered over a colorful prosthetic arm, couldn't hear. Her hand on Britt's arm was warm and a little damp.

Britt twisted her arm to loosen Teddy's grip and took Teddy's hand, squeezing gently. "I wouldn't let you down. I said I'd be here."

Teddy visibly relaxed, her eyes brightening. "Home from War?"

Britt squeezed Teddy's hand again. "Twelve million."

Teddy brought her free hand to cover her mouth in a surprised gesture. "Oh my God. Twelve million? That's amazing." She pulled Britt into a tight hug and whispered into Britt's ear, "I'd kiss you if we were alone."

"I wish you could have been there." Britt stepped back when Teddy released her. "There's a lot more to tell, but I'll save it for later. Let's get this done."

Teddy led Britt to a chair placed next to a table full of computer equipment and the bionic arm the men had been examining. "We need you to sit in this chair and take off your outer shirt."

Britt still wore the Oxford shirt she'd purchased in Louisville, but as usual, it was a size or two too large because of the T-shirt and shoulder harness she wore underneath. As always, Teddy didn't offer to help her shed the shirt. She wouldn't unless Britt asked. Teddy did, however, remove her standard prosthesis and pressure sock, then examined Britt's residual limb. Finally, she turned to the men still bent over the new arm.

"We're ready when you are," Teddy said.

Colonel Winstead looked up and smiled. "Excellent." He nodded to Dr. Thomas, who picked up the digital arm. They both approached wearing large grins.

"Dr. Thomas, Colonel Winstead." Britt kept her greeting professional, even though she wasn't in uniform, but smiled slightly and held out her hand to shake theirs in a welcoming gesture.

"I know you have to address him by rank, but I'm just Will, remember," Dr. Thomas said.

Britt nodded. "Right. Will."

He held up the bionic arm, predominantly black, but with red, green, and yellow wires visibly running between, ducking under, or fused into silver circuit boards. "And I'd like you to meet Lucy."

"Lucy." Britt deadpanned the name and raised an eyebrow. Had he really named that thing like it was a person? Okay, maybe she had started to think of her clicking-hook arm as Joe, but she'd never actually admit that to anyone.

Will shrugged. "I name every custom-made prosthesis. It's easier to remember than a number. I mean, I know that when they go into widespread production, we'll have to identify them by a serial number, but with so few now, I prefer names. All the left limbs get one starting with L. All right limb names start with an R."

"Custom-made?"

"While you were in surgery to have your left arm amputated, we took digital scans of both your right limb and what remained of your left one, then used them to reconstruct—with up to ninety-eight percent accuracy—an exact replica of your left arm and hand before it was injured." He held the new prosthesis out to her. "Lucy."

Britt stared at the digital limb, too stunned to move. "That's my hand?" She had flashes of her damaged hand, flopped across her chest and tied down before the medic and two soldiers from her unit lifted her onto a stretcher and double-timed it to a waiting helicopter. She blinked and was staring at the bionic arm again.

Will's answer was gentle, as if he understood the emotional impact of what he'd revealed to her. "A nearly identical replica."

Of course that bundle of gears and electronics wasn't her lost limb, but it eerily felt like a reincarnated version. She recognized the long, slender fingers, the shape of the forearm. Will was still waiting patiently for her to touch it, to take it. Shaken, Britt glanced at Teddy, who nodded. Britt reached for the hand end of the prosthesis, and Will laid the other end across her knees.

She expected the mechanical arm to be heavy and feel like plastic. Instead, it was deceptively light and the covering as soft as skin. It was…warm? Britt frowned up at Will.

"Yeah. The covering is almost indistinguishable from real skin. A Swiss toy company developed it. We enhanced it a bit by figuring out how to warm it to your average body temperature. Unfortunately, it won't vary with the outside temperature like your real body parts do. So, when your other hand gets cold or sweats, this one will remain at about ninety-eight degrees."

"I can live with that."

Will took the arm back. "Ready to try it on?"

Britt was both eager and nervous. She held out her hand to Teddy, who took it.

"You can do this, Britt." Teddy squatted beside her. "You adapted to your first prosthesis quicker than anyone I've seen."

"It's weird. Those are…I recognize those fingers." Britt didn't need to explain further. She knew Teddy would understand.

"I know. It will feel weird at first."

Britt nodded to Will. "Okay. I'm ready."

Will paused to hold Britt's gaze. "Before we start, I need to caution you that this is only a preliminary fitting. Unlike the more rudimentary arm, Lucy is a delicate instrument that connects to your brain through the nerves in your arm. Today, we'll start mapping her movements to your brain messages. It takes a lot of patience and determination and a hundred small tweaks."

Britt blew out a breath, then turned to Colonel Winstead and Teddy. "Hoo-ah," she said quietly.

Colonel Winstead gave her a thumbs-up and dragged a chair over for Teddy to sit next to Britt for moral support.

Will rolled up Britt's T-shirt sleeve and explained she didn't need a compression sock. After he pressed a few buttons on the outside of the arm, a computer automatically sought out and aligned with the nerves that had been surgically placed just under the skin on the inside of her residual limb, then expanded the gel liner inside the cup to fit snugly. Teddy removed Britt's shoulder harness and replaced it with a lighter mesh harness without the cable and pulleys that had operated the hooks on the other prosthesis. Lucy attached to the new harness with a Velcro flap. Easy on, easy off. Less bulk and barely noticeable under a shirt. That was nice.

Lucy bent at the elbow, jerking upward toward Britt's face. She reached to stop Lucy with her real hand, but the bionic hand had already stopped short of her face. Will looked as surprised as she felt. "Will this thing go rogue and kill me in my sleep?"

Will opened and closed his mouth a few times, as if he couldn't decide what to say. Then something dawned in his eyes. "What were you thinking about right before Lucy moved?"

Britt frowned down at Lucy's bionic parts, tiny lights blinking inside like something alive in the long fingers. She hesitantly raised her real hand to finger the crescent-shaped scar near the base of the thumb. "I wanted a closer look at this. The computer replicated my hand so closely that it copied this scar where I broke my thumb when I was sixteen and it was surgically repaired."

"Excellent. Wow." Will was jubilant. "This might not take as long as I thought." He began scribbling notes on his clipboard. "Lucy is already communicating with your brain. We just need to smooth out her response."

An hour later, Teddy called an end to the session where Will had asked Britt to flex individual fingers, make a fist, rotate her wrist, and various other movements. She'd been appointed timekeeper and monitor over Britt's tolerance levels, since she knew the patient best. Britt was relieved. Sweat ran down her back, and her back ached from the tension of trying to get Lucy to respond to her thoughts.

"This is excellent progress," Will said, scanning his notes. "We never expected such compatibility with the army's first subject." He looked up at Colonel Winstead. "I'd say the army's program is a lock. It has a high probability of success, and I'll be happy to testify to that before Congress."

"We should have several more subjects soon. How long before we can actually test her under simulated combat conditions?" Colonel Winstead asked.

"Whoa, hoss." Britt's tired brain screamed *incoming*. "I haven't signed up for that." She ripped the Velcro fastener open and pressed the controls Will had shown her to contract the gel cup and release her residual limb. "Lucy is a really cool toy, but I refuse to be the army's bionic toy soldier." She stood and jerked off the shoulder harness, throwing it into the chair where she'd been sitting.

Britt strode out of the lab, not thinking about where she was going. Minutes later, she found herself in the parking lot, shaking with rage and with no escape. Pop had dropped her off. Shit. She'd forgotten her old harness and arm, her shirt and her phone on a table in the lab. Shit, shit, shit. Britt closed her eyes and took a deep breath, counting to ten as she let it out slowly. She'd never experienced fits of temper this strong before this last deployment. The fury that had engulfed her and propelled her out of the lab began to drain away. She turned back to the hospital. Teddy stood on the curb, studying her. She held the items Britt had forgotten.

Britt unconsciously started to cross her arms, then realized a stump wasn't enough to complete the defensive posture. She felt ridiculous. Again. She'd been so enamored with Lucy, she'd followed their carrot right up to the door of the army's trap. Like a rookie private. Is that why Teddy had been so distant on the way back from Louisville? Had she known they planned to lure her to a point where the army would give her no choice?

Her hand in her pocket, her eyes on the pavement, she walked slowly to where Teddy stood. "I can't do this." She couldn't meet Teddy's eyes for fear of what she might see there. Disappointment. Disgust at her weakness. Because, honestly, Teddy would know. Principle wasn't the only thing holding her back.

"I know." Teddy cupped her cheek, and Britt leaned into its warmth. Only then did she chance a look, and the understanding in Teddy's eyes made her throat tighten. She needed Teddy so much. She hungered for the calm that flowed through her when Teddy's arms were wrapped around her, when Teddy's heart beat against hers. "Let's go to my office, where we have a little privacy, to get you armed and dressed," Teddy said, leading her back inside the hospital.

The offices, including Teddy's, that ringed the huge rehab gymnasium were all glass on the interior wall with incapsulated mini blinds. Teddy didn't close the blinds. When she'd said privacy, she meant the implied privacy of a therapist working with a client in an open gymnasium but among others who were concentrating on their own therapy. She closed the door to indicate she was with a client and shouldn't be disturbed without good reason, but she intentionally didn't close the blinds. She couldn't be really alone with Britt. She was too weak. Torn between shame and desire, she was afraid she'd give in to the desire that screamed for her to grab Britt and kiss her until they both were breathless.

Instead, she methodically inspected Britt's arm, dressed her in the shoulder harness, and installed the prosthesis. Britt watched her quizzically. Teddy hadn't done this since Britt had mastered doing it for herself. She only glanced at Britt a few times, afraid her own eyes would lay bare her confused emotions. When she held up Britt's shirt, Britt slipped her prosthetic arm in first, then leaned forward so Teddy could bring the shirt around Britt's back to slip her right arm into the other sleeve. The move brought their faces close together, and Britt brushed her cheek against Teddy's.

"Teddy." Britt's breath was warm on Teddy's ear.

"Don't, Britt. I can't." Teddy stared at the floor when Britt slid her arm into the sleeve and sat back to button her shirt.

"Sorry. Of course. I forgot where we were. Will you have dinner with me? At my hotel? Pop's already headed back to the farm, but I thought I'd stay another night. We can eat in the restaurant or order room service. Whatever you want." Britt's eyes blazed like blue flames that heated Teddy so hot, she had to turn away.

"I...I can't. Colonel Winstead invited me to dinner with him and his wife. Afterward, we plan to catch up on the status of the prosthesis project. We haven't had a chance to do that with me at the farm for the past month." She could feel Britt's eyes boring into her back. She hated herself for being one more person to disappoint this beautiful wounded warrior and for being unable to let go of the past. Her desk phone rang, and she welcomed the interruption.

"Lieutenant Alexander."

"This is the reception desk in the lobby. I have a man here with some papers for you."

Teddy had no idea what papers they could be, but she wanted desperately to jump at this excuse to cowardly avoid the talk she needed to have with Britt. She needed to explain that her vows didn't die when Shannon did, and prolonging that talk would only extend her misery. "Ask him to leave them there at the desk. I'll come pick it up before I leave today."

"He says he has to deliver them to you in person."

"Really?" Teddy let out an impatient huff. "All right. I'll be right there." She hung up the receiver and turned back to Britt. "I have to go to the reception desk to pick up something I must have to sign for. I'll be back in a few minutes."

"I'm not going anywhere. I don't have a ride."

Teddy stopped just as she reached the door. "What?"

"Pop dropped me off. I thought we'd...I can call an Uber," Britt said, her face flushing and eyes shifting away from Teddy's.

"You were in the parking lot."

"Yeah. I was so mad I kinda forgot that. That's why I was just standing there when you came out. Once I got out there, I realized I didn't have my truck or my phone to call for a ride."

Teddy wanted to laugh and hug away Britt's embarrassment. For someone so smart and confident, Britt could be a big goof sometimes. But she didn't laugh. She couldn't hug her. She had to remember to keep her distance from Britt. It was the only way to cut the bond that had formed between them. "Don't leave until I get back. We need to talk."

❖

"We need to talk."

The words echoed around Britt's brain like a ricocheting bullet. You never wanted to hear that phrase from a girlfriend. Was Teddy her girlfriend now? They'd spent a lot of time together over the past month, sharing nightly walks, therapy sessions, interrupting each other's nightmares. They'd shared occasional kisses and one romantic, passion-filled night. But neither had talked about their deepest feelings, fears, or past hurts. All Britt knew for sure was that she'd finally met the one person with whom she wanted to share those things.

A woman in scrubs poked her head in the office, looking directly at the empty desk chair, then startling a little when she noticed Britt. "Oh, I was looking for Teddy. Lieutenant Alexander. Is she around?"

"She said she'd be right back." Britt frowned. Was Teddy always in such high demand?

"Oh. Okay. Would you tell her that Colonel Winstead wants to see her in his office right away? General Banks is on a very tight schedule and wants to talk with her before he leaves."

Britt nearly growled. What the hell did that ass Banks want with Teddy? She was medical and not under his command. But the woman didn't wait for an answer. She apparently was just carrying a message and not privy to Banks's purpose.

Britt checked her phone. Did she have new orders? Maybe Banks wanted a report on her medical progress. She scrolled through email and text messages. A text from Marianne said Home from War would be heading to South Carolina early the next morning. Various other business emails were related to the week's sale of other yearlings. One email in her personal account was from her mother, asking when she planned to visit. "You can always come visit me, Mother," Britt muttered to herself.

Bored with her phone, she stood and reviewed the photos on the wall of Teddy's office. She studied the faces of the people in Teddy's unit. She didn't recognize any of them. That wasn't unusual. Teddy appeared to have been attached to a policing unit. Britt's unit was a ground unit of army intelligence—advance scouts. Drone units were slowly taking over their jobs. She paused at the photo of Teddy kneeling by her medic pack. She was closer to the camera in this picture, so close Britt could read her nametag. T. DICE. Wait. Why was her name different? She went to Teddy's desk and was reaching for the photo of the tall blonde when she jerked toward the door at the sound of a knock.

"Sorry. Didn't mean to startle you. I was looking for Teddy. Uh, Lieutenant Alexander." The husky female soldier wore a modified mohawk and the insignia of a staff sergeant on her desert camos.

"She went to sign for a package at the reception desk. She should return soon."

"Do you mind if I wait? I only have a few minutes. I'm with a convoy passing through on our way to Bragg. We stopped for a break and early chow about a mile from here, so I'd thought I'd surprise her."

"No. Not at all, Sergeant." Britt held out her hand. "Britt Story."

"Alisha Denning." Alisha shook Britt's hand. "Captain Story, right?"

"Uh, yes?"

"Relax. No rumors or anything. I have a friend still in Afghanistan who says you're the best captain she's ever served under."

"Tell your friend I said thanks." Britt suddenly felt conscious of her prosthesis and turned so it wasn't in Alisha's line of vision. "How do you know Lieutenant Alexander?"

She gestured to the photos on the wall and smiled. "We went through basic and advanced training together, then deployed in the same unit that first time." She shook her head. "We were so damn young and naive. Got our cherries popped pretty quick." She went to the photo and touched one of the figures smiling at the camera. "That's me. It's hard to tell because of the shadow across my face." Her fingers slid over the other faces. "Only about half of us came back after eighteen months over there."

Britt gestured to the photo on Teddy's desk. "Did you know her?"

"Shannon? Oh, yeah. Everybody knew Shannon. She was like the unit Wonder Woman. We all thought she was bulletproof because she acted like she was. Sharpshooter, fastest runner in the unit. If there was a hot spot, she was there. She could throw a grenade like a major-league pitcher. She and Teddy were the big love story of the unit. There's a long story about how they met over a game of craps that I won't bore you with, but Teddy always said Shannon was her lucky seven."

Britt stared at the photo, remembering Teddy's words at the hotel. *Seven's always been lucky for me.* "Where's Shannon now?"

Alisha looked up from Shannon's photo, surprise replacing her sad expression. "You don't know?"

Britt shifted uncomfortably. Should she? "No. I don't."

"Killed. By a suicide bomber on her last deployment about five years ago, just days before the Supreme Court struck down the Defense of Marriage Act. Teddy had a bad feeling about Shannon going back to Afghanistan, and Boston, where Teddy's parents lived, was still Teddy's home on record with the army. So they'd driven up to Massachusetts and got married before Shannon deployed. A national group of LGBTQ service members took up her cause, and backed by her and Shannon's own unit, they filed a lawsuit to have Teddy granted survivor's benefits following Shannon's death. There was lots of media about it. I'm surprised you didn't see any of it."

"That circus must have been hard to go through while she was grieving." Britt was lucky she was already serving when her father decided to run for the senate. Duty had saved her from the worst of the campaign dog-and-pony show. Still, the army had encouraged her participation in the hope that his success in Congress would translate to more money in the military budget. And she'd hated every minute in the spotlight.

"Shannon was her true love. Don't get me wrong. Teddy's dated. She dated another widow for a while, but she said they both knew it was just for comfort and wasn't going anywhere. And she spends a night or two with other women now and then. I mean, she's only human. We all understand that she's still a young woman with needs."

"We?"

"Her family, Shannon's family, her military family. We're all still tight, you know? Teddy's like a daughter to Shannon's parents. But we're okay with her doing what she needs, because she'll always and forever love only Shannon." Alisha glanced at her watch. "Damn. I've got to go, or the convoy's going to leave without me. Their thirty-minute break is almost up." She grabbed a sheet of paper from the computer's printer and rummaged in the desk for a pen, then scribbled a quick note for Teddy.

"Nice to meet you, Cap." She gave a quick salute, even though Britt wasn't in uniform.

"Safe travels." Britt returned the salute.

When she reached the doorway, Alisha looked back at Shannon's photo. "I hope that one day I'll find my one great love like Teddy did."

She must have left, but Britt didn't notice. She was staring at the same photo. *...She spends a night or two with other women now and then. ...She'll always and forever love only Shannon.*

❖

The only person at the reception desk was a civilian worker, as were most of the VA hospital employees. But her meticulously neat attire and severe bun and rigid posture screamed retired military.

"Hello. I'm Lieutenant Alexander. You called and said there was a package I needed to sign for."

"I don't know if you have to sign anything, ma'am. But the man over there insisted he must put a document directly in your hands." The woman stood from her chair and leaned across the circular desk to whisper. "I had one of our security officers speak with him, and the officer said it was okay. Still, he's standing by over there." She pointed discreetly, and Teddy glanced over to see a lean man with a steel-gray crew cut and wearing a security-guard uniform. He stood at the ready, a few feet down a hallway that led away from the lobby, purposely out of sight of the man she noted was approaching from her left.

"That's him wearing the yellow golf shirt," the receptionist said, sliding quietly back into her chair.

Teddy almost laughed. This day had been an emotional roller coaster, and now she felt like she was in a bad spy movie. Maybe she was dreaming, and she'd wake up in bed next to Britt's sexy body and start the day all over again, happy. No. Euphoric. She sighed. In love. Why couldn't she just let go and enjoy it?

"Lieutenant Theodora Alexander?"

"Yes."

The man held out an envelope. "You've been served."

Teddy reflexively took the envelope, staring at it while the man turned and headed for the hospital entrance. She shook her head and ran after him. "Wait." When she caught up with him, she grabbed his arm. "Just wait a minute. Do I have to sign something?"

He cocked his head for a second. "No. You just have to show up."

"Show up for what?"

He stared at her, then spoke like he was talking to a child. "For court. It's a subpoena."

"Really?" She narrowed her eyes and imagined them emitting a laser ray that burned his eyebrows off. "It's not my fault I've lived an exemplary life and never been arrested or hauled into court to testify about anything. I have no idea what this could be about."

"Look. I just get paid to track people down and deliver these things. You can't imagine how hard that can be. I've been stalking you for three weeks." He pointed at the hospital. "All your buddies in there would say was that you were on special assignment. I finally got a call from your landlady this morning to let me know she'd seen you leaving your apartment earlier in uniform so you might be here."

"My sweet old landlady gave me up?"

"I might have insinuated that she'd be in big trouble if she was harboring a fugitive."

"Oh my God. Now she's going to think I'm a criminal. Thanks a lot."

"I do what I gotta do. Besides, I don't know what's in there either. Maybe you are a criminal. Maybe you're being subpoenaed to testify in a big mob trial or something. You gotta open it to find out."

Teddy glared at him but slid her fingernail under the sealed flap to pry it loose, then unfolded the documents inside. She scanned them quickly, then folded them back into the envelope when she realized her confessed stalker had edged closer in an attempt to read over her shoulder.

"Damn. They must have found out about the guy in Alabama. I guess that bear decided he smelled too bad to eat much of him. I should have gone ahead and put him through the wood chipper. But I was wearing a new outfit that I really liked, and wood chippers can be so messy. My handler is going to give me some real shit over this one. Might was well grab the go-bag. I'm sure the army will make me go dark in some Middle East sandpit until this blows over."

She turned back to her stalker, but he was gone. Not a yellow shirt in sight.

❖

Britt tugged at the neck of her T-shirt. Sweat was trickling down her temples, along her jaw, down her back, soaking her shirt. She couldn't breathe. She needed air. She needed to be outside. She walked fast, skirting around others in the hallway, until she finally broke into a trot. Her lungs felt like they were closing. The hallway seemed to narrow, closing in on her. Darkness swam in the edges of her vision. She wasn't going to make it. Then she remembered. Taking a sharp left at the next hallway, she burst through the glass doors into an open courtyard and threw her head back to suck in great gulps of fresh outdoor air.

Her heart finally began to slow, and she looked around. Thankfully, she appeared to be alone. She sat on a bench in the sunlight. The sweat that had been pouring off her minutes ago was drying quickly, and she began to shiver.

The night terrors had gotten better. Not every night now. And she had hardly any daytime flashbacks. Well, except for the one today when she was introduced to Lucy. Teddy had made that go away. But she'd just experienced a full-fledged panic attack. She'd read about them. They'd all sat through the pre-deployment talks about PTSD and other side effects of serving in a war zone. Panic attacks had been one of them. They hadn't sounded as bad as this felt.

She was getting better, wasn't she? Hell, who could tell? It was like the war had just followed her home. Maybe that was why so many guys kept going back. They thought they'd left something unfinished in that godforsaken desert, but they were unconsciously trying each time to leave it all over there and return without the war baggage. Instead, the baggage just piled higher and higher.

And she'd never be done until she'd unloaded hers. She straightened, her battle plan clear now.

She would hire a lawyer to force the army to release her, then testify at Senator Elsbeth's hearing. Cpl. Jessica Avery deserved her due. And, if asked, she'd tell *The New York Times* why Gen. George Banks should not be elected to fill her father's senate seat if Brock's candidate did win the presidency in the next election and appoint him Secretary of Defense.

Britt woke her phone, opened the Uber app, and arranged for a ride to the hotel to collect her things and her truck. Then she stood, gave herself a minute to map in her mind the quickest path to where she'd promised to meet the driver, and set out.

Story Hill Farm was what she needed now—her grandfather's steady presence, the smell of hay and horses, long rides on Mysty, and a good training year for her new racehorse. Then she'd be truly home from war.

CHAPTER EIGHTEEN

Five minutes and a maze of hallways, stairs, and elevators later, Teddy found her way back to the rehabilitation department.

Her head was too full. Why was she being subpoenaed to appear before a Congressional hearing led by Sen. Amanda Elsbeth? What was the hearing about? Finally, she was headed back to her office so she could sit down and google it. Wait. Could this have something to do with Britt? Damn it. She needed to focus. First, she needed to talk to Britt. What would she say? I'm married? I can't love you because I'm supposed to love someone else forever?

Teddy slowed as she approached her office. It was empty. Teddy scanned the gym. Maybe Britt was talking to another veteran who was there for treatment. No sign of her. Maybe she'd gone to the bathroom. Teddy sat down to boot up her computer and saw the note Alisha had left.

"Oh, no. I missed her. Damn." The hearing and its purpose forgotten, she dug her phone out of her pocket and was about to call Alisha when Colonel Winstead waved from her doorway to get her attention.

"Sir?"

"I'd like to see you in my office."

Teddy stood. "Now?"

"Yes, Lieutenant."

"Let me jot a quick note for someone I'm expecting, and I'll be right there." The fact that Colonel Winstead had addressed her formally indicated this was important. She flipped Alisha's note over and penned a quick *In the boss's office, be right back* note for Britt.

Teddy was surprised to find a one-star general standing in the colonel's office.

Colonel Winstead made the introductions. "Lieutenant Theodora Alexander, this is General George Banks."

"General Banks, sir." Teddy saluted and held it until General Banks returned her salute.

"At ease, Lieutenant," he said. "I've been hearing good things about you, young lady." He smiled, but something about his smugness and the way his eyes swept over her felt condescending and invasive.

"I strive every day to be the best soldier I can be." She could quote army propaganda to him all day, but she wasn't going to suck up by giving this man anything personal.

He raised an eyebrow. Maybe he'd gotten the message.

"Yes, well, apparently your best has been exceptional lately. I was in town to visit with a friend, so I thought I'd drop by to pin these on you personally." He took a small box from his pocket and opened it to reveal what was inside.

Teddy snapped to attention again as he stepped toward her, removing the single silver bars from her uniform and replacing them with the double bars of a captain. Then he stepped back and saluted her. "Captain Alexander. The army appreciates your dedication, your loyalty, and service to your country."

She returned his salute and broke into a smile. "Thank you, General. This…this is unexpected." She looked to Colonel Winstead, who looked as surprised as she was, but recovered quickly.

"Congratulations, Teddy. You deserve this more than any soldier I know," Colonel Winstead said. "You've been an invaluable asset to the prosthesis project so far. I seriously doubt we'd be nearly this far along without your organizational skills."

"Not to mention your recruiting skills. Brock Story is a personal friend, and he says he has no idea how you did it, but you have his tiger of a daughter purring like a house cat. I understand from

Colonel Winstead that Captain Story's adapting very quickly to the prototype appendage. Bionic implants could be the future of our military."

"General Banks, I'm afraid we might be getting ahead of ourselves." Teddy glanced at Colonel Winstead. Hadn't he told General Banks about Britt walking out on the project?

General Banks narrowed his eyes, staring at Teddy. "What do you mean?"

Colonel Winstead laid his hand on her shoulder and squeezed when she opened her mouth to answer. "Teddy's just being cautious. We did only the first mapping today to synch Captain Story's brain with the digital prosthesis and still have to do a lot of delicate work and testing. The patent ultimately belongs to Duke researchers, and they won't release it to the market or the government until they're confident it's one hundred percent operational."

General Banks considered this information but didn't look like he was buying it. "That's your job, isn't it? To make sure it works well enough for us to get our hands on it." He looked at his watch. "I've got a steak dinner, then a poker game waiting with some men that have the influence we need in Congress to pump up our budget."

He left the office but took only two steps before he returned to the doorway. "One more thing. Captain Story has been subpoenaed to appear before a Congressional hearing chaired by that bitch Senator Amanda Elsbeth. She's been ordered not to respond. I want you two to make sure she follows those orders."

Britt was to testify at the same hearing? What had happened that they were afraid for Britt to talk about? "Sir, I don't know what we could do if she's determined."

General Banks looked at his watch again, then glared at Teddy. "Hell. I don't care what you do. You have my permission to use anything in your arsenal. Alter her calendar, take her to Durham where they have the bionics lab, drug her, seduce her, damn it. I understand you both like girls, and Brock said you two were getting rather cozy at the farm. Whatever you need to do, do it!"

Teddy's face heated with guilt, but mostly with anger. "Sir, I would never—"

"Lieutenant Alexander has never failed to follow orders," Colonel Winstead said.

General Banks ignored him and stepped forward to push his sausage-like finger close to her face. "Yes, you will, Captain. Or we won't just drop Captain Story from the project. We'll cancel it completely. Story might be too much of a little girl to return to combat, but a lot of men would gladly return if they had arms and legs. You'll be letting all of them down if this project doesn't go forward."

Stunned, Teddy stared after General Banks as he stormed through the gymnasium, past the rehabbing veterans who straightened. He ignored more than a few offered salutes.

"Teddy." The soft voice came from her friend and mentor, Tom, not from the man who minutes ago had been Colonel Winstead, her boss.

She turned and glared at him. "I'll be in my office, Colonel."

Teddy marched to her office and closed the door. How had her day gone off the rails so badly? She'd woken that morning next to Britt, floating in a cloud of happiness. Now she'd lost everything. She'd broken her promise to love Shannon forever. She'd lost confidence in her mentor as he'd fallen in line with army politics. She was losing out on a project she loved and hoped would be the future of her career. But her biggest regret, her deepest shame was getting caught in a political web and unwittingly betraying Britt.

She knew what she had to do. She booted her laptop and began.

Britt paid the Uber driver and dug the ticket for her truck out of her wallet. When she stopped at the valet desk to tell them she was checking out, she asked them to have her truck brought up in twenty minutes. Then she started across the large hotel lobby in long strides. The sooner she got on the road, the better. Lexington was getting a little too crowded for her taste.

She was halfway there, the elevators in sight, when she contemplated ignoring the voice that rang out.

"Britt. Wait up." Despite her long legs, her father was still taller and caught up with her easily. His smile was broad. "Wow. You've bought yourself a racehorse. And what a colt. Dad says it's the best he's ever bred. I've been looking for you. I want you to have dinner with us."

It didn't take much to deduce the "us" guest list because General Banks was barreling across the lobby, heading straight for them.

"Thanks, but I was just going up to my room to check out and head back to the farm."

"You've got to eat," he said. "Let's get a good steak in you, and then you can hit the road. Go ahead and check out, if you want, and you can leave from the restaurant. I've got some people who'd really like to meet the owner of the next Triple Crown winner."

"Half owner. And your prediction is premature. I'm tired and really just want to leave."

"Nonsense." General Banks finally reached them, breathing heavy. Apparently, his desk job hadn't kept him as physically fit as her dad and she were. "And give your little lieutenant a call. Wait, I meant captain. She was promoted today. Bet you didn't know that. Pinned the bars on her myself just a little while ago." He actually winked at her. "We'd love to have two attractive ladies join us, and I'm sure she'd want to have dinner with you."

Britt narrowed her eyes at him. What did he mean by that remark? She'd been trying to be polite, but her patience was wearing very thin. She glanced at General Banks and gave her father a look she knew would convey her disgust for the company he had in mind.

"I'm going home," she said quietly. Her father dropped his gaze and nodded.

"You're staying, Captain Story," General Banks said, his face reddening. "That's an order. The men we're dining with are important to army appropriations. It's time you quit focusing on yourself and showed some concern for every soldier in this army."

"George—" Her dad scowled at General Banks, but Britt interrupted whatever he was going to say. She didn't need her father to shield her.

"Respectfully, sir, I could offer you the same advice." She knew she was being insubordinate, but she'd plead incompetency due to recent battle trauma if he brought her up on charges. Surely, he wasn't too stupid to know that. "I am on medical leave, General Banks, and I've had an exhausting therapy session this afternoon. My doctor's orders are for me to go home and rest. Another time perhaps."

General Banks's ruddy color deepened, and he had opened his mouth to reply when a slender man with salt-and-pepper hair approached with a phone, notebook, and pen in hand.

"Britt. Sorry to interrupt, but do you have a moment?"

"Hey, Emmet. I was heading up to my room to pack and check out. What's up?" She smiled at the well-known journalist who contributed to several horse-racing publications. His reporting was always accurate and well-sourced, earning the respect of everyone in the business.

"You know nothing is secret for very long around the barns. I understand you and Marianne are co-owners of your grandfather's colt that went for twelve million earlier today."

She laughed and shook her head as she looked at her feet. "And you're sure of your sources?"

He chuckled. "Very sure. Roberto's wife, Melina, is crowing all over the barn about how Marianne bribed Ross to let her steal Roberto for a month to get that high-dollar colt settled in his new home and train one of her grooms how to best handle him. But when Melina refused for her husband to be gone so long, Marianne offered their whole family use of her beach house at Edisto Island the entire month and promised Roberto could join them on the weekends." He leaned close and lowered his voice. "And she might have let it slip that to convince her that he should go, Roberto told her this colt was triple blessed because he was bred by a Story, co-owned by a Story, then co-owned and to be trained by Marianne. Melina does not ignore numerology."

Britt offered her father an unapologetic half smile. "Another time. Business calls." She seized both the opportunity and Emmet by the arm. "Come up to my room, and I'll talk to you while I pack."

Two elevators opened as they approached. A waiting couple took the one on the right, so Britt steered Emmet to the one on the left. She blew out a breath when the doors closed on her father and General Banks still staring after them.

"Thanks for rescuing me," she said to Emmet. She'd known him since she was a kid and he was a young man with a notebook jotting down as much of Pop's wisdom as he could while he breakfasted with them at Keeneland, or in Louisville at Churchill Downs. He'd even been to the farm a few times.

"I've seen that expression before. You looked like you wanted to rip those stars off that general's shoulders and shove them up his ass." They both chuckled. "But I really do want a story from you, if you're willing."

"Sure. It'll come out eventually, so I'd rather give it to you than have somebody else write it and maybe get it wrong, because the IRS is going to eyeball really close where the money came from." They'd have to be careful with the money transfers so it didn't appear Pop had bought his own horse.

She ran through the story, from his bloodlines to the auction, then answered his questions. She asked and trusted him to leave out the part about Pop deciding to use her trust he administered to throw in with Marianne because she would have approved it anyway. But she let him use the part she'd kept secret from her family—the several million she'd made investing her own money and had added at the last minute to hold off the other high bidder. When she was packed and the interview done, they headed downstairs.

"You okay if I run with this tonight?"

"Do me a favor and check that Marianne is okay with it first."

He smiled and held out his hand. "I talked to her before I chased you down. She said the same about checking with you. Good luck, Britt. Hope to see you in the winner's circle next year."

"Thanks, Emmet. I have to warn you, though. I'm going to turn my phone off for the rest of the night. I know once you break this, everybody else will be calling to confirm it."

He grinned. "Won't hurt my feelings if you put them off. That just means they'll have to credit my story with the news."

He headed out, while she dropped off her room key and asked them to email her billing receipt for tax purposes, then made a quick side trip to the vending room for a bottle of water. Britt was surprised to hear a familiar voice when she passed a hallway that led to some private dining rooms. She cautiously peeked around the corner, relieved to see General Banks had his back turned as he held his cell phone to his ear.

"I'm telling you, Story is headed back to the farm. So, you call your bait and tell her to get her cute ass out there and get to work." He was quiet for a minute. "No. All you or she needs to know is that Story holds me responsible for something that happened way down my chain of command. Women just aren't reasonable creatures. That's why they shouldn't be in the military. Now tell her to get out there and keep Story on the farm and out of DC until those hearings are over."

Britt turned and nearly ran for the door.

"Hey, thanks!" The valet traded her keys for the twenty-dollar bill she held out. She answered with a nod, jumped into the truck, and sped off. Her mind spun into overdrive, stopping and starting, flashing from one thought to the next.

That night in Louisville, had she been stupidly courting the enemy? No. Nobody could fake what she'd seen in Teddy's eyes. Could they? Did she? Had her father been a part of this, too?

The knock at her door was little more than a courtesy, because Colonel Winstead didn't wait for a reply before opening the door and stepping inside. Teddy hit the print key for the second time as he closed the door behind him. Instead of greeting him, she turned her back and gathered the papers in the printer's tray, along with the last few spitting out into her hands.

"Teddy."

"Sir." She stapled four pages together and held them out to him. "Captain Britt Story's rehab is complete. Her wound is healed, and she has adapted well to the standard prosthetic arm provided by the

Veterans Affairs Medical Services. She still suffers, however, from common symptoms of PTSD, so I cannot recommend her either physically or mentally fit to return to any MOS that would require her to be deployed in combat zones. All of that is in this report."

"Isn't your report premature, Lieutenant? She's just begun working with our project."

"She has informed me that she will not continue with the army's project to create bionic soldiers, sir."

"I think General Banks made it clear that you aren't to stop until you convince her."

Teddy stapled, then held out the rest of the papers in her hand. "I'm requesting a transfer, volunteering for deployment."

"I won't approve it."

"If you don't approve it, then I intend to report myself to the medical board for an ethics violation. I'm sure it will mean I'll lose these nice captain's bars I just got, but it would also get me transferred out to Alaska or a desert somewhere."

"Ethics violation, my ass. You and I both know you've never even failed to put a used needle in the proper medical-waste receptacle."

"I slept with her."

Colonel Winstead stared at her for a long, silent moment. "You slept with Captain Story." It was a statement, not a question.

"I did."

"But you are so goddamned pissed at General Bank's suggestion that you do it again, you want to transfer out or turn yourself in to the medical board and sabotage your career."

"He wanted me to use the…the bond…between us to persuade her to do something she feels is wrong." Teddy straightened her shoulders and looked him in the eye. "I will not do that."

He held her gaze until she felt his stare too penetrating and looked away. "I felt like something was off between you two at the session with Will today. Has she gotten too attached to her therapist? Is that it? We both know you've had to deal with that before, Teddy."

She shook her head, involuntarily glancing at Shannon's photo and mentally cursing the tears filling her eyes.

"You've become attached to her." The soft words came from Tom, her mentor, the man who had flown with his wife at the last minute to serve as witnesses at their wedding. The man who'd been a second father to her when Shannon's death had left her crippled with grief. The man who'd cleared the path for her to exit the army as an enlisted medic and reenlist as an officer with a degree and double certifications.

"I love Shannon."

Tom turned and closed the blinds to shield them from surreptitious glances that'd been cast their way since General Banks had stormed out. Then he wrapped Teddy in his arms. "Teddy, honey. We all know that. But you're still a young woman. I know Shannon wouldn't want you to be alone the rest of your life."

"When I married her, I promised to love her forever." Teddy wanted to still be angry with him, but she needed him and his connection to Shannon right now.

He hugged her a little tighter. "I was there and heard her promise the same. If it'd been you, not her, attacked by that suicide bomber, would you have wanted her to spend the rest of her life alone?"

"No." Her voice sounded small, even to her. "I wouldn't."

"I'm going to tear up those papers, and I want you to delete that transfer request out of your computer." He gave her back a few rubs before he released her and stepped back. "I'll do what I can to protect you. Banks is only one star. I've got a few other generals I can call on if it comes to that, but I'm not sure how willing they'll be to take on Senator Story if Banks is his boy."

Britt didn't stop at her usual spot to pay homage to Story Hill Farm. Mysty had been there, a lean, gray figure in the gathering dusk. The mare whinnied a greeting, then ran along the fence when Britt didn't stop the truck.

Pop stood on the porch, watching as she parked and got out, grabbing her suitcase from the backseat of the crew cab and closing the door with her hip. "You gonna bring in your mare and feed her?"

"Jill should have done that before she left."

"Brock called and said you were on your way home. I told Jill to leave her out for you."

"I didn't stop." The steps seemed like eighteen instead of six, and she plopped her suitcase onto the porch when she reached the top. "And why did he call?"

"He said you were really tired, and he was worried about you falling asleep at the wheel."

"I'm not just tired, Pop. I'm drained."

"You want to talk about it? I got two rocking chairs right here, and it won't take but a minute to grab a couple of mugs of coffee."

"Thanks." She surprised herself and Pop by stepping forward and pulling him into a long hug. They were the same height now, his frame shrinking with age and hers still in its prime. "I do want to talk, but tonight I just need to chew on it all and get some sleep."

He hugged her back. "You don't have to carry this alone. Anything we talk about stays between you and me."

"I know, Pop. I couldn't do without you." She gave him another squeeze before releasing him and stepping back.

"I can tell you what you're going to do without me." His blue eyes were bright in the dim light. He pointed toward the barns where Mysty's whinnies still echoed across the paddocks. "You're going to march down there to feed and put that big-mouthed mare to bed." He peeled off the flannel-lined vest he wore and held it out for her. "Here. It's getting chilly already. I'm going inside to watch my shows."

She snuggled into the vest. It was warm from his body heat and smelled of Old Spice and horses, her favorite scent. "Anything to eat?"

"Lynn left some beef stew in the fridge for you." He picked up her suitcase. "I'll leave this at the bottom of the stairs for you."

He didn't need to remind her of the unwritten rule on a farm where the cheapest horse was worth thousands of dollars and the most expensive worth millions. Horses eat first.

"Thanks. I'll be back in a bit."

Britt detoured through the barn where Mysty was assigned, where she checked her stall to make sure it had clean bedding and a full water bucket. That was another rule. Never put a horse in a stall without checking first. Mice were a persistent problem in barns where some horses liked to look around while they ate and dribbled sweet feed as they chewed. It wasn't often, but sometimes a mouse would climb up to drink from a water bucket, fall in, and drown, fouling the water. Britt poured Mysty's nightly measure of sweet feed into her bucket, then reached for her halter and lead. Rethinking that move, she replaced them on the hook and walked to the paddock where Mysty still called for her.

"Hey, hey. What's all the racket? Are you mad because everybody else has had dinner already?" She went to the fence, expecting Mysty to show her usual impatience by staying by the gate to clang the metal shoe on her hoof against it. Instead, Mysty abandoned the gate and came to her. She nuzzled Britt's cheek, then rubbed her long, slender head against Britt's chest. Britt's throat tightened at the mare's care to be gentle, rather than butting Britt in her normal manner. Britt kissed the soft hair on the hard forehead. "Come on."

Mysty followed Britt down to the gate and stepped through when Britt opened it. She knew the routine—which barn, which stall was hers—and should have trotted off to her waiting dinner. But she waited while Britt closed and latched the gate, and she remained still when Britt leaned against her shoulder and scratched Mysty's withers.

There were no flag-draped caskets, no barking generals, no betraying fathers, no heart-breaking therapists here. Just warm, silent support from this big mare she'd raised from a skittish baby. She didn't need to read the scientific studies to know that horses can read and recognize human emotions. She'd grown up with them, and their body language was clear. She breathed in the horsey scent she loved best and finally let go, sobbing her torn and confused emotions into Mysty's shoulder. The mare reached back and held the tail of Britt's vest in her mouth, something she'd been prone to do as a foal—like she was holding on to her person.

The night was growing darker around them, so Britt pulled herself together, wiping her face on her shirt and giving Mysty a final hug. "Thanks for that. Now let's both get some dinner and sleep." Mysty bobbed her head as if she understood and walked with Britt to the barn. They didn't need a halter or a lead, because they were forever tethered by that invisible bond between horse and woman.

❖

Teddy dialed Britt's number again and hung up when she got voice mail. They needed to have this conversation in person.

She'd called the hotel and asked that they ring her room, but the desk clerk said Britt had already checked out. Damn, she wished she'd gotten E.B.'s mobile number. The only landline at the farm was in the office. She knew that during office hours, that line forwarded to E.B.'s mobile. But between five thirty in the evening and eight in the morning, those calls forwarded to a voice-mail system.

She dialed again, deciding to leave a message after all.

"Hi. This is the voice mail of Captain Britt Story. At the tone, please leave a message." The tone sounded, and a robotic voice recited: "Voice mailbox full."

Teddy threw her phone onto the sofa in her small apartment. "What the hell's going on?" Her frustration had been building all day, and she was at a boiling point. She snatched the television remote from the coffee table and flopped onto the sofa, next to her phone. She clicked the television on, anything to distract her from the thoughts churning her brain and her stomach. Maybe she'd watch one of those house-rehab shows. She liked those. She'd clicked through several channels when a photo of the Keeneland auction on the eleven o'clock news stopped her.

A video of a colt and the auction ran on-screen, the announcer talking about a near-record sale at the Keeneland September Yearling Sale today. Although it had been reported earlier that South Carolina trainer Marianne Woodard had won the colt with a bid of twelve million dollars, the news just breaking was that she was not making the purchase for a consortium of investors as rumored, but for only two people—herself and Britt Story, granddaughter of the breeder E.B. Story of Story Hill Farm and daughter of Sen. Brock Story.

"That was Britt's news. She bought Home from War." Wow. No wonder her voice mail was full. And Teddy had crapped all over her good news. She'd freaked out that morning and was silent during the drive back, then didn't stay for the auction. Then when Britt had showed up for her appointment, Teddy had left her sitting in her office until Britt finally just left. If possible, her shoulders slumped more than they'd been all day.

She had been hip-deep in shame that morning when she imagined she'd seen Shannon in the hotel lobby. Tonight, she felt hopelessly tangled in a political web and drowning in regret for how she'd treated one of the two most wonderful women who'd ever entered her life.

Teddy sighed, turned off the television, and slumped into the curve of the couch. Her gaze wandered around the room while her mind tried to organize the disjointed events of the day—making love to Britt, not attending the auction, Britt's amazing therapy session, getting the subpoena, missing a visit from Alisha, being promoted to captain, being threatened by General Banks, her conversation with Tom. She focused on the spine of a photo album sticking out from the line of books on one shelf and got up to retrieve it.

It was filled with photos of her and Shannon. Boot camp, then separate advanced training, but at the same military base in Georgia. Pictures of their first leave together, rough camping because it was cheap at a state park on the beach. There were lots of photos of them in bars, beers in their hands, and one of Shannon diving off a cliff while Teddy stood below with her hands covering her face. More than one showed Shannon geared up for a patrol, heavily armed and deadly sexy.

Shannon had been her beautiful wild child. She liked to party, ride motorcycles, and seek thrills. She was a fierce, brave, and talented, but mission-to-mission soldier. She didn't want any job that involved paperwork or planning. She just wanted to take point every time her patrol went out or swoop in and save the soldier pinned down by crossfire. The wild child in Shannon had attracted Teddy.

But Britt was all that, too, and more. She was responsible, smart, a great leader, brave, noble, and so beautiful. She was an adult with a solid foundation and a plan for her life. She was so tough on the outside but sweetly vulnerable on the inside. That combination completely disarmed and charmed Teddy.

Yes. She was in love. But the odds were against them.

She didn't know but was beginning to suspect the nature of Britt's beef with General Banks. Somehow, Teddy had found herself tangled in the same mess and saw no way to predict how that would turn out.

If Britt could free herself from the army, Teddy would be relocated in about six months to Fort Bragg or DC, and Britt would be here in Kentucky. Teddy's enlistment ended next year. She hadn't given it much thought until now, but her experience would easily translate into the civilian job market. Besides, now that she'd had a taste of military politics, she wasn't sure she could choke any more down.

It was nearly midnight, but she pushed the speed-dial for Britt's number again. Voice mail. Still full. If Britt wouldn't answer, her only option would be to drive out to the farm. She wasn't ready to do that. Not yet.

First, she needed to clean up some of the mess her life had churned up in the past twenty-four hours.

CHAPTER NINETEEN

B ritt first became aware of the rhythmic throbbing of a motor that both pulled her toward consciousness and lulled her back into a deep sleep. When something tickled her left cheek and ear, her shortened limb didn't stop her reflex to raise her left arm and brush it away, but a heavy weight held it down. She was instantly awake. The motor sound faltered at her movement but didn't stop. And something soft rubbing against her cheek replaced the tickling. Oh, God. She wasn't alone. She opened her eyes and frowned. "Hey, how'd you get in here?"

The orange bobtailed kitten, she couldn't remember what Teddy had named him, rubbed his cheek along hers again in answer.

"No, no, no. I gave you to her. She'll have to come get you." Or maybe she'd ask Jill to deliver the kitten to Teddy's office, along with anything else Teddy might have left at the farm. Britt had returned items to Jill's ex-lovers several times for her after Jill tired of them.

The familiar sounds of Pop banging around in the kitchen meant breakfast would be ready soon, and Britt welcomed the comfort of the farm's routine. Besides, she and Pop had breeding schedules to map out and stud choices to make now that the auction was over and they could concentrate on a budget for next year.

Then she had to make plans for herself. Right after breakfast, she'd call her friend in Washington who was a JAG officer once and could help her get released from the army. Maybe she'd talk to her about her subpoena, too. But putting the army behind her had to be a priority so she could focus her life on horses again. She didn't want anything from her life in the military. Almost nothing.

She was undecided about Lucy, the bionic arm designed for her and already partially synched to her brain. Maybe she'd talk to Will about how much it would cost to buy it outright and participate in the program outside the army's project. As long as she didn't have to see Teddy.

Teddy. Well. That was just a kick in the teeth. Oh, she believed Teddy did feel something for her—sympathy, friendship, even undeniable lust. But Britt had fallen for her. Fallen hard. She hadn't realized Teddy didn't, couldn't love her back. *She'll always and forever love only Shannon.* Best to let that filly go, with no buy-back clause.

Britt pulled on her bathrobe and headed downstairs. She'd tossed and turned most of the night, then overslept. She'd miss breakfast if she showered and went through the exercise and preparation routine to wear her prosthetic arm. Getting a sore on her stump would land her right back in the rehab program and under Teddy's care. She would not let that happen.

Pop turned to her, spatula in his raised hand, when she shuffled into the kitchen and went straight for the coffee. "Ha. Now that you're a fancy racehorse owner, you think you can just sleep in and lounge about the mansion until race time?"

"I might get a little bored doing that for a whole year until Home has his first race, don't you think?"

"You reckon?"

They both peered out the window, then shared a smile when Lynn's truck skidded past them and slammed to a stop in her usual parking spot. Pop spooned grits onto a plate, then plopped two over-easy eggs next to them and handed the plate to Britt. "Bacon's on the table."

Lynn stumbled into the house, coming through the door while still toeing off her muddy boots. "Hot damn! You're gonna race the colt."

Pop cracked two more eggs into the frying pan. "Not me. Not Story Hill Farm." Pop pointed the spatula at Britt. "Britt and Marianne bought him."

Lynn looked at Britt's plate. "Fry me a couple of those, too, please. I was so excited when I heard the news this morning, I left before breakfast."

Pop shook his head. "I figured. That's why I fixed extra bacon. These are your eggs in the pan now. You can make some toast for everyone."

This time, Britt and Lynn shared a smile. The plate of bacon on the table did indeed hold a third more strips than usual. Pop paid attention. Lynn went to work and had a plate of buttered toast ready by the time they were all seated at the table.

"What are you thinking of doing with your colt?" Pop asked, cutting his bacon and eggs to mix with his grits, like they all were doing.

"I'm going to let Marianne take the lead on his training. My first priority is to get free of the army and testify at this hearing I got a subpoena for. Marianne's the expert on racing. Not me. I want to stay fully informed and see how he comes along, but I'm going to trust her to make the right decisions."

"You should spend some time down there. You can learn a lot from her and her son Jace."

"I plan to. I'll also be spending time here, helping you."

Lynn nodded her approval. "It's hard to find the extra help we need in the spring, during foaling season. The old man here nearly runs himself in the ground."

"What about long-term?" Pop asked.

"Long-term?"

"With the colt."

"If he races as good as we expect, I expect we'll keep him for stud service."

"Good racer doesn't mean he'll pass those genes along."

Britt held her grandfather's gaze. "I know the gamble, Pop. You've had me studying bloodlines ever since I was old enough to read. If he doesn't pass along his good genes, he'll be the first in his line to fall short."

Britt tilted her chair back to see the source of a growl and hiss from near the pantry door. Mama Cat was munching some bacon scraps in a bowl next to a water dish obviously set out for the cats. A swat of her gray paw sent the orange kitten scampering away. Mamma Cat apparently didn't intend to share her bacon.

Lynn started breaking up her last piece of bacon, glancing around the kitchen as if finally taking notice of something. "Hey, where's Teddy?" She put her plate on the floor next to her chair, and the kitten immediately appeared and began scarfing down the bacon bits.

Pop looked to Britt for an answer.

"We're done."

The others still stared.

"With my rehab. I've met all the army's check marks. I still have a month of medical leave, but I also have to have an army psychiatrist clear me to be ordered back to duty. I'm calling a lawyer friend this morning to see if I can get free of the army before that happens."

"Teddy's coming back to get this kitten and all her equipment that's still upstairs, isn't she?" Lynn asked.

"Actually, I'm going to ask Jill if she'll take everything to the hospital today, so Teddy won't have to drive out."

Lynn looked at Pop, who shook his head. He made a shooing gesture at Britt. "Go do what you need, then holler if you want any help bringing her stuff downstairs. I'll be in the office, checking the accounts to see what's come through from the auction so far." He rose from the table. "Lynn, the kitchen is all yours."

One of the many things Britt loved about Pop was he knew when to stop asking questions. She trudged up the stairs and showered quickly and went into the room they'd used for rehabbing. She dragged the weight bench into her spacious bedroom, which gave her plenty of room to complete her light weight-lifting and stretching routines. Then she inspected her stump—not residual limb, she stubbornly thought—for any signs of redness, massaged it with cocoa butter to soften the scar, and covered it with the compression sock. Slipping on the harness, then attaching the prosthesis, was easy now. On to the next task.

Britt smoothed her hand over the portable massage table. She closed her eyes and could almost feel Teddy's strong hands gliding over her skin, firmly kneading the tight muscles in her shoulders, digging into stiff back muscles. She could feel Teddy's gentle fingers massaging cocoa butter into her incision scar and carefully applying antibiotic ointment to irritated areas of her residual limb. She jerked her hand off the table. *Stump. Not residual limb.* Britt flipped the table onto its side and released the latches on the legs, then folded the table in half. She transferred a few tubes of antibiotic ointment, a jar of cocoa butter, and several compression sleeves to her bathroom. Then she shoved the bandages, medicines, and the small TENS unit into the black duffel. She still needed the TENS unit occasionally, but she could order one online. And she had her own prescriptions.

She moved the duffel and table to the bottom of the stairs, then took a deep breath and rubbed the heel of her hand against the pounding inside her forehead.

"Hey, kiddo. I can do that for you." Lynn's hand squeezed Britt's shoulder. True to the military way, Lynn didn't ask questions or suggest they talk about the problem. She simply offered support.

"Thanks, but I need to do this," Britt said. "Can you ask Jill to come up to the house?"

"Sure. I can do that."

"Thanks."

Stepping into Teddy's bedroom nearly broke her. The scent of Teddy was everywhere. Britt opened the closet and grabbed the army-green duffel that sat in the corner, still filled with the uniforms Teddy never wore. Britt pulled blouses and a couple of dresses from the hangers to stuff them inside the duffel with the rest. She shoved the shoes and boots into one of several cloth grocery bags she found on the closet shelf. Once the closet was empty, she moved to the dresser. One drawer contained several pairs of jeans. Another had a couple of sweatshirts. The top drawer was full of underwear and socks. Britt fingered the silk panties and smiled despite the pain squeezing her heart. Not exactly army issue. Footsteps clomped up the stairway, and Britt quickly scooped up the underwear and stuffed it into the duffel, followed by the socks and sweatshirts. She was folding the jeans to add on top when Jill stepped into the room.

"Hey, pal. You summoned? Whatever you need, I'm your wingman, uh, woman," Jill said. "As long as I don't have to go to prison for it. I hear the food is really bad and the women aren't very pretty."

Britt snorted and shook her head. "Same thing I've done for you a couple of times, and I haven't gone to prison yet." She narrowed her eyes at Jill. "Although I remember one chick I thought was going to cut me with a fillet knife."

"Ah. The chef. I should have warned you to make sure she wasn't cooking at the time. It could have been worse. She might have been holding a pan of hot grease."

Britt stuffed the last pair of jeans into the duffel. When she finished closing it, Jill wrapped her arms around Britt from behind and rested her chin on Britt's shoulder.

"Maybe we should just quit this futile hunt for perfect women and settle down with each other," Jill said.

They stared at their reflection in the dresser's mirror, then spoke in unison. "Not!" They burst into laughter as Britt turned and snapped the hook device several times at Jill, who slapped at it to fend off the threatened pinch.

"Shit. I didn't realize they'd armed you permanently with that thing," Jill said, her tone joking.

Britt stopped, the reality of the army's true intention crashing back. "That's exactly what they intended."

Jill stiffened, all efforts to lighten Britt's mood gone. "What do you mean?"

Britt pointed to the duffel. "Can you take that down?" She held up the remaining cloth grocery bag. "I'm going to check the bedside table, under the bed, and the bathroom for anything else. Then I'll meet you, Lynn, and Pop downstairs. I'll tell you what I can."

Jill hefted the packed duffel, then put it down and went to the bed. She lifted the mattress off the box springs.

"What are you doing?" Britt asked.

"Just checking," Jill said. "She might have had nudie pictures of you under there that she jerked off to at night. You wouldn't want Lynn finding them when she changed the sheets, would you?"

"What makes you think Teddy would have nude photos of me?"

Jill shrugged. "If she did, you'd never tell me, so I figured I'd just better go ahead and check. Not even a dust bunny there." Jill picked up the duffel again. "Always looking out for my best buddy."

After Jill left, Britt rummaged through the bedside table and found a bottle of eyedrops and the copy of *Seabiscuit* she'd loaned Teddy. She almost put it in the bag until she remembered it was the last birthday gift her grandmother had personally inscribed and given her, so she laid it on the bed. If Teddy wanted to finish it, she'd have to buy her own copy.

Jill, Lynn, and Pop were waiting for her in the living room. She was ready and cleared her throat.

"The army won't let me tell you everything, but I'll share what I can. Something happened in Afghanistan that cost a young soldier's life. I was injured trying to prevent it. Army command had been advised there was a problem but refused to respond. Their negligence apparently has been widespread enough that a Senate hearing is being held on the issue. I've been subpoenaed to testify. The army won't release me even though my enlistment is up because I've been ordered not to speak about the incident. Once I'm a civilian, they have no authority to stop me."

Pop swore under his breath, and Lynn's expression was grim. Britt held her hand up to forestall questions or comments.

"The next thing I'm going to tell you is all I'm going to say about this matter. Then I'm taking Mysty out for a ride...alone. I'm sorry, Pop, but I need some horse therapy today. I'll be ready to work first thing tomorrow."

Pop nodded but said nothing. Britt opened her mouth to continue but paused when her throat tightened. She closed her eyes to gather her thoughts and harden her heart.

"Teddy and her assignment as an in-residence therapist are part of the army's plot to keep me from testifying. General Banks and Dad hoped she and the offer of an advanced bionic prosthesis would persuade me to stay away from Washington. I don't agree with their tactics or their hidden intent to create a squad of bionic soldiers. So, any further relationship between Teddy and me, personal or professional, would be detrimental to her career, her prosthesis project, and the lawsuit I'll be filing to force the army to release me from service."

They were all quiet for a long minute, grim faces all around.

"No worries," Jill said. "You sure we got everything of hers out. No coffee mug in the kitchen, boots on the porch, clothes in the laundry room. Anything like that?"

"I'll double-check," Lynn said, and hurried off to the kitchen.

"Take your phone with you," Pop said. "Call that lawyer while you're out communing with nature." He started toward the office, then stopped. "And ask her about getting restraining orders against your father and that general." He hesitated, his tone changing from strident to resigned. "And get one for Teddy. Then General Asshole can't blame her for not swaying you." He cupped her jaw and brushed his callused thumb over her cheek. "Just until you testify."

The very thought made Britt sick, but he was right. "Okay, Pop."

Teddy glanced up at the pitiful caterwaul coming from the group crowded together a short distance from her office door. She straightened, rolled her stiff shoulders, and stared up at the ceiling. The sound definitely came from an animal, which was not permitted in the hospital unless certified as a therapy animal. Colonel Winstead could handle it. He was the boss, so it was his job to enforce the rules in that department.

Her blinds had been drawn and her door closed all day because she didn't want to be bothered. She had put in a call to the lawyer who had helped her win survivor benefits after Shannon was killed. She hadn't told anyone in her chain of command that she'd been subpoenaed. She knew her friend Tom would stay quiet and have her back, but Colonel Winstead's career would suffer if General Banks found out that he knew beforehand and still let her testify.

She hunched again over the spreadsheet she was slowly working her way through, searching for possible candidates for their program. The yowl sounded again, but closer and accompanied by a sharp knock on her door. She scowled, looked up, and blinked, surprised to see Jill through the window in the door. She rose and quickly opened the door.

"Hey." She smiled. Maybe Britt had sent Jill because she was so tied up giving interviews. Her smile faltered when Jill didn't offer one. Her brain instantly flashed through a hundred scenarios—Britt hurt, Britt devastated because Pop was hurt, barns burning and horses dying at the farm. "What's wrong? Is Britt okay?"

"She's fine. I'm not." Another cry sounded from the pet carrier Jill held next to her leg. "I've had to listen to this Satan's spawn howl like someone's removing his tiny little balls with a dull knife all the way from the farm." She plunked the carrier down on Teddy's desk. "He's all yours now. I've got the rest of your stuff in my truck. Do you want it in your car, or should I haul it all in here?"

Teddy realized her mouth was hanging open, and she closed it with a snap. "My stuff?"

"That you left at the farm."

"I was coming out to pick it up later." She peered into the pet carrier and saw the orange kitten, who mewed pitifully and thrust his paw through the wire door in an imploring gesture.

"No need now. I've got it here."

"I need to talk to Britt." The kitten's caterwauling was growing so insistent, Teddy had to raise her voice to be heard.

"She said she's fulfilled the therapy required for amputees. She only has to see the army shrink now. I don't suppose you have that certification, too?"

Teddy didn't like this cold, snippy side of Jill. Not at all. "It has nothing to do with her therapy." She opened the carrier, and the kitten ran up Teddy's uniform to snuggle as close as possible against Teddy's neck, trembling and glaring at Jill.

"What then?" Jill glared back at the kitten.

"It's personal and none of your business."

Jill stepped closer, so close that Teddy had to force herself not to back away. "That's where you're wrong. Britt Story has been my best friend since we were kids. I can list on one hand the number of people she's let get close to her. But somehow you wormed through her defenses. Then she finds out yesterday that you're just an enemy spy, part of the army's plot to manipulate her in a cover-up. She doesn't want to talk to you."

Teddy's heart dropped into her stomach. Somebody must have said something. Had General Banks caught Britt in her office before Teddy returned? Is that why Britt was gone when she got back? She grabbed Jill's arm. "No. I have to talk to her. I didn't know myself. Not until yesterday."

"She said it didn't matter if you knew or not. She's talking to a lawyer today to get a restraining order against you, General Banks, and her own father until after the hearing. E.B.'s getting a judge to ban the three of you from the farm property. Delete her number from your phone. Forget how to get to the farm. Forget you ever knew her."

Teddy covered her mouth but couldn't stop the sob that escaped.

The office door swung open, and Rachel entered. She was wearing her bionic hand, which was clenching and unclenching as she moved to stand between Jill and Teddy. "Do you need some help in here, Captain?"

Jill raised an eyebrow and stared down at this intruder. Rachel stood about five-four, and Jill was approximately six feet tall. Except Teddy knew Rachel was a trained killer and had calmly claimed many lives as a top army sniper before losing her left hand.

The ridiculousness of the situation gave Teddy a few seconds to collect her thoughts. She wiped the tears from her cheeks and grabbed a tissue to wipe her nose. "Yes, Rachel. I do need some help, if you don't mind." She fished her car keys from her uniform pocket. "This is Jill. She's a friend of Captain Story."

"Oh." Rachel looked back at Jill, her expression going from guard dog to confused. "Captain Story called a friend and got me a good job at a local gun range."

Jill nodded. "Big heart, that one."

Rachel nodded but scowled. "So why are you in here yelling?"

Jill narrowed her eyes, so Teddy jumped in before another argument started.

"Because there's been a misunderstanding, Rachel. I won't go into detail because it's personal, but I've hurt Captain Story's feelings badly, and Jill was just defending her best friend." She handed her car keys to Rachel. "Could you go with Jill? She's brought some things I left at Captain Story's farm, and I need them transferred from her truck to my car." She pointed to the kitten. "I don't think I'll be able to get him back in the carrier right now, and I don't trust the terror in my office alone."

"Sure. I can do that for you."

"Thanks. And Rachel?"

"Yeah?"

"Jill really is a friend. I'd be very upset if she was harmed in any way."

Rachel grinned. "Gotcha. Hands off."

Jill smirked. "Really?"

"Jill, look at me." Teddy gave Jill a very serious stare. "Do not aggravate Rachel. She might look small, but she's an expert killer. Among army snipers, she's in the top five for number of kills. She's in the top ten among all US government snipers, including armed services, FBI, CIA, and a few the public doesn't know about."

Jill looked at Rachel with new respect. "No fooling?"

"Even better with this new hand. I can lay a M-24 barrel in this hand, and it's rock steady."

Jill touched the hand. "Wow. That's really cool. Is that what Britt's going to end up getting?"

Rachel shrugged. "I think so."

Teddy closed her door again and slumped into her chair as Jill and Rachel disappeared around the corner, chatting like new friends. The kitten had stopped shaking and purred in her ear, rubbing his face against her ear.

Her cell phone rang, the caller ID indicating it was the lawyer.

"Elizabeth, hey. Thanks for calling me back."

The conversation was to explain the subpoena and that Teddy had no idea what they wanted her to testify about, but she hadn't told her superiors about the subpoena. To explain why, she had to tell about Britt and the army's underhanded manipulations to prevent her from testifying at some Congressional hearing. No, Teddy didn't know if it was the same hearing as the one she was being called to. It was all so very complicated.

"This is very intriguing. I'll be glad to represent you."

Teddy hesitated. "There's just one thing. I don't have a lot of money, and I imagine your hourly billing is pretty high."

Elizabeth laughed. "Honey, if this is the Elsbeth hearing I think it is, I'd do this pro bono just for the publicity. But a lot of groups are sponsoring representation for those who do come forward and testify, so you don't have to worry about that. This won't cost you a penny."

"Great. Thanks."

"I'll be in touch, but Teddy?"

"Yes?"

"I have to advise you to stay away from your friend Britt until I find out if she's also testifying. We don't want to hurt your testimony or hers by having the media report that you might have been collaborating."

That empty pit in her chest opened wider. "Don't worry. No chance of that."

The kitten hopped down to her lap and stared up at her while he kneaded her stomach and purred. Tears filled her eyes again. Damn, would this hollow feeling in her chest ever go away? Would she ever stop crying?

A soft paw patted at a tear that was making its way down her cheek, and she looked down to stroke his silky fur. "I really need to give you a name." She picked him up and kissed his head while he batted at her face. Then she set him on the desk to play while she turned back to her computer. Britt had blocked her phone calls and texts, so she'd probably blocked her emails, too. She could try.

She typed a quick email: *Please let me talk to you.* She hit send.

If this doesn't work...the email bounced right back as unable to deliver. Her tears threatened again.

"What am I going to do? I can't visit. I can't call. I can't text. I can't email." She frowned when the kitten batted a pencil into her lap. She opened her desk drawer and started to put the pencil away when another item dropped into her lap. A letter from her mother, who loved to write old-fashioned letters rather than email or call on the phone. Or visit. That was it. She'd write a letter. Of course, Britt could throw it away without opening it, but she had some ideas for that.

"You're a genius, my little friend," she said to the kitten. "I'm going to name you..." She was about to say Einstein, but then she saw the fuzzy dice one of her clients had given her to hang from her rearview mirror. The kitten lay on his side, wrestling with the soft, oversized dice with his feet. The dots facing her on the dice added up to seven, her lucky number. "Seven," she said. "Your name is Seven."

The kitten sprang to his feet and sent the dice rolling across the desk when he leapt to the floor as Rachel opened the door and tossed Teddy's keys to her. "Hey, look what that cat just rolled."

Sure enough, face up, the dice added up to seven.

"That's his name," Teddy said, producing a real smile for the first time all day. "Lucky Seven."

CHAPTER TWENTY

Britt paced the room nervously. Congressional hearings weren't like court hearings. She could have watched Teddy's testimony on the television in her father's office, but she didn't want it to possibly affect her testimony.

Four long weeks had passed with the media dredging up speculation and every angle possible once the witness list became public record and the hearings began. She could barely leave the farm, so Marianne sent video of Home from War with weekly updates.

Four long weeks, and she still missed Teddy more than she'd ever missed her left arm. Every minute of every hour of every day. Her heart had nearly thumped out of her chest the day she'd ripped open the plain, long envelope addressed to Story Hill Farm with no return address and found Teddy's letter addressed to her inside. She held onto it all day, arguing with herself about whether to open it or throw it away. Finally, she'd saddled Mysty and ridden to the highest hill on the farm and read it.

Teddy explained in the letter that she hadn't known about the hearing until General Banks showed up the afternoon after they came back from Louisville. And she didn't know until the next day that she'd been subpoenaed to the same hearing. But she had known one thing for certain that morning when they'd left Louisville. She was wrong when she thought she'd never fall in love with another woman after Shannon, because she'd fallen hard for Britt. She'd asked two things.

Let me know that you read this letter. If you feel the same, wait for me.

Britt addressed a plain white envelope to Capt. Theodora Alexander at the hospital and put a single sheet of ornate Story Hill Farm stationary inside. On it she wrote in careful cursive, "I'm waiting."

Teddy had testified yesterday, and whatever she'd said had stirred a media storm. Her face was everywhere—on televisions in the hotel bar and the hotel gym, in newspapers, and on websites. It took everything in her to turn away from them all.

Britt would testify today, then go find Teddy. She had waited long enough.

Sen. Brock Story strode into the room. "Ready?"

Britt took a deep breath. "Ready to get it over."

He clasped her shoulders and looked into her eyes. "I am so sorry I was such a self-important ass and nearly chose a friend—one I apparently didn't know as well as I thought—over my family. I might have never come to my senses if you and Pop hadn't filed court actions to keep me away from you and the farm."

Britt hugged the man who was both her senator and her father—a man who had ultimately stepped up and done the right thing.

He'd gone straight to Teddy, then to Colonel Winstead and learned that George had tried to order Teddy to prostitute herself to cover his ass and had threatened to shut down a project that would benefit handicapped soldiers, civilians, and the army if he didn't get the coverup he wanted.

Then, he'd followed Teddy's advice to write a letter to her and Pop, and they'd had the restraining orders against Teddy and her dad lifted. Brock came to the farm and made amends. Teddy stayed away until she and Britt could testify.

Britt released him and stepped back to straighten her uniform again. "You're here now, Dad, and I'm really glad. I'd rather be staring down a gun barrel than facing all those cameras."

"Relax. You're a friendly witness for this panel. They want to hear what you're here to tell them. Just watch out for the neckless guy on the end. Senator Mitchell." He brushed a bit of lint from her uniform and pulled his handkerchief out to polish the new major's insignia on her shoulders.

Today was the last day she'd wear the uniform. At midnight, she would be a civilian again. He took her hand and tucked it in the crook of his arm to lead her through the maze of hallways to the hearing room. The closer they got to their destination, the more crowded the hallway was. Cameras began to flash as they passed.

When they reached the double doors to the hearing room, he stopped and stepped back to salute her. "I'm so proud to be your father, Major Story. Go kick some ass."

"Sir." She returned his salute, even though he was no longer in the service. "You aren't coming in?"

"I'll be upstairs in the gallery. I thought Captain Alexander would like some company. She's saving me a seat."

"Teddy's here?" Britt's stomach did a double flip-flop. She was going to throw up for sure.

"Steady. She'll be to your right, on the second row and close to the end. You won't even have to turn your head much to see her."

Britt nodded. "Okay." As she watched her father go, she felt another hand on her arm.

Her friend and attorney, Renee, smiled. "They're ready for us."

Britt followed Renee to the witness table, where they settled in, and an aide adjusted their microphones.

"These are directional mics," he instructed. "If you want to talk privately, just cover yours with your hand like this." He cupped his hand over the end of the microphone.

After going through the usual "state your name" routine, Senator Elsbeth began the questioning.

"Major Story, you were in command of the unit in which Corporal Jessica Avery was assigned."

"Yes, I was."

Senator Elsbeth held out some stapled papers to an aide and pointed for him to hand them to Britt. "Is this a copy of the report you filed on the incident Corporal Avery reported on June 2, 2018?"

Britt accepted the papers and scanned them. "Yes. It is."

"Can you summarize it for the committee?"

"I was awakened at approximately oh-three-hundred by a call from the military-police sergeant on duty and informed that Corporal Avery was in his office filing a report saying three men had sexually assaulted her when she went to the latrine around twenty-two-hundred. I dressed and personally interviewed her after I made sure she received proper medical attention from a female physician and female nurses or medics."

Senator Elsbeth looked up from the report Britt was referencing. "Excuse my interruption, but how did Corporal Avery appear to you when you first saw her?"

"Appear?"

"What was her physical and emotional state?"

Britt wanted to grind her teeth as images of that night flashed before her eyes. "She was curled into a fetal position on a wood bench while male soldiers came and went from the room. Her T-shirt was ripped down the front, so that she had to hold it closed with her hands. Her face was swollen and bruised. She had multiple abrasions and small cuts on her arms, legs, and face. She had clearly resisted and been beaten. Her pants were gone and her underwear bloody."

"What did you do when you saw that?"

Red lights began to flash up and down Britt's prosthetic hand, and then it went completely dark. Great. She should have kept it in her lap. Now she wouldn't be able to move it until she calmed down.

"Major Story?"

Britt licked her lips. "I took my shirt...I had a T-shirt underneath...and I covered her. Then I reprimanded that duty sergeant, wrote down the names of the officers responsible for him, took custody of Corporal Avery, and transported her to the medical unit."

Senator Elsbeth's eyes glinted like dark shards of glass. "I hope your reprimand was harsh, Major Story."

"That reprimand was brief. My priority was to get medical aid for Corporal Avery. She had been found and brought in by a female

MP on patrol around twenty-three-hundred hours. She had been on that bench until I was notified more than four hours later."

A moan came from the gallery, and Britt glanced up to see Julie Prescott, Corporal Avery's sister who had visited Britt before to ask her to testify, weeping. Britt's father, who was sitting beside Julie, wrapped his arm around her and murmured something in her ear and handed her his handkerchief. Britt's eyes immediately tracked to Brock's other side. Teddy. She was as beautiful as the first day she'd stepped into Britt's world, soothed the pain in her arm, and ultimately healed the wound in her heart.

Senator Elsbeth leaned toward her microphone, fury etched across her face, so Britt hurried to continue.

"I did return later to discuss the issue with the duty sergeant. I'm pretty sure the man defecates through two rectums now."

Senator Elsbeth smiled and sat back in her chair. "Please continue, Major Story. What happened at the hospital?"

"I requested a female physician but was told the only doctors on duty were male. One was operating on a mess-hall cook who'd nearly cut his thumb off chopping up chickens. The other doctor was removing a vibrator from another soldier's rectum that some men in his unit thought would be funny to insert while the guy was passed out drunk."

Titters ran through the audience and media covering the hearing.

"I also was told that rape kits had not been a priority on the clinic supply list, so they had none."

Senator Mitchell, the one her father had warned her to watch, cleared his throat. "Your report indicates a rape kit was, in fact, completed."

"While we waited, a female physician showed up. She wasn't scheduled for duty, but one of the nurses called her and explained our case. This was not her first deployment, so she was familiar with how clinics at the smaller bases were stocked. Her husband, also an army doctor, had shipped a box of rape kits directly to her. She and the nurse who called her were experienced in working with sexual-assault victims. I turned Corporal Avery over to them for processing. And I filed my report, naming Private Dirk Smallwood as the man she identified as her rapist. She didn't know the other men, who had held her down. She said they got scared because she was bleeding when he was done and ran off when he offered for them to be next. She said Private Smallwood was the only one who beat and raped her."

Britt felt her prosthesis vibrate as it rebooted and came back online.

"And Private Smallwood was arrested after you filed your report?"

"Yes. But he was charged only with assault, then released from the brig two days later and returned to duty."

Senator Elsbeth removed her reading glasses and put down the report. "I'm sorry. I thought I heard you say he was returned to duty."

"Yes. In the same unit as Corporal Avery. Smallwood identified the two men who were with him, and they testified that Corporal Avery had consensual sex with him."

"How did they explain her beating?"

"Jessica was a lesbian, married to another soldier in the mechanics unit at the same base. Smallwood claimed that she was curious about men, then scared that her wife would know what she'd done when she bled after intercourse. She asked him and his pals to mess her up a little. They didn't like it, but they did it because she kept telling them to hit her again. It was his word against hers, even though the doctor's report detailed vaginal trauma typical of rape."

"And what did you do when he was returned to duty?"

"First I gave orders that they should always be put on separate patrols and separate duty rosters. And I assigned him to clean latrines several times when I caught him making inappropriate gestures to her when they crossed paths in the mess hall or around the base. I asked her group of friends and some of the male soldiers I trusted to keep an eye on her and Smallwood. There are many more good, honorable men serving their country than there are deviants like Smallwood."

"Still, on the day she was killed, Corporal Avery was assigned to the same patrol as Private Smallwood."

"Yes. Allow me to backtrack a bit. The rape kit disappeared. It was logged as leaving in the outgoing mail, addressed to Landstuhl Medical Center for processing, but it never was logged in as arriving. The evidence was lost."

The red lights in her prosthetic hand began to flicker again, and Britt paused to take a couple of deep breaths to calm her mind. The lights stopped.

"Corporal Avery was growing more and more withdrawn from everyone. I blame myself for not transferring her out for a mental evaluation, but that kind of thing is a blot you never get off your record. Even after you leave the military." Britt took a sip of water from her glass to collect herself. "I spent weeks going up the chain of command about this case and the overall lack of safety for women soldiers among their own troops. Many hovered on the edge of dehydration because they wouldn't drink water after a certain time, fearing they'd wake up and need to go to the latrine after dark. Walking to the latrine at night isn't safe for women."

"How high did you go?"

"I spoke with General George Banks."

Senator Mitchell laughed loudly. "That's pretty high up for a captain."

"Yes, sir. It is. But General Banks was a friend of my father. He and his wife visited my family's home many times as I was growing up. He was more to me than just the top of my command. I had hoped he would listen."

Senator Elsbeth glared at the rude senator. "Please continue, Major Story."

"I returned to base to find that a patrol with both Corporal Avery and Private Smallwood was almost ready to pull out. I confronted the lieutenant leading the patrol about violating my orders by putting both of them on the same patrol. He said Smallwood was a last-minute substitution when another soldier got a sudden bellyache and reported to sick call. I relieved the lieutenant, ran to my container unit, and geared up to lead the patrol myself."

Flashes of that day began to surface, and she closed her eyes. She could feel the desert heat, the sand between her collar and neck, and the weight of her rifle slung over her shoulder.

Renee, who had remained silent until now, rested a hand on Britt's arm. "We would like to request a ten-minute break, Senator Elsbeth."

Britt shook her head. "No. I'm okay. I need to finish."

Senator Elsbeth nodded, and the rest of the committee stared in silence.

Britt took a big gulp of air. "Avery was huddled in the very back of the personnel carrier, like she might jump out at any minute, and Smallwood sat directly across from her. He was alternately making kissing noises and flicking his tongue at her in a suggestive manner. I grabbed his collar and yanked him down out of the carrier, then dragged him to the front of the truck where the others couldn't hear us and used the weight of my body to pin him against the truck. He wasn't a big man, no taller than me, and I was still wearing my forty-pound pack. I told him that if he so much as looked at Corporal Avery one more time, he was going to be cleaning latrines for the rest of his deployment." She smiled. "He knew nobody could hear us, so he wasn't afraid of being insubordinate. He said he liked a woman who wanted to get rough and that I was giving him an erection."

Senator Elsbeth's eyebrows shot up, and the other women on the panel gave each other knowing looks. Yeah. All women had heard similar lines from men. Fun maybe with a lover. Not so much from an unwelcome Lothario, and clearly insubordinate. Most of the men had the grace to appear embarrassed. Senator Mitchell chuckled.

Senator Elsbeth cocked her head, her expression amused. "I'm sure you had an appropriate reply."

"I told him I couldn't detect a thing, so maybe that's where he got his last name—small wood."

Most of the men smiled behind their hands, but the room filled with the light, delighted laughter of women—in the gallery, among the press corps, and on the committee. She needed that lighter moment to get through the final part.

"Without recounting a long blow-by-blow of the patrol, at one point we were pinned down by enemy fire but secure enough to hold our position while we waited for air support. It was two minutes away. I was looking around, attempting to get a head count to see if we were missing anyone, when I saw Smallwood crouched behind a half wall, making the lewd gestures at Avery again. We were under fire, and he was sticking his tongue out at her and humping the stock of his M16. She was a few feet away, standing at the corner of a building. I saw her point her rifle at him and begin firing as she walked out into the open toward him. I yelled at her to get down and ran to stop her, but I was too late. She had killed Smallwood, and enemy fire killed her and nearly killed me." She felt like stone, cold and walled off, when she finished speaking.

The room was silent.

She unconsciously threaded the fingers of her hands together in front of her and waited. The prosthesis so closely duplicated her lost hand, even its warmth, that she was beginning to sometimes forget that it wasn't real. Dr. Will Thomas had begged her to let him have the covering matched to skin tone so it would look natural, too. But she wanted the reminder. Women like Corporal Jessica Avery, and the bravery of soldiers like Shannon Alexander, deserved to be remembered.

She looked up when Senator Mitchell cleared his throat again.

"Ms. Story. Wouldn't it be fair to say your rapid advancement in your military career has been helped by your father's substantial influence as an officer and more recently as a senator with a strong hand on the military budget?"

"No, Senator. If anything, it's been more difficult. Like you, most expected that type of favoritism to happen, so I had to work twice as hard to prove myself worthy of each advancement in rank. I graduated top of my class at West Point and ranked third in my class on the physical requirements. I've logged more combat time than most of the other officers competing for promotion. I completed the course work for the rank of major last year, but requested that my promotion be delayed until I fulfilled my schedule of deployment. The promotion would have kept me stateside, and my deployment slot would have been filled by another captain—perhaps someone with a wife or husband and children they'd have to leave behind."

"That's very noble of you, Ms. Story. But it's fortuitous that your promotion should come through right before you retire from the service…today, isn't it? That makes a significant change in your retirement income."

Renee keyed her microphone. "Mr. Mitchell, if you want to question my client, you will address her by the rank indicated on her uniform." She slapped her forehead. "Oh, I apologize. You probably don't recognize it since…what was it…a weakness in your spine kept you from serving your county. Anyway, it's major. Major Story."

The senator's face turned red, and his nostrils flared. "A curvature of my spine."

"Doesn't keep him off the golf course," someone from the gallery shouted.

Senator Elsbeth banged her chairman's gavel. "Let's get this hearing back on track. Did you have a point to make, Senator Mitchell?"

He sat forward in his chair, the loose skin under his chin wobbling as he spoke. "Major Story's testimony is an impeachment of General Banks's character and his command. It's well known that he does not support women in combat roles or queers among the ranks. It just causes chaos. Major Story…" He sneered out her name. "…obviously identified with Corporal Avery because she's never made it a secret that she, too, is a lesbian. Of course, she believed that girl and not Private Smallwood."

He bristled when the mention of Smallwood's name generated a fresh wave of titters. He pointed to Britt. "General Banks has generously promoted her and made sure she got one of the army's newest, most expensive bionic prosthetic limbs. Now she's ruining an exemplary soldier's career with a questionable testimony that reflects poorly on the culture he allows under his command."

One of the other male senators spoke up. "I would think Captain Alexander's testimony yesterday would damage General Banks's career more than Major Story's testimony today might."

"Those two women obviously conspired against him."

"Until Captain Alexander was assigned as my therapist, I had never met her. The last time I saw or spoke to her was the day she signed off on my medical file. Yes, we formed a close friendship during the time she worked with me. But after we separately discovered that General Banks intended to use her to keep me from testifying today, we agreed the only way to remove that opportunity from him was for us to break off our connection. I have not corresponded or spoken with Captain Alexander since the day after she signed off on my medical file."

"That prosthesis should have been given only to a soldier willing to return to service." Senator Mitchell's tone was accusing.

Both Renee and Senator Elsbeth moved toward their mics to speak, but Britt stood and raised her bionic arm, hand turned palm out to stop them. She clenched her jaw, her chest heaving with anger. Her command voice was deep and cold, carrying perfectly across the room without amplification.

"Do you see the red lights blinking in my hand? That's a warning. My brain is telling the prosthesis that my anger is about to reach an unsafe level, so the bionics are preparing to shut down." She flexed the fingers. They were almost clenched into a fist when the hand went dark and the fingers froze in position. The elbow joint would stay fixed until the bionics rebooted, but she lowered her residual limb.

"The army did not pay for this arm. I did. I've lived frugally in the years that I've been in the service, taking advantage of military housing and the mess hall. And I got very lucky with some investments I made in several start-ups. Very lucky. The army has a project underway to build a squad of bionic warriors. Their prosthetic limbs will encase weapons, much like comic-book artists dreamed up years ago. I still suffer from PTSD and do not qualify as a candidate for that program. That said, my prosthesis still is capable of a grip that could crush someone's neck or a headlock that could smash their skull. That's why it's programmed to shut down when it detects my anger rising to a dangerous level."

She felt the familiar vibration, and the hand began to come back to life. She held it up for them to see. "When my brain reads appropriate levels of serotonin, or calmness, in my system, then it reactivates the bionics. Dr. Thomas worked very hard on that modification before I would accept the prosthesis."

"Amazing," Senator Elsbeth said.

"Will there be any other questions, Senator?" Renee asked.

Senator Elsbeth looked left and right, but only one committee member indicated a question.

"Senator Lewis?"

"How can we learn more about that remarkable arm you have?"

"I'm just a test subject," Britt said. "The man you want to talk with is Dr. Will Thomas at Duke University Medical School's research labs."

"Thank you, Major Story," Senator Lewis said. "And we all thank you for your service and sacrifice for your country."

"It's been my honor," Britt said.

CHAPTER TWENTY-ONE

When Britt and Renee turned to leave, they met a wall of media: phones thrust forward to capture video, photos, and sound bites. Questions were shouted from every quarter. Two huge marines broke through the crowd, and one smiled. Only then did Britt realize she was an Amazon of a woman, besting Britt's six feet by three or four inches and at least thirty pounds of muscle heavier.

"Need an escort, Major?"

"It would be much appreciated, Sergeant."

The two marines spun on their heels and carved a path, with Renee and Britt following close behind. Outside, Renee steered Britt to a door a short distance down the hallway.

Renee looked up at the marines. "Damn, you guys are tall. I'm going to the ladies' room. Can you guard this door until I get back?"

"Yes, ma'am," they replied in unison.

She pinched the cheek of the male marine. "You're so cute."

"Renee."

"Well, you know I don't play for your team. That's why you were the perfect roommate at the Point. I didn't have to worry about you stealing my dates, and you didn't have to worry about me stealing yours." She opened the door and pushed Britt inside. "We'll be out here to give you some privacy for a while. Just open the door when you're ready to leave."

Britt stared at the closing door. What the hell? Then she turned and saw the familiar figure silhouetted against a huge window. "Teddy?" Was it finally her?

The figure turned, and Teddy took a tentative step toward her.

Adrenaline had carried Britt through the hearing, but seeing Teddy drained all of it away. She didn't have to be strong for Teddy.

Tears filled Teddy's eyes, and when she held her arms out, Britt went to her. She buried her face in Teddy's shoulder and let it all go. Teddy held her close, stroking her back. "Oh, baby. I had no idea how awful the secret was that you were carrying. You might not have been able to save that girl, but you tried your best. You're still my hero."

Britt shook her head. "I should have sent her to psych."

"No. Those units are awful. You would have sent her from purgatory to the depths of hell. The army doesn't ignore just women. They ignore men who suffer from depression, male victims of sex assault, gay service members who are harassed and assaulted. Those patients don't need to be thrown in with the hard-core schizophrenics and brain-damaged patients."

"Really?"

"I'm in the medical field, remember? I've seen them."

"Okay."

They stared at each other.

Teddy brushed away some of Britt's tears with her fingers, then pulled a handkerchief from her pocket to dry the rest. Britt caught a glimpse of the initials embroidered on one corner and grabbed Teddy's wrist to stop her.

"Oh my God. Is that Dad's handkerchief?"

Teddy looked at her suspended hand holding the handkerchief in question. "Yes. He gave it to me earlier. I couldn't help but cry at some of your testimony."

"I think he's loaned that to everybody in this building at some point today." She turned and grabbed a box of tissues from the desk behind her. Taking two, she held the box out to Teddy. "Take one. You don't know who else has wiped their nose on that hanky."

Teddy laughed. "You're a germaphobe."

"Am not. I'm just going to be that one person who lives when everybody else dies from contagion."

Teddy wiped at new tears with a fresh tissue, tears from her laughter. She reached up to cup Britt's face in her hands and, still laughing, said, "I love you." A nanosecond later, her eyes widened with the realization of what words had spilled from her lips.

Britt drew Teddy into her arms, lowered her head, and caressed Teddy's lips with hers. She drew back only slightly, sharing heat and breath.

"I'm glad. Because I love you, too."

A rapid knock sounded, and the door opened.

"Okay. You've had enough time," Renee said. "I said a few minutes of privacy. I didn't say you had time to bed her."

"You can't say that in front of her father."

"Oorah," the female marine said.

Britt and Teddy tore their gaze from each other, then walked toward their audience of five—two marines, Brock, Renee, and Julie Prescott.

"Dinner's on me," Brock said.

"Thank you, but I have to get home to the kids," Julie said. "I'm sure they're driving Sam crazy by now." She stepped forward and caught Britt in a tight hug before stepping back. "I just wanted to thank you for everything you tried to do for my sister. And for your testimony today."

"She deserved better."

"Yes, she did. But at least she got our best."

EPILOGUE

One year later

Britt paced in their box at Keeneland, pausing only when she spotted Teddy making her way toward her.

"I thought I was supposed to meet you at the paddock?" She stretched to give Britt a quick peck on the lips.

"Marianne sent me away. She said I was going to make Home nervous."

Teddy smiled. "I know, baby. I left Pop down there with her." Teddy needlessly straightened Britt's collar, but she allowed it. Any connection with Teddy helped calm her.

"She'll probably send him away, too. He's been strutting around the barns like an old peacock all morning. You'd think he owned the colt."

"He did breed him, and he did get twelve million for Home before he ever set hoof on a racetrack." Teddy moved to Britt's right side and kissed her hand as she draped Britt's right arm over her shoulder. She wore a thick cable-knit sweater over a silk, long-sleeved T-shirt, jeans, and stylish boots. It was perfect for the chilly but not cold early November weather. Britt wore her usual jeans, button-down shirt, and tweed sports jacket.

A waiter appeared with two Kentucky Mule cocktails. "Good afternoon, Major Story. Here are the cocktails you ordered." He set the drinks on the table in their owner's box. "Would you like something to eat?"

"Not for me. I'm too nervous. Teddy?"

"Thanks. I'm fine."

"You've got a horse running?"

"Home from War, in the next race."

"Is he looking good?"

"This is just his second race, but he won the first by four lengths. We've had to find a more experienced jockey who can hold him back some in the longer races."

The young man held up the seven dollars Britt had tipped him. "I'll have to put this down on him then."

"Good luck," Britt said. "Oh, and really, I'm retired from military service. It's Ms. Story, or just Britt. I think I'd prefer Britt."

"Of course, Major Story." He snapped his best imitation of a salute and hurried off.

Teddy smiled. "You're superstitious."

"No, I'm not."

"You tipped him seven dollars."

Britt pursed her lips in an effort to disguise the smile she was holding back. "I did. Except for that maniac cat of yours, it seems to be a lucky number for us. Did I ever tell you that Home's hip number in the auction was double-zero double-seven?"

"No. You're kidding."

"Swear on the stack of breeding records in Pop's office."

"Wow, that's serious." Teddy slipped a hand under Britt's jacket and tickled her ribs.

Britt dodged away, then slipped behind and wrapped her arms around Teddy. She rested her chin on Teddy's shoulder. "I can't believe you don't have to go back."

Teddy turned her head to kiss Britt's cheek. "I spent all day Wednesday and yesterday out-processing and left at the stroke of midnight, the very second it was official."

"I love you," Britt said. Teddy was a salve that seemed to heal everything in her life. She still had occasional nightmares, but it wasn't so bad when Teddy was there to hold her and soothe them away. And her temper still erupted every now and then. Her bionic limb shutting down each time turned out to be like a bucket of cold water on that fire. They hadn't anticipated that valuable side effect.

"I love you back," Teddy said, pressing her cheek against Britt's. "So much."

"Okay, you two. See if you can pry yourselves apart for two minutes to watch the race," Pop said as he and Marianne joined them. "They're putting them in the starting gate."

Teddy stumbled to keep her balance when Britt sprang away and snatched up her drink to drain it before the last horse was loaded.

"Oh my God. Hand me the binoculars, babe."

Teddy handed over her cocktail instead, waited while Britt drained that one too, then traded the empty glass for the binoculars. She retrieved a second pair from her shoulder bag for herself.

Marianne shook her head and looked at Teddy. "Are you sure that's the same woman who calmly led troops through enemy fire? She falls to pieces every time we lead that colt near a starting gate."

Teddy smiled and rubbed Britt's back. "She's a lot more protective about her horses than soldiers. Aren't you, honey?"

"Uh-huh." Britt heard her, but the words didn't register. Didn't matter. She usually agreed with Teddy. She would start paying closer attention if Teddy painted their bedroom Barney purple because Britt had agreed to it. But at this moment, her attention was laser-focused on the fourth horse from the rail, who was moving restlessly in the starting gate. Home began to rock, shifting front to back, front to back, as if he was considering rearing up. She'd seen more than one horse's career end in the metal starting gate before he ever had a chance to race. "Steady, steady." Britt's quiet words were for herself more than the horse. She felt Teddy's hand slide under her jacket and curl around her belt at the center of her back. It steadied her more than words.

"He's okay," Marianne, watching through her own binoculars, said. "It's a thing he does."

The last horse loaded, and the next second seemed to hang in the air forever. Then the starter bell rang, and the doors flew open. Home from War, having rocked back on his heels, leapt from the gate almost a full stride ahead of the other horses. His jockey moved him quickly toward the rail, but not so close he could be hemmed in.

Home had won his first race handily. But the difference in how he responded to that jockey and this more experienced one was easy to see. The colt settled into a smooth glide. The jockey rode with his body and talked to the horse with his hands. They stayed a neck ahead, even as three different colts moved up to challenge around the first turn and down the backstretch. But when they rounded the second turn into the homestretch, the jockey extended his arms out over the colt's neck and let him loose. Without even a tap of the whip to keep the young racer focused, Home lengthened his stride and pulled away like the others were only out for a stroll.

"And it's Home from War still in front, Savory Fox battling for second with Twist a Whirl, and Dancing Cat fourth. Home from War is pulling away, one length, two lengths. Savory Fox drops back as Phar Turn makes his move on the outside."

The track announcer's voice rose with each length the pack dropped behind.

"Home from War now four lengths in the lead, trailed by Twist a Whirl, Phar Turn, then Dancing Cat, Gallant Man, Expresso and Cha-Cha Russo.

"And across the finish line, it's Home from War by six lengths." A short pause. "Phar Turn places second by a nose, with Twist a Whirl third, and Dancing Cat places fourth."

For the first time, the jockey appeared to struggle with Home to slow him and turn him back toward the winner's circle. But he was laughing and rubbing the colt on the neck.

"By God, I think he wanted to go around again," Pop said, breaking the stunned silence.

"And I was worried about finding a jock who could hold him back for the long-distance races." Britt laughed. Pop and then the rest joined in until Teddy stopped them.

"Don't you have to go to the winner's circle and get your trophy?"

"To hell with the trophy," Marianne said, already heading for the stairs. "I want the check that goes with it. We'll need it to keep that jock riding for us the rest of the year."

Britt grabbed Teddy's hand. "Come with me." She hesitated. "Pop? You coming?"

"Nah. You know I hate the crush of crowds. This is your moment. You've earned it. Go."

The race announcer had been replaced by an enthusiastic racing commentator broadcasting over a website channel and displayed on large screens throughout the track facilities.

"What a display of speed today, folks. This two-year-old colt was sired by War Front, out of Unbridled Storm. This is his second race in the Road to the Kentucky Derby series. He won the Iroquois at Churchill Downs last month by four lengths."

"That's right, Jim," his co-announcer said. "It's still early, and there are a lot of races to come, but it's a safe bet we'll see this colt again when they load the starting gate in May for the world's most famous horse race, the Kentucky Derby."

Britt woke slowly, aware the darkness in the room was fading to gray. Naked and sprawled on her back, she sighed with absolute contentment. The source of her bliss was Teddy, also naked and snuggled against her side.

They'd left Home from War at Keeneland to be tucked in by his favorite groom, Roberto. The colt would board there until his next race, which was scheduled in four weeks at Churchill Downs in Louisville. She wondered if the black colt the California trainer had purchased would be there. She was anxious to see how he'd match up against her colt.

She moaned when a warm mouth closed over her nipple, then sharp teeth gently squeezed until electric jolts ran from her breast to her crotch. "I love the way you say good morning."

"I love that you're still in bed and not already in the shower and going out to play with your horses." Teddy moved on top of Britt, and Britt wrapped her leg around Teddy's so she couldn't leave the bed. She realized her mistake when Teddy's thigh slipped between her legs and pressed against Britt's very wet sex and swollen clit.

"Hmm. Somebody has a morning stiffy. You know, some of the nurses were in the hospital cafeteria taking one of those magazine surveys the other day, and one of the questions asked how many orgasms a woman can have in a lifetime. You know, like you can reach a limit, then there's no more. So, I told them that a woman can have an infinite number…as many as there are blades of bluegrass in Kentucky."

Britt's breath hitched when Teddy undulated her hips and her thigh massaged her aching clit. "I think we killed off a couple of acres last night."

Teddy had been at Fort Bragg for the past three weeks, arriving back in Kentucky yesterday just before the race at Keeneland. They were exhausted when they'd finally fallen into bed last night, but their need to reconnect was stronger than their need to sleep. They'd made love for hours before they finally gave in to restorative rest wrapped in each other's arms.

Teddy rolled her hips again and kissed Britt, her tongue dominating Britt's. Teddy drew back, then kissed along Britt's neck before whispering in her ear. "I'm thinking we should set higher goals…like a whole pasture."

She slid down Britt's body, nipping an earlobe, licking a nipple, rimming her navel, and scraping blunt fingernails across the sensitive nerves of Britt's lower belly as her tongue found and teased Britt's plump clit to rock-hardness.

"Teddy. Don't tease." Britt tangled her fingers in Teddy's hair. "Please."

Teddy sucked her into her mouth and entered her with two slender fingers. Pumping and sucking. Pumping and sucking. She played Britt like a concert violin, the tension gathering as quick as a summer storm. One scrape of her nails across Britt's belly, and the storm exploded. Lightning shot through every limb, holding her arched and breathless for long seconds. Then Britt collapsed.

Teddy crawled up and kissed Britt briefly, then slid across the bed on her belly, reaching for the bedside table.

Britt rolled over in swift attack, using her body to pin Teddy to the bed. This was one of their favorite positions, especially when Britt was prepared with an extra bit of equipment that freed her hand. Teddy said it was some erogenous spot inside that was always missed when she was penetrated from the missionary position. Britt liked it because it made her crazy hot. Teddy groaned and opened her legs wider when Britt reached between them.

Britt loved how responsive and uninhibited Teddy was when they made love. She would top Britt one minute, then become a complete bottom the next. It gave Britt the freedom to do the same. She skimmed her hand through Teddy's slickness a few times. Her lover always produced plentiful lubrication. Then she plunged her thumb inside and forked her fingers on either side of Teddy's clit, stroking that bundle of nerves each time she withdrew her thumb and thrust inside again. She sucked at Teddy's neck and bit down on her earlobe.

She bucked her hips against her hand, thrusting her thumb deeper as Teddy raised her hips to meet each stroke. They easily found their rhythm, but the pressure was never quite enough for Britt, so Teddy reached behind her, offering her hand. Britt shifted so that Teddy's fingers stroked her as her hand stroked Teddy. She was going to come again. She bore down with her thumb and thrust faster, harder. Teddy's breath began to hitch. She was about to come, and not a moment too soon.

"Come with me, Teddy. Come on, babe." Britt barely had time to recognize the flood of warmth spilling into her hand and the clench of muscle around her thumb when her own orgasm nearly paralyzed her. Somehow, she managed to thrust through it until Teddy went limp, and she gratefully followed. They panted together, and then Britt planted a few kisses between Teddy's shoulder blades. She removed her thumb slowly, nipping at Teddy's perfect ass. She felt like a big cat, wanted to rub herself all over Teddy. Instead, she rolled to the other side of the bed and slipped her hand inside her pillowcase. Yes. It was still there.

She glanced at the clock. Six thirty. "Hey, look at the time. I haven't heard Pop downstairs yet." Britt started to get up, but Teddy pressed her back down.

"That's because I hung a big DO NOT DISTURB sign at the bottom of the stairs last night."

"You did?"

"Yes. I told E.B. I needed some private time with you because we needed to discuss some things."

Britt smiled. "I like the way you discuss things."

"Stop. I really mean talk. Will wants me to continue working with the prosthesis program, but only the civilian part. The VA in Lexington also wants to hire me. They're having to contract out more and more work to therapists they don't know because of the volume of patients being sent to them. So I've been thinking that maybe I should start my own practice and take patients referred to me from the VA here. In Durham, I wouldn't be working with patients, just going down there once or twice a month to teach other therapists about the digital limbs."

"I'll have to take trips, too. Homey will have to race sometimes in California. He might be the only racehorse I own, or I might find another to invest in. I don't know." Britt reclined against the pillows and tugged Teddy down to cuddle against her. "Spending a few nights apart isn't as bad as wondering if you're coming back from some patrol in Afghanistan."

Teddy sat up and retrieved something she kept hidden in her hand from the drawer in the bedside table. Tears ran down her cheeks. Britt reached for her, but Teddy shook her head.

"Don't, or I'll lose my nerve, and it's taken me a long time to work up the courage to ask this." She opened her hands and popped open a small jewelry box. "Britt Story. Would you consider…will you marry me?"

Britt was stunned, unable to believe Teddy was doing this. She looked into those tear-filled eyes and said, "Not if it's going to make you cry."

Teddy's crestfallen expression told Britt her joke had fallen flat, so she hurried to set things right. She felt under her pillow to retrieve an identical jewelry box. She popped it open and held it out to Teddy.

"And I'll say yes only if you do."

About the Author

D. Jackson Leigh grew up barefoot and happy, swimming in farm ponds and riding rude ponies in rural south Georgia. She is a career journalist but has found her real passion in writing sultry lesbian romances laced with her trademark Southern humor and affection for horses.

She has published 13 novels and one collection of short stories with Bold Strokes Books, winning three Golden Crown Literary Society awards in paranormal, romance, and fantasy categories. She was also a finalist in the romance category of the 2014 Lambda Literary Awards.

Friend her at facebook.com/d.jackson.leigh, on twitter @ djacksonleigh, or learn more about her at www.djacksonleigh .com.

Books Available from Bold Strokes Books

A Love that Leads to Home by Ronica Black. For Carla Sims and Janice Carpenter, home isn't about location, it's where your heart is. (978-1-63555-675-9)

Blades of Bluegrass by D. Jackson Leigh. A US Army occupational therapist must rehab a bitter veteran who is a ticking political time bomb the military is desperate to disarm. (978-1-63555-637-7)

Guarding Hearts by Jaycie Morrison. As treachery and temptation threaten the women of the Women's Army Corps, who will risk it all for love? (978-1-63555-806-7)

Hopeless Romantic by Georgia Beers. Can a jaded wedding planner and an optimistic divorce attorney possibly find a future together? (978-1-63555-650-6)

Hopes and Dreams by PJ Trebelhorn. Movie theater manager Riley Warren is forced to face her high school crush and tormentor, wealthy socialite Victoria Thayer, at their twentieth reunion. (978-1-63555-670-4)

In the Cards by Kimberly Cooper Griffin. Daria and Phaedra are about to discover that love finds a way, especially when powers outside their control are at play. (978-1-63555-717-6)

Moon Fever by Ileandra Young. SPEAR agent Danika Karson must clear her werewolf friend of multiple false charges while teaching her vampire girlfriend to resist the blood mania brought on by a full moon. (978-1-63555-603-2)

Quake City by St John Karp. Can Andre find his best friend Amy before the night devolves into a nightmare of broken hearts, malevolent drag queens, and spontaneous human combustion? Or has it always happened this way, every night, at Aunty Bob's Quake City Club? (978-1-63555-723-7)

Serenity by Jesse J. Thoma. For Kit Marsden, there are many things in life she cannot change. Serenity is in the acceptance. (978-1-63555-713-8)

Sylver and Gold by Michelle Larkin. Working feverishly to find a killer before he strikes again, Boston Homicide Detective Reid Sylver and rookie cop London Gold are blindsided by their chemistry and developing attraction. (978-1-63555-611-7)

Trade Secrets by Kathleen Knowles. In Silicon Valley, love and business are a volatile mix for clinical lab scientist Tony Leung and venture capitalist Sheila Garrison. (978-1-63555-642-1)

Death Overdue by David S. Pederson. Did Heath turn to murder in an alcohol induced haze to solve the problem of his blackmailer, or was it someone else who brought about a death overdue? (978-1-63555-711-4)

Entangled by Melissa Brayden. Becca Crawford is the perfect person to head up the Jade Hotel, if only the captivating owner of the local vineyard would get on board with her plan and stop badmouthing the hotel to everyone in town. (978-1-63555-709-1)

First Do No Harm by Emily Smith. Pierce and Cassidy are about to discover that when it comes to love, sometimes you have to risk it all to have it all. (978-1-63555-699-5)

Kiss Me Every Day by Dena Blake. For Wynn Evans, wishing for a do-over with Carly Jamison was a long shot, actually getting one was a game changer. (978-1-63555-551-6)

Olivia by Genevieve McCluer. In this lesbian Shakespeare adaption with vampires, Olivia is a centuries old vampire who must fight a strange figure from her past if she wants a chance at happiness. (978-1-63555-701-5)

One Woman's Treasure by Jean Copeland. Daphne's search for discarded antiques and treasures leads to an embarrassing misunderstanding, and ultimately, the opportunity for the romance of a lifetime with Nina. (978-1-63555-652-0)

Silver Ravens by Jane Fletcher. Lori has lost her girlfriend, her home, and her job. Things don't improve when she's kidnapped and taken to fairyland. (978-1-63555-631-5)

Still Not Over You by Jenny Frame, Carsen Taite, Ali Vali. Old flames die hard in these tales of a second chance at love with the ex you're still not over. Stories by award winning authors Jenny Frame, Carsen Taite, and Ali Vali. (978-1-63555-516-5)

Storm Lines by Jessica L. Webb. Devon is a psychologist who likes rules. Marley is a cop who doesn't. They don't always agree, but both fight to protect a girl immersed in a street drug ring. (978-1-63555-626-1)

The Politics of Love by Jen Jensen. Is it possible to love across the political divide in a hostile world? Conservative Shelley Whitmore and liberal Rand Thomas are about to find out. (978-1-63555-693-3)

All the Paths to You by Morgan Lee Miller. High school sweethearts Quinn Hughes and Kennedy Reed reconnect five years after they break up and realize that their chemistry is all but over. (978-1-63555-662-9)

Arrested Pleasures by Nanisi Barrett D'Arnuck. When charged with a crime she didn't commit Katherine Lowe faces the question: Which is harder, going to prison or falling in love? (978-1-63555-684-1)

Bonded Love by Renee Roman. Carpenter Blaze Carter suffers an injury that shatters her dreams, and ER nurse Trinity Greene hopes to show her that sometimes love is worth fighting for. (978-1-63555-530-1)

Convergence by Jane C. Esther. With life as they know it on the line, can Aerin McLeary and Olivia Ando's love survive an otherworldly threat to humankind? (978-1-63555-488-5)

Coyote Blues by Karen F. Williams. Riley Dawson, psychotherapist and shape-shifter, has her world turned upside down when Fiona Bell, her one true love, returns. (978-1-63555-558-5)

Drawn by Carsen Taite. Will the clues lead Detective Claire Hanlon to the killer terrorizing Dallas, or will she merely lose her heart to person of interest, urban artist Riley Flynn? (978-1-63555-644-5)

Every Summer Day by Lee Patton. Meant to celebrate every summer day, Luke's journal instead chronicles a love affair as fast-moving and possibly as fatal as his brother's brain tumor. (978-1-63555-706-0)

Lucky by Kris Bryant. Was Serena Evans's luck really about winning the lottery, or is she about to get even luckier in love? (978-1-63555-510-3)

The Last Days of Autumn by Donna K. Ford. Autumn and Caroline question the fairness of life, the cruelty of loss, and what it means to love as they navigate the complicated minefield of relationships, grief, and life-altering illness. (978-1-63555-672-8)

Three Alarm Response by Erin Dutton. In the midst of tragedy, can these first responders find love and healing? Three stories of courage, bravery, and passion. (978-1-63555-592-9)

Veterinary Partner by Nancy Wheelton. Callie and Lauren are determined to keep their hearts safe but find that taking a chance on love is the safest option of all. (978-1-63555-666-7)

Everyday People by Louis Barr. When film star Diana Danning hires private eye Clint Steele to find her son, Clint turns to his former West Point barracks mate, and ex-buddy with benefits, Mars Hauser to lend his cyber espionage and digital black ops skills to the case. (978-1-63555-698-8)

Forging a Desire Line by Mary P. Burns. When Charley's ex-wife, Tricia, is diagnosed with inoperable cancer, the private duty nurse Tricia hires turns out to be the handsome and aloof Joanna, who ignites something inside Charley she isn't ready to face. (978-1-63555-665-0)

Love on the Night Shift by Radclyffe. Between ruling the night shift in the ER at the Rivers and raising her teenage daughter, Blaise Richilieu has all the drama she needs in her life, until a dashing young attending appears on the scene and relentlessly pursues her. (978-1-63555-668-1)

Olivia's Awakening by Ronica Black. When the daring and dangerously gorgeous Eve Monroe is hired to get Olivia Savage into shape, a fierce passion ignites, causing both to question everything they've ever known about love. (978-1-63555-613-1)

The Duchess and the Dreamer by Jenny Frame. Clementine Fitzroy has lost her faith and love of life. Can dreamer Evan Fox make her believe in life and dream again? (978-1-63555-601-8)

The Road Home by Erin Zak. Hollywood actress Gwendolyn Carter is about to discover that losing someone you love sometimes means gaining someone to fall for. (978-1-63555-633-9)

Waiting for You by Elle Spencer. When passionate past-life lovers meet again in the present day, one remembers it vividly and the other isn't so sure. (978-1-63555-635-3)

While My Heart Beats by Erin McKenzie. Can a love born amidst the horrors of the Great War survive? (978-1-63555-589-9)

Face the Music by Ali Vali. Sweet music is the last thing that happens when Nashville music producer Mason Liner, and daughter of country royalty Victoria Roddy are thrown together in an effort to save country star Sophie Roddy's career. (978-1-63555-532-5)

Flavor of the Month by Georgia Beers. What happens when baker Charlie and chef Emma realize their differing paths have led them right back to each other? (978-1-63555-616-2)

Mending Fences by Angie Williams. Rancher Bobbie Del Rey and veterinarian Grace Hammond are about to discover if heartbreaks of the past can ever truly be mended. (978-1-63555-708-4)

Silk and Leather: Lesbian Erotica with an Edge edited by Victoria Villasenor. This collection of stories by award winning authors offers fantasies as soft as silk and tough as leather. The only question is: How far will you go to make your deepest desires come true? (978-1-63555-587-5)

The Last Place You Look by Aurora Rey. Dumped by her wife and looking for anything but love, Julia Pierce retreats to her hometown, only to rediscover high school friend Taylor Winslow, who's secretly crushed on her for years. (978-1-63555-574-5)

The Mortician's Daughter by Nan Higgins. A singer on the verge of stardom discovers she must give up her dreams to live a life in service to ghosts. (978-1-63555-594-3)

The Real Thing by Laney Webber. When passion flares between actress Virginia Green and masseuse Allison McDonald, can they be sure it's the real thing? (978-1-63555-478-6)

What the Heart Remembers Most by M. Ullrich. For college sweethearts Jax Levine and Gretchen Mills, could an accident be the second chance neither knew they wanted? (978-1-63555-401-4)

White Horse Point by Andrews & Austin. Mystery writer Taylor James finds herself falling for the mysterious woman on White Horse Point who lives alone, protecting a secret she can't share about a murderer who walks among them. (978-1-63555-695-7)